To Adrian Public Library
Enjoy!
Brenda Humphrey
Meisels

Family at Booknook

Brenda Humphrey Meisels

authorHOUSE®

AuthorHouse™
1663 Liberty Drive, Suite 200
Bloomington, IN 47403
www.authorhouse.com
Phone: 1-800-839-8640

First published by AuthorHouse 6/5/2009

ISBN: 978-1-4389-1793-1 (sc)

Library of Congress Control Number: 2009905679

*Printed in the United States of America
Bloomington, Indiana*

This book is printed on acid-free paper.

Acknowledgements

I have always been entranced by the unfolding of people's stories. As a psychotherapist I have heard many personal narratives and have been privileged to play a part in helping people grow and change their lives. My clients tell me their stories and together we work to make sense of their issues. When I started this novel, I had in mind the characters and the journey they would take. But I found that, just as with my clients, as each character appeared all I could do was follow.

Family at Booknook was conceived and birthed with the support and help of my writing colleagues Susan Scott Morales and Margaret Fuchs Singer, two talented women each writing a book of her own. When I tried to impose my will on my characters, it was they who said, "Would she do that?" I could not have written this without them.

The idea that I could write a novel began with Laura Kasischke, a prolific author and tactful writing teacher, who gave me hope when she said, "You have a story to tell." It was through her that I learned of the Bear River Writers' Conference. Each summer, in an ideal setting, practicing authors share their expertise and motivate aspiring writers. At Bear River I have had the opportunity to meet and learn from successful writers and teachers, especially Elizabeth Cox, Anne Marie Oomen, and the very personable Richard McCann. This conference introduced me to another writing group which includes Clare Cross, Rachel

Nelson and Diane Kimball. These women helped keep me grounded. Often they would ask, "What is it you really want to say?"

I appreciate my supportive friends who read *Family at Booknook* in its various drafts and encouraged me to persist: Sally Seymour, Susan Pierson, Debora Heskett, Roni Moncur, Madelon Possley and Sally Brush. Heartfelt thanks to Ellen Toronto for listening and lending a hand with her editing skills.

My children and their spouses have tolerated my preoccupation with the novel and urged me to finish it. They knew it was important to me. To them I say, "Thanks. I did it. Now, you have to read it."

In the end I am tremendously indebted to my knowledgeable editor and mentor Elizabeth Kirchen, who has been continuously available, has challenged me on grammatical correctness and helped flesh out details and make the parts into a whole.

Lastly, I dedicate this book to my husband, Murray Meisels, who encouraged me to follow my heart. And although he is not a fiction reader, he has read and reread this book. And says he likes it.

Contents

An Unwanted Guest
October 1959

*D*ave Stanley had to get out of the house. With yesterday's Adrian *Daily Telegram* tucked under his arm, he walked to his shop, Booknook. He had misplaced his belt again; his jeans, which had become too large, were riding low on his hips, hems skimming the cement. His shoulders were hunched, eyes unseeing. Winter Street was deserted, which suited him just fine—too early for church. He wasn't going to open the store. He could work on accounts, but had no intention of doing so.

At sixty-six Dave felt old, used, worn out and ready for the junk heap. Although not a handsome man, he had had a rough sort of charm. His once wavy silver hair, now a dull gray, hung uncut over his plaid shirt collar. Two bushy brows met and became one, accenting eyes dark with pain. He no longer smiled, and the straight line of his lips hid his almost perfect teeth.

At the book store Dave pulled the key from his pocket. It slipped through stiff fingers and clattered onto the cement. "Damn!" Inside the store the phone

1

rang. "It's Sunday, isn't it? Why the hell is anyone calling now? Oh, stop your bleating! I'm coming." As he plucked up the key, his knuckles scraped against rough cement. He unlocked the door, hastened to his desk and grabbed the phone.

"Booknook—not open!"

"David, I tried to reach you at home. What are you doing at work today?" Clare Washington's tone was accusatory.

Bossy Clare, he thought. She may have been the youngest kid in the family, but she certainly made her presence known. "Where should I be? Sitting at home?"

"No, David, you shouldn't. You should be fishing, at church, here with me, anywhere, but not alone."

"You've got all the answers for everything, don't you, little sister?" He would have slammed the phone into its cradle, but knew if he did she'd be pounding on his door in an hour.

"I didn't call to fight. I called because I need your help."

"*You* need *my* help?"

"Yes…there's a girl here, a really sweet girl. She needs a place to stay for a while. I was thinking of that little apartment above the store. The one you and Emily lived in when you were first married. She could earn her keep…clean, and wait on customers."

"Someone here in my store?"

"Yes, and there's more…she's pregnant."

"No!"

Clare continued. The girl was sixteen, a straight-A student, scared of her shadow. She was a good worker and wouldn't give anyone any trouble.

"But she *is* in trouble!"

"She's shamed and humiliated, needs to get out of town. She'd be much better off in Adrian, where people don't know her."

"What are you talking about? Milan's less than an hour away. She can't hide here."

"No one knows, and she's not showing yet. As soon as there's space in the unwed mothers' home in Detroit, she'll be gone. You aren't the only one in the world with problems. Can't you think of somebody else for a change?"

Dave held the phone from his ear and shook his scraped, raw hand.

"Are you there?" asked Clare.

"Yeah, I'm here."

Clare's voice softened. She explained about the girl's family, how they lived in Dick's shack. "Our own brother rents that hovel!" Clare said that the girl's face was swollen, that she may have been beaten. "How would you feel if something happens to her, when you could have helped?"

"But I don't even know her!"

As though he'd not spoken, Clare continued. "Besides, Dave, you need help. Booknook is filthy. Why, when you pick up a book, you have to wipe off the dust before you can read the title."

Emily had cleaned every day, arranged the books and made displays. He knew that since she'd died he'd let things go, but he could barely put one foot in front of the other. Perhaps he should close the place and live on Social Security. He was exhausted and tired of arguing. He knew Clare wouldn't let go of this. She'd keep at him. When she wanted something, she was like a dog with a bone.

"Do her parents know she's leaving? I can't be harboring a runaway."

"Running away? Don't you understand? They kicked her out. They don't want anything to do with her."

"What kind of parents would kick a kid out because she's pregnant?"

"Abusive! That's what kind."

In the end Dave simply gave up. "Just for a few days. I'm not going to babysit a pregnant adolescent."

Without saying goodbye, Dave banged the phone down. "Damn that Clare. She won't let me be. I sure as hell am not going to let some abused kid live in my apartment!"

Dave went to the bathroom, ran cold water on his aching hand, then dried it roughly. He paced to the front of the store, where he collapsed on the window seat. He stared at the paper. Although he'd read it yesterday, he could remember nothing from it. But then, he couldn't remember a lot of things these days. The *Telegram* didn't put out a Sunday paper. Each morning Dave bought a *Detroit Free Press* from Sam at the newsstand, but this morning he couldn't bear to speak to anyone. Trying to orient himself, he stared at the date—Saturday, October 17, 1959. A year had passed. He flipped open the paper and scanned the headlines: "General Marshal 78, Leader War and Peace Is Dead." "Mamie Has Cold."

"Good God!" His rage echoed against the books. "It's October, General Marshal died in March, so why in the hell would they run a headline like that? And Mamie—who cares if the president's wife has a cold and can't have dinner with the president of Mexico? This paper's worthless."

Dave would have boycotted the *Telegram*. "There's nothing in it," he had said. "Just a lot of gossip." But his wife, Emily, was firm: they must support the community. Since her death, he hadn't had the gumption to cancel the subscription. And the paper, dropped in front of Booknook each day, seemed to taunt him with memories of her.

Dave flung the paper in the trash and went to the back of store, where he poured a cup of cold, stale coffee, sniffed it, then put it down. He returned to the entrance and watched the righteous in their overpriced cars drive to church. He had not been there since Emily's funeral. If there was a God, he was a cruel God; he had let Emily suffer. The doctors had removed the tumor, zapped her with radiation, filled her with poison, and rationed the morphine. They'd tortured her until she lay between stark white sheets, body emaciated, head bald like the Jews at Auschwitz. He had prayed, "Let it be me. Spare her the pain." But Gestapo God had turned away.

The Methodist women kept bothering him with casseroles that he did not want and could not eat. The dishes stacked up on the kitchen counter. After a couple of weeks, when he noticed the smell, he dumped the food and rinsed the dishes, being careful not to remove the tape that identified each cook. Then he got in his '49 Ford pickup and delivered them to their respective owners. He wondered whether, if he tossed the dishes, the flood of tuna casseroles would stop. However, he remembered Emily taking food to bereaved friends and her pleasure at being thanked when they returned her bowl or plate. If he couldn't, wouldn't, eat the stuff, he could at least take back the damn dishes.

Over the months the "care packages" reduced to a trickle. Still, each week a widow would knock on his door bearing her specialty—Swiss steak, rich chocolate cake, delicacies that he no longer enjoyed.

She would stand at the door, angling for an invitation to step in. He would mutter a gruff hello, say thank you, then shut the door. In the privacy of his kitchen, he would run his finger through the frosting and lick it, remembering how Emily had chided him for doing this. He might even have a sliver of cake, but he did not savor it as he once had.

Now, when his mind was whirling with memory and longing, when he could barely make out the outline of the person in front of him, when words were thick on his tongue, a girl—a pregnant girl—was coming to Booknook. Clare had said that she was fragile. He would have to be civil. Damn, she should just get an abortion. Well, but it would have to be in some filthy office, or at home, maybe with a coat hanger. She might not survive.

Had she been raped? No, he did not want to know about her, the circumstances of her predicament. But thoughts nudged him, interrupting his warm, murky preoccupation with his dead wife. He sat at the table trying to call up her face, her gentle brown eyes. "Oh Emily, what have I gotten myself into?"

That afternoon Dave watched a Chevy convertible squeal around the corner and bounce to a stop, one wheel nudging the curb. The right front fender was dented, rust beginning to eat through the blue paint. A big, broad guy dressed in jeans and plaid shirt and wearing a baseball cap stepped out of the car. He needed a haircut. Dave wondered if he was the father of the baby. A girl got out, her navy skirt reaching her ankles, long wavy hair hiding her face. Each picked up a couple of grocery bags, and the girl followed the fellow toward the bookshop. As they got halfway up the walk Dave noticed the bulge of the fellow's chest. "What the hell? He's a woman!" When they reached the door, he noted that she had a smooth pleasant face and was just a teen herself.

"Hi," said the big one, taking a step to the side, revealing the girl behind her. "I'm Mary. I brought Sparrow." She extended her hand.

"Yeah, I can see." Dave kept his hands in his pockets.

The little one stood staring at the wide wooden floorboards, hair shielding her face.

Dave glared at the girls. Damn, he thought, what shenanigan has Clare gotten me into now? "You can only stay for a few days."

The girl did not look up.

Hell, she's just a kid, thought Dave. He said, "Well, the place is not fit. You'll have to clean it up." He led the way up the narrow stairs. As though protesting the intrusion, the door at the top groaned.

The room served as both kitchen and living area. Four narrow, floor-length windows faced the street. A couch and chair, both with slipcovers, were huddled together near an end wall. A tall antique stand with a tarnished lamp seemed to hover over the chair. A gray Formica table pressed against one window. Two chrome chairs with cracked red vinyl seats were tucked under the table and faced a bar across the road—EL CHAPULIN GRASSHOPPER MEXICAN BAR AND GRILL. On the opposite wall were a half-size stove, 1940s refrigerator, and cupboard. The counter held a chipped enamel sink with a scant foot of working space on either side. Dust sprinkles floated in the sunlight; spider webs like forgotten lace hung from the lampshade and ceiling. The air was thick and stale, with a hint of tobacco and coffee. It occurred to Dave that he should have opened the windows.

On the kitchen side of the room a door led into an oversized bedroom, where a faded chenille bedspread covered the sagging bed and an antique oak dresser stood in a corner. Faded blue wallpaper with pink roses adorned the walls; pine boards appeared half-dressed by a round braided rug.

The apartment held memories of love, but today Dave saw it through the eyes of the girls. It was just plain shabby. It didn't matter; it was better than the girl being on the street. Through the quiet he could hear the cars on the road below.

Dave had been content living in the apartment, building the business, saving for a family. Emily had not complained, but he knew she had been uneasy when she got up at night and navigated the dimly lit stairs to the bathroom. He wondered if the girl would be scared to go down to the bathroom. But he didn't want her to be too comfortable. He didn't want her here in any case.

He cleared his throat. "That's all, storage in back. You'll have to use the bathroom downstairs."

"Does it have a tub?" whispered the girl.

"What? Yeah, sure, needs cleaning." Strange question, he thought.

The girl lifted her head and peeked out through the strands of hair. "I'll do it."

Frightened eyes met Dave's, brown, the color of Emily's. He reeled. "That's all. I'm going now. I'll lock the door. Shop opens at ten." He bolted down the stairs.

"Goodbye," Mary called after him. She grinned at Sparrow. "Wow, he moves fast for an old guy."

"Yeah, like I'm the plague."

Mary shrugged. "Nah, he's just grouchy. He'll like you. Everybody likes you."

"Sure, like my mom."

"Sparrow, your mom's crazy mean."

"And what about this guy?"

"He's Mrs. Washington's brother. He's not going to hurt you. Come on. Let's try and get this place cleaned up." Mary picked up the sacks and set them on the bed

Sparrow stood staring at the striped mattress covering metal springs. She ran her hand down the iron bedstead. Although the room was large, it was bare and reminded her of a prison cell. Mr. Stanley had locked the front door, and she wondered if she could get out without a key. Later, when Mary left, she realized that she could simply unbolt the door from the inside.

Mary's voice penetrated her thoughts. "You make the bed. I'll vacuum."

Sparrow willed her rigid muscles to move. She picked up a sheet, shook it and watched it float down onto the bed. The sound of the vacuum whirred in her head, drowning out her thoughts. Robotically she dusted the scarred furniture and put her meager clothes in the wardrobe, six hangers in all.

Mary made supper, Kraft macaroni and cheese. With an eye to equality, she divided the yellow lumps on mismatched plates and poured two glasses of milk. The smell of pungent cheese joined with the oily scent of Pledge. Sparrow's stomach rebelled. She lifted her fork and impaled three of the slimy objects. Bile rose in her throat, up to her mouth; she ran down the steps to the bathroom and retched into the toilet. Mary brought her a glass of water, moistened a washcloth and wiped her face.

While Sparrow, imprisoned in her fears, lay on the bed, her friend started the dishes. She scraped

Sparrow's dinner into a small bowl to save for lunch the next day. Then, leaning against the counter, she ate a spoonful, and then another and another until it was gone.

When there were no more excuses for staying, Mary went to Sparrow and touched her arm. "Will you be okay?"

Sparrow sat up and lifted the corners of her mouth. "Sure."

"I'll call." Mary walked to the door, turned, raised her hand in the semblance of a wave, turned again and hurried down the stairs.

With great effort, Sparrow went to the window. She watched Mary slide into the car. The door slammed; the car started and sped away. Her friend was gone—just like Rob Roye, the boy she loved.

Hanging onto the rail, she crept down the narrow stairs. The streetlight gave the cavernous shop an eerie look. Books were lined up on the shelves like soldiers waiting for their marching orders. A mouse scurried across the floor, paused and looked at her as though to say, "What are you doing here?" On the used-book table a title caught her eye, *A Tree Grows in Brooklyn*. She dusted it with the tail of her blouse, tucked it under her arm, and took it upstairs. She readied herself for bed, and although it was a warm night, she cocooned herself in the soft blue blanket. Hands cradling the tiny bulge of her stomach, she slept.

Romance at the Drug Store
July 1959

Summer's sun had not yet burned through the gray of the Michigan dawn when Sparrow's family left for Wamplers Lake. Dirt clinging to bare feet, Sparrow Avery stood in the driveway, clutching her faded nightie around her, watching the old Buick pull out of the drive. She waved until she could no longer see eight-year-old Robin or twelve-year-old Jay returning her wave from the back seat. She had difficulty breathing. Putting her hand to her racing heart, she sank down onto the warm earth. Sifting soil through her fingers, she watched the car until it rounded the bend. After a while, she roused herself and went into the house to get ready for her first day of work at the drug store.

For as long as she could remember, each summer the family had spent two weeks at Wamplers Lake. Sparrow looked forward to the vacation, to swimming, building sandcastles and hiking. During those times, when the family lived in a tent, her mother was different. She'd settle herself in a lawn chair, under the shade of a straggly maple, and read romance

11

novels. The children roasted wieners over an open fire or wrapped hamburgers and potatoes in foil and cooked them on the coals. Sparrow played with Robin and Jay, intercepting problems before their mother became involved. Sparrow could pretend that she was a normal girl from a regular family.

This summer, the summer of Sparrow's seventeenth year, she would be working at Milan's drug store. The owner, Mr. Jensen, needed help, and his neighbor, Clare Washington, had recommended one of her students. "She's shy, but bright and a hard worker. Her family's poor. She needs the job."

During the interview the girl had clasped her hands in her lap and studied them. Her voice was almost inaudible; continually he had to ask her to repeat herself. It didn't seem normal that she would be so frightened, but finally she peeked at him with sad brown eyes, and he decided to give her a chance. He hoped that Clare was right and the girl could overcome her shyness.

On her first day, Sparrow worried that Mr. Jensen would notice how shaky she was. Mostly he saw the top of her head and a ponytail drooping down her neck. If she had lifted her head, he could not have seen her eyes for the bangs hiding them. She was a pathetic little creature, in a faded cotton dress, concealing herself behind the counter. Mr. Jensen kept his voice steady as he gave instructions. But Sparrow's heart pounded so loudly that she found it difficult to understand him. Her eyes darted about the store.

The shop was an unimpressive rectangle with the usual sundries: comics, magazines, hair products, greeting cards and a prescription area in the back. Sparrow's job was to keep the store clean, ring up sales and work the soda fountain, a marble-topped counter with four stools. In a fog, moving in slow motion, she washed the counter, then the glasses and placed them on the open shelf. Mr. Jensen, distressed by her discomfort, sequestered himself in the back filling prescriptions. It was a slow day, and she managed to serve a few Cokes and ice cream and to blend a malt without mishap.

In the early afternoon, an overflowing banana split slipped from Sparrow's perspiring hands and clattered to the floor. Stifling a cry she watched as chocolate oozed between the holes in the rubber mat and red-blood strawberry syrup trickled over her white sandals and between her toes. Mr. Jensen walked, with measured nonchalance, from the back of the store.

The druggist spoke softly. "It's okay. These things happen. I'll handle the counter while you clean up."

Sparrow scooped up the ice cream and banana, moved the mat and washed the floor. She scrubbed her sandals, leaving pink cotton-candy splotches on her toes. She wished that like the syrup she could dissolve and run liquid through the holes in the mat. She thought of Robin and Jay at the lake. They would be swimming now. If she were there, she could put her feet in the cool water and be free of the red. She sank to the floor and leaned her head against the cabinet. In her mind's eye she could see her mother standing over her, berating her for her clumsiness. But he's not screaming, she thought. He's not like Mom. He's not going to hit me. She grasped the handle of the cupboard and pulled herself up.

Sparrow had reason to fear her mother, Elvira. The townspeople thought of her as a timid woman, a recluse, who sent her docile husband Oliver to buy groceries and run the family errands. But in the privacy of her home she was a tyrant. A certain look, cocking her head to the right, a twitch of her hand, would send the children scurrying. Sometimes the smack came without warning. Although Sparrow never gave any trouble, her mother acted as though she would. Elvira had been adamant that Sparrow should not stay home alone, but the need for money had won out. "Don't you get into trouble!" she had threatened.

Sparrow's feet felt sticky, toes glued together. Her sandals made a squishing sound on the mat. The door of the drug store seemed to invite her out. She longed to run home and shower, to cleanse herself. But she stayed and went through the motions—pouring cokes, scooping ice-cream.

Shortly before closing Mrs. Washington, hair in an ever-tidy French roll, sleek black dress camouflaging her weight, strode purposefully toward the drug store. A couple of high-school dropouts with greased-back hair and cigarette packs rolled into their T-shirt sleeves were smoking by the entrance.

The teacher cleared her throat. "Good morning, boys."

Instantly at attention, hiding their cigarettes, they responded in unison, "Good morning, Mrs. Washington." Once she'd entered the store, they slouched and resumed their smoking, exhaling smoke rings into the air.

The teacher eased her ample hips onto the tall stool and smiled at Sparrow. "I see you took my advice? Earning some money for college?"

"I don't think I'll be goin', ma'am."

"Why? What are you talking about? I told you that with your grades you can get a full scholarship to a state college."

Hands clutching the rim of the sink, Sparrow studied the bubbles in the water.

Mrs. Washington leaned over the counter. "I could talk to your mom."

Sparrow's head jerked up. "No! No, please don't."

Mrs. Washington nodded. "Not if you don't want me to. But I could tell her what a good student you are, how you're doing such a fine job on the school paper."

"No, ma'am. Please no!

"She doesn't know about your working on the paper?"

"She said I couldn't."

"I didn't know."

Mrs. Washington remembered the conversation she had had with Sparrow early this past year. Impressed by her work, the teacher had asked the girl to stay after class.

"Sparrow, your essay on capital punishment was quite stirring. Your arguments were clear and your examples evocative. You *almost* convinced me that we should abolish the death penalty. Have you ever considered writing for the school newspaper?"

Sparrow held her English book close to her chest. "No, ma'am."

"Would you like to?"

"Can't. I have to go home right after school and help."

"Nonsense." Mrs. Washington explained that the newspaper staff met seventh hour and Sparrow could get home at the usual time.

Sparrow joined the news staff and proved to be a skillful writer and editor. Her essay "Evils of Slavery" won first place in the school competition. Mrs. Washington was fascinated with this silent girl who could write well researched and thoughtful essays. College would give her an opportunity to become an independent and productive young woman, and the teacher was determined to facilitate this transition.

But at the moment, Sparrow seemed to be trying to scrub the C-o-k-e off a glass.

"Well, I see you're busy with the dishes. We can talk about this later. I'll take a nickel Coke."

Deep in thought, Clare Washington sipped her drink. Her brother, Dick, owned the dilapidated house that Sparrow's family lived in. Originally for migrant help, the structure stood next to an abandoned cornfield. Mrs. Washington had told her brother that to rent such a shack was a disgrace; it was the 1950s and no human should live in such abominable, antiquated conditions. There was no indoor toilet and only a makeshift shower in the basement, a primitive wooden platform built over a drain in the dirt floor, with a hose attached to a showerhead. Four rooms comprised the house: kitchen, living room and two bedrooms. During the winter, the house seemed to hibernate. Plastic covered the windows, and bales of straw huddled against the foundation. In summer, it came to life. Birds clustered at feeders that hung precariously from the sunken porch roof; zinnias hugging the foundation added a bit of color to the landscape. To the east of the house, marigolds surrounded a lush vegetable garden. Next to the garden was a clothesline composed of two poles and a wire, where on windy days sheets waved at passing cars.

Mrs. Washington twirled the straw in her drink and gave one last pull on it, producing an unladylike slurp. She smiled more in surprise than embarrassment. Sparrow's lips turned up in something like a smile.

"You think about college. There are ways to do things. You might feel differently after you've worked this summer." Mrs. Washington pivoted off her stool and left the store.

Sparrow rolled her shoulders back and gazed at the ceiling. She picked the dripping dishrag out of the sink, squeezed it, folded it into quarters and methodically scrubbed the spotless gray counter.

A young man entered the store and took a place on a stool. Broad nose, full lips, and round face were incongruent with his gangly body and long neck. Sparrow, head bent, continued rubbing the counter, back and forth, back and forth, in the same spot.

"Are you busy?"

"Oh!" Sparrow dropped the rag into the sink.

"Well?"

Sparrow stared at him.

"Aren't you going to ask me what I want?"

"I'm sorry, what…?"

"I'll have a chocolate shake—chocolate shake—double chocolate."

Sparrow flushed scarlet; her eyes closed. She is seven years old, alone on her way home from school, bundled up in a brown coat, stocking cap covering her eyebrows—frozen in a circle of bullies. Snowballs pelt her face, her bare legs. The boys jeer. *The bird lives in an outhouse, outhouse, outhouse!*

Sparrow hears only the cadence—*outhouse, outhouse, outhouse.*

"Are you all right?"

The scene faded. Sparrow opened her eyes. "Oh… yes, chocolate shake…double chocolate."

With trembling hands, she scooped ice cream into the metal container, squirted the chocolate, poured

17

milk from a bottle labeled "MILAN DAIRY" and hooked the container to the mixer.

The fellow spoke loudly above the noise of the motor. "I didn't mean to scare you."

Sparrow scrubbed the ice cream scoop. "No, you just startled me." She stopped the mixer, poured the shake into a glass and set it and the half-filled container on the counter.

"Now, if I can have a straw I'll be set."

As she handed him the straw, Sparrow dared to look at him. He smiled. "Rob Roye, that's the name."

"Sparrow."

"Neat."

Her eyes smiling, Sparrow touched her parted lips.

The week continued with Rob Roye making a habit of showing up late afternoon and ordering a chocolate shake—double chocolate. Needing an immense amount of space, leaning on the counter, legs extended into the aisle, he created an obstacle to harried customers hurrying through the store. Sparrow expected that at any moment someone would trip and fall. However, in the nick of time, the lanky fellow would yank his legs out of the way and fold them under the counter. Secretly Sparrow called him Ichabod Crane, not because he seemed bizarre to her but because he appeared to be all arms and legs like Ichabod.

Rob was a sophomore at Colorado State University, majoring in business. His home was Englewood, a suburb of Denver. He was easy, talkative and proud to be earning good money. "It's cheaper boarding here in Milan than in Ann Arbor. I can save more for college. My dad's teaching me to refinish the lanes of bowling alleys. It's hard work running that sander, but a lot of money!" His face shone with pleasure. "You got to do it just so. Got to get all the bumps out—clear down to the bare wood. If you don't control it, the sander jumps all over the place and makes grooves and nicks." He flexed his biceps and winked. "No bumps in the lanes."

On his visits to the drug store he gulped his malt, then chatted until Sparrow got busy or until Mr. Jenkins came to check on her. Leaving, he'd grin and say, "See you tomorrow." It was a promise.

Sparrow found herself anticipating Rob Roye's visits and was relieved that he didn't seem to mind her lack of words. Smiling and nodding seemed to be sufficient. She wanted to laugh and talk with him as other girls would. She wished that she could be like Mary, who was always full of clever comments. But when she saw him her heart thumped, her hands shook and her thoughts were jumbled. Alone at night she looked in the mirror, put on a smile and had imaginary conversations with him.

On the fourth day he entered, eyes seeking Sparrow's.

She beamed and said, "Chocolate shake—double chocolate?"

"Thought you'd never ask!"

Sparrow giggled. "How's the sanding going?"

Later that week, after a rush at the soda counter, Sparrow was washing glasses, swishing them one by one through the soapy water. Her feet were firmly planted and her hands steady. She was humming softly and thinking of Rob Roye.

Mary sauntered in and perched on the stool directly in front of Sparrow. Mary leaned across the counter. "Okay, so what's going on? Who's the guy?"

Sparrow pushed a sopping dish rag over the counter in front of Mary. "What guy?"

"The guy I just saw leaving. Hey, you're splashing me!"

"Oh, sorry." Sparrow grabbed a towel and dried the counter.

Mary took the towel from her and made a show of wiping her arms. "So, you've been avoiding me. Your folks go on vacation, and you finally get some freedom, and we could hang out, go to a movie, but by the time I get off work, you've left the drug store. You don't have a phone, and somebody tells me you're hanging out with a guy."

"I'm sorry. I didn't think...I didn't know."

Mary sighed. "Oh, I was only teasing. You take everything so seriously. I think it's great. Who'd of thought—you taking up with some strange guy."

Sparrow grimaced. Her mother would be enraged if she knew. She wondered if Mary was mad at her. "He's not so strange. He's real nice, and I think he likes me."

"Course he does. Everybody likes you."

Sparrow pursed her lips. Perhaps Mary wasn't angry with her.

"You just think people don't like you." Mary smiled. "Calls for a celebration. Make me a turtle."

Sparrow filled a tulip glass to the brim with vanilla ice cream, chocolate, butterscotch and peanuts. She squirted a mountain of whipped cream on top and added three maraschino cherries. Mary dug in. Sparrow sipped a Coke.

"He's gentle-like, cute." Sparrow giggled. "He's all arms and legs. Reminds me of Ichabod Crane. That's what I call him, but not to his face. We don't do that much. We go to the Dairy Barn and get a shake and burger, drive around, talk, and he takes me home."

"Well, he'd better treat you right, or he'll answer to me."

"Yeah, what would you do? Hit him with your lunch pail?"

"No, I don't need a lunch pail. I can handle Ichabod."

Mary had been a tomboy and could terrorize the boys. In third grade a bully had made the mistake of calling her "Fatso." The altercation culminated in his running for cover. In fourth grade she came upon a group of boys taunting Sparrow. She ran them down and flung her lunch pail at the ringleader, hitting him just above his eye. The cut had been deep and required stitches. Although the boys had been the instigators, it was Mary who had had to stay after school.

This incident cemented the girls' friendship. They were inseparable at school, and on rare occasions Sparrow was allowed to play at Mary's house. Mary, however, had never set foot inside Sparrow's. Still, it was not a one-sided friendship. Mary, who was the editor for the school paper, had been delighted when Sparrow joined the staff.

"Has he kissed you?" Mary asked.

Sparrow blushed.

"Ooh, go Sparrow. It's about time you had some fun. Too bad your folks will be home in a few days." As she pointed the long-handled spoon to emphasize her point, peanuts, chocolate, and whipped cream dripped onto the counter.

Sparrow handed her the dishrag.

Raising Dust
October 1959

*A*fter leaving the girl and her friend, Dave paced down the street. "Damn it! What has Clare talked me into?" His words floated along the empty street. He missed Emily; he needed to talk with her. There'd been a frost the previous night; the wind had picked up and newly fallen leaves seemed meant to torment him as they swirled about his feet. At home the red maple was shedding its splendor. Kicking leaves strewn on the path, he walked toward the house. He did not need that girl complicating his life. Why, she could run off with the till. Not that there was much to run off with, but he should have locked up the cash. No, she was not a threat in that way. She was just a kid, having a kid. She'd be terrified to stay in the shop alone, and she didn't have his phone number. He'd probably find her all in a heap tomorrow.

Dave preheated the oven, popped in a frozen potpie and sat down in his recliner, surrounded by newspapers and books. Well, they'd just have to let her in that home for unwed mothers. That's where she should go. He'd tell her in the morning, and that giant of a friend, or better yet Clare, could come and get her. Resolved, he laid his head back on the cushion, closed his eyes, and dozed.

He felt a warmth on his shoulder, and in his mind's eye he saw Emily, not the Emily at her death, gray and shriveled, but the girl of her youth. *Dave.* Her voice was soft. *Think about this. Remember when we were courting? President Wilson had just gotten us into the First World War. You were working your way through college. I was about Sparrow's age, just graduating from high school.*

"What's that got to do with anything?"

You signed up, left me, shipped out.

"Oh, Emily, don't…"

Zinggggg, zingggg, zingggg! He bolted upright, rushed to the kitchen and yanked the towel from the hook, which came loose, fell, bounced and skittered across the floor. When he grabbed the potpie, the end of the towel grazed the flame and ignited. "Ouch!" He dropped the burning towel. Cursing, he stomped out the flame. "Of all the stupid…!"

He threw the towel into the trash and glared at the pie sitting upright on the floor. This time, he took a hot pad from the drawer, picked up the pie, dumped it onto a plate and sat at the kitchen table. Fork poised, he watched as gravy oozed across the daisies on the plate. After what seemed a long time, he laid his fork on the table and shoved the pie away.

In bed, Dave tossed and turned. Rising early, he left his comforter in a tangle and waded through dirty sheets and clothes that lay crumpled in the corner. He looked in the closet, then shrugged and donned yesterday's clothes. Better not let Clare see this, he thought. In the kitchen, he stepped in the ashes of the towel, leaving a trail of black. He gulped a bowl of Grape Nuts and left his bowl, half filled with milk, on the counter. He wanted to get to Booknook by eight, brew some coffee and prepare for the confrontation.

Hoping the cool fall air would clear his head, Dave walked to work, past modest homes on Winter Street, across the busy intersection and down the block to the corner of Maumee and Winter. He stood in front of Booknook for a moment and braced himself. He unlocked and opened the door. Smoke filled his eyes and nostrils. His mind raced. No, wait, it didn't smell like smoke. He looked up toward the apartment, and a cloud of dust settled on his face.

He coughed. "What the hell is going on here?"

The girl was sweeping the dust off the tallest bookshelf, brandishing a feather duster with one hand, clinging to the rickety old ladder with the other. This was no small feat, as the shelves were built nearly to the ten-foot ceiling. She whirled to face him and lost her grip. Dave, with a speed that he would later marvel at, rushed over and steadied the ladder. Recovering her balance, she stepped down.

Dave removed his dusty glasses and shook them at her. "What in tarnation are you doing up there? What's all this mess?"

The color drained from Sparrow's face. She retreated to the opposite side of the ladder, keeping it between them. "I'm sorry. I couldn't find the vacuum."

"The vacuum? What are you talking about?"

"To clean, so's not to raise the dust." Although Sparrow's feet were on the floor, she clung to the ladder.

"I didn't tell you to clean!" Dave wiped his glasses on the tail of his shirt.

Sparrow looked directly at him. "I'm supposed to clean."

"Says who?"

"Mrs. Washington said you needed help."

"She did, did she? Well, this is my place, not hers. I run it my way."

"I'm sorry Mr. Stanley." Her eyes pleaded.

Dave wondered if she thought he might hit her. "Dirt never hurt anyone as long as it stays put. You're just swishing it around. This ladder's got a loose hinge, and you shouldn't be up on it in the first place, young lady! Especially in…in your…"

"I'm sorry. I couldn't find the vacuum."

"Quit saying I'm sorry. Couldn't find it 'cause it quit and I tossed it." Dave paused. Truth be known, she'd given him quite a scare, swaying up there on that shaky ladder. "Okay, so how am I going to open the store with all this filth? Can hardly breathe."

"You said Booknook opens at ten. It's just eight. I meant to have part of it done and aired by the time you got here."

Dave took a good look at the girl. She was wearing a pair of faded jeans, with a white T-shirt stretched across the acorn of her tummy. A triangular scarf tied at the back of her neck held her hair; he could actually see her pinched face. Pretty scrawny, he thought.

He relented. "Oh, well, then do it, but just do what you can reach and stay off the ladder. I'm going to make coffee, read the paper. I like a little peace and quiet in the morning."

"Coffee should be done."

"You made coffee?"

"Yes, sir. Mrs. Washington said you like it first thing."

"Damn, what else did Mrs. Washington tell you about me?" Dave banged the ladder together and carried it down the narrow aisle, the loose hinge dangling like a disconnected limb.

Dave sat at the old round oak table, holding his cup in both hands, the pungent aroma filling his nostrils. It smelled good. It did not occur to him that Sparrow had scrubbed the scum out of the pot before brewing the coffee. The *Detroit Free Press* lay unopened on the table. He watched as the girl used a damp rag to dust the lower shelves. Standing on tiptoe, she wiped the backs of the books and then the lip of the ledge. He didn't know that, had time permitted, she would have taken the books out and scrubbed each shelf.

The air was beginning to clear. It was 9:50. The girl spoke. "Can I keep cleaning, or do you want me to stop when you open?"

"Suit yourself." Dave folded the paper and went to unlock the door.

Late morning Sparrow approached Dave and thrust a piece of paper at him. "What's this?" he asked as he took it.

Sparrow cleared her throat. "Cleaning supplies. We need cleaning supplies."

"What do you think I am, a delivery service?"

Sparrow pivoted and hurried away, but not before he saw the look of terror in her eyes. "Oh, okay," he grumbled. Unable to bear her presence for a moment longer, he left immediately for the grocery.

An hour later Dave returned with Murphy's Oil soap, Spic and Span, Ajax and vinegar. He had also picked up a few things for her, peanut butter, bread, eggs, milk and hamburger. He supposed she had to eat.

Sparrow spent the afternoon washing the grime off the windows with vinegar and hot water. Dave walked to Ace Hardware and bought a hinge to repair the ladder. While at Ace, he looked at the vacuums, but was in no mood to buy one. After thinking it over, that evening he drove back and purchased a Hoover upright and a small Hoover canister with long cleaning tools. The canister would be good to get the high shelves. If the girl was to give the place a good cleaning, she needed the right equipment.

On Tuesday afternoon, Dave finished his crossword puzzle in the *Free Press* and picked up the *Telegram* from the front sidewalk. "Wonder what nonsense they're writing about now."

Sparrow, on her knees scrubbing the mopboard, glanced up.

Dave thought, I can't even talk to myself anymore without that girl looking at me like I'm strange. Irritated, he flipped through the paper. Page 5. "How Salvation Army Helps," he said. Damned if he'd quit talking to himself just 'cause she was there. "So, they're starting the United Fund Drive. Every year they want more. Used to be, people took care of themselves." He read again. "Unwed Mothers Are Aided."

Dave continued to read to himself. The Salvation Army had a home in Detroit where unwed mothers could live, and there was a hospital where they could give birth. Good, but there was a catch. The home would only take expectant mothers when they were seven months along. No way was the girl going to stay here that long. One week—that was it. In the article a girl was interviewed. At the home she'd received counseling about keeping or giving up the baby. Since she was seventeen and had no way to support a baby, she chose to give it up. One statement gave him pause. "In Detroit I was just another girl waiting to have a baby." Dave wondered what that meant. Was the home like a factory churning out babies, or did being unknown lessen her shame?

Dave circled the article and walked over to Sparrow. "I think you should read this." He tossed the paper on the table. "I'm going home."

Sparrow sat back on her haunches and watched as Mr. Stanley locked the door and left the shop. Shoulders bent, head down, uncut hair fluttering in the wind, he strode down the sidewalk.

The water in the bucket had cooled. Her back ached, and her legs had gone to sleep. She was besieged by grimy, oversized, old-fashioned molding that wrapped around the floor, the doors and the windows. As she dumped the filthy water, she inhaled the scent of Murphy's Oil Soap, a smell she usually thought of as fresh and mellow. This time she gagged and retched into the toilet.

After rinsing her mouth, she sat at the table, took off her oxfords and massaged her swollen feet. She was frightened, alone in this strange place. But the books were comforting. At home her trips to the library had been few and far between. Her mother had criticized her mightily for sticking her nose in a book, for neglecting her work. Here, after Mr. Stanley had gone home, Sparrow had all the books she could ever read. She could shut out her own thoughts and live in the book. And at the moment she was thinking about the girl in *A Tree Grows in Brooklyn*. She was wondering how she was making out in her new school, the one where the teachers were kind.

As her last duty of the day, Sparrow picked up the paper to read the article. Words swam in her head: *unwed mothers...home in Detroit...chose to give up my baby.*

She could not grasp the meaning. She didn't feel well, needed to rest, to get something to eat. She dumped the paper in the trash and dragged herself up the stairs. After supper she would read more in the book, maybe finish it.

But later Sparrow couldn't concentrate. She could not get Rob Roye out of her mind. She pictured the two of them walking down Main Street hand in hand, he shortening his steps, she lengthening hers.

His touch had awakened an insatiable longing. She had wanted to stay in his arms forever, to meld with him. She had tried to form the word "no." But she had had no breath, no will. And now, he was gone... disappeared, leaving only memories—memories that she must banish if she was to survive. But her body kept remembering.

The week passed with Sparrow vacuuming, dusting and mopping. When she was not cleaning, she kept out of the way. For his part, Dave Stanley skulked around the shop, resenting her presence, thinking she should say something, thankful that she didn't.

A Change of Plans

*C*lare Washington breezed into Booknook; luxuriant hair, liberated from its French roll, flowed down her shoulders. Filling the narrow aisle, bigger than life, she looked right and left, up and down, her eyes following the line of bookshelves. Checking for dust, she picked up a book and ran her fingers over its cover. She grinned at her brother. "What a transformation! The place is clean. The windows sparkle."

Dave, sitting at the table eating tuna out of a can, did not respond.

"Say hello, David."

He took a bite. "Aren't you supposed to be teaching school?"

"No, it's Saturday." She poured a cup of coffee and sat down.

"You come to get her?" He scraped the last bit of tuna from the can.

"Not exactly. I've come to see how it's going."

Dave slammed the can on the table. "It's time for her to *go!* You said a week."

As though he were one of her slow students, Clare responded with exaggerated patience. "Yes, I did….

31

But there are complications. The home will make an exception in her case, but there aren't any openings, not for a month. And she can't go back to Milan. Her parents won't have her, and even if they would, everyone would know. She's fragile. It would be too humiliating for her."

Dave glowered. "If she stays here, people won't know she's pregnant? Milan's only forty-five minutes away. She can't hide here." He tossed the tuna can into the wastebasket.

"She's not showing yet. We can just say she's working for you. Look at this place!" Clare pointed to the shelves. "It hasn't looked this good since Emily got sick. I told you Sparrow was a hard worker…. Dave, please. In a month she can go to the home."

"She hardly talks. She does what I tell her to do and then scuttles away. She nearly fell off the ladder the first day." His eyes met Clare's. "I can't be responsible for her! What if something happens to her?"

"Oh, Dave. Nothing's going to happen in a month. She'll only be four months along. You just can't send her away."

"But the store's not bringing in enough. I don't have money to be paying anyone!"

"Money isn't the problem. It's you. You're withdrawn, reclusive! Can't you think of someone else for a change?"

"So, you think I'm a selfish S.O.B."

Clare smiled. "You have been acting like one." She reached for his hand. Her voice softened. "It's more than a year. You've pushed everybody away. You've got to get out of yourself. You can help this girl."

Dave did not recoil. Instead, he seemed to study Clare's plump, smooth hand. At last he sighed.

"Perhaps you're right." He managed a lopsided grin. "But it does feel like another one of your messes."

Dave remembered when Clare was born. He had been a teen, just beginning to lust after girls and well aware of the possible consequences if his passion should get out of control. Then his mother turned up pregnant. There she was at his basketball games, with her belly sticking out, a billboard, advertising what she and his dad had been up to! Reluctantly, Dave went to the hospital to see the baby. His mom, weary but triumphant, held this little doll with a tiny face and a head full of black hair. He pulled back the bunting to have a look and opened her hand. Miniscule fingers curled around his. He was smitten.

Occasionally, when the baby cried at two a.m., Dave's mother would be slow to wake, and Dave would bolt out of bed. By the time she reached the room, he would be rocking the baby. After his mother heated the bottle, it was he who fed Clare. Dave adored her, played and tussled with her. She grew into a bright, headstrong girl, and when she became an adolescent, he had advocated for her with their parents.

Clare took a sip of coffee. "So, you'll let her stay the month."

That week, whenever there were no customers in the store, Dave spent much of his time sitting at the table, the crossword puzzle laid out before him. Sparrow, ever watchful for any sign of reproach, continued her cleaning: vacuuming, removing and dusting books, scrubbing shelves and polishing tables. Dave had forbidden her to clean the highest shelves. However, he suspected that she was doing it in the evening after he left.

On Friday morning Dave found the girl pulling junk out of the storage room under the stairs. "What are you up to now?"

Sparrow stammered. "I've, I've pretty well cleaned the store, and, and I thought I could tidy this up."

Dave put his hands on his hips. "Just like a woman. You clean just to mess things up again."

Head bent, hair hiding her face, Sparrow stood mute. Like a puppy, Dave thought. Like a puppy that's been caught in the act.

Indeed the area was a mess. There were stacks of old newspapers and magazines, damaged books, a box of old and broken tools, a sewing machine with a box of fabric and a wicker baby bassinette containing shirt boxes.

Dave took a long slow breath. "As long as it's out, we might as well sort it."

He squatted and began to go through the box of tools. As he recognized the castoffs, his anger abated. "I always wondered where this wrench went, and there's my old hammer." For several moments he was lost in memories. He picked up the heavy box and tried to hoist himself up. Grimacing, he dropped the box, just missing his foot.

"Damn it, I think I've knocked my knee out of joint." Shifting his weight to the right leg, he stood up, hobbled to a nearby chair and plopped down. He sat for some time, with Sparrow staring at him wide-eyed. Then he stood, easing his weight onto his right leg, and inched his way to a chair by the table.

"Well, don't just stand there. Go get me some ice."

Sparrow hurried to the refrigerator, took out a tray of ice, thumped it on the table and wrapped the cubes in a dishtowel. Dave jerked it out of her hand and applied it to his knee. Sparrow hovered over him. The doorbell jingled. A teenage boy stood at the entrance. Sparrow started toward the boy, then turned and looked inquiringly at Dave.

The boy hollered, "Anyone here?"

Dave tried to rise, moaned and clutched his knee. He nodded to Sparrow.

Sparrow walked to the front of the store. Her voice clear, she spoke. "May I help you with something?"

Five minutes later Sparrow was ringing up the sale. She placed a bookmark in the novel and put it in a bag. "Thank you. Come back soon."

Her face a mask, she crept back to Dave. "Is there anything I can do for you?"

"How'd you know to do that, run the register?" Dave wondered more how she had managed to speak to the customer.

"I worked at the drugstore this summer. And I've watched you do it."

Dave had not simply knocked his knee out of joint. Years of basketball and walking had taken their toll; he'd torn his meniscus. Dr. Bentz recommended surgery. She explained that cutting away the torn part of the meniscus would be a straightforward procedure, with a quick recovery. If he chose against that and relied on physical therapy, the knee could mend itself, but it might take months, rather than weeks, to heal. She added that older people were slower to recover.

Dave's hand sliced the air, then dropped to his knee. "So, a young punk gets to keep his meniscus, and an old codger gets to walk around with no glider on his knee, just bone on bone. No thanks, I'll go to physical therapy."

Settling In

Sitting in his chair, leg propped on the hassock, Dave had been arguing with Clare for an hour. She told him that although he could get around on crutches, he couldn't possibly run Booknook by himself. He was just being obstinate and endangering his health. Sparrow needed a place to live for the next few months, and Dave needed help. The girl was a godsend. She'd proved that she was responsible. In fact, she was in charge of the shop right now while they were talking and drinking coffee. Dave blustered, but in the end capitulated. Sparrow could stay till he got on his feet. Then she would have to go to the home.

The two settled into a routine. Each morning, greeted by the aroma of fresh-perked coffee, Dave hobbled into Booknook with his newspaper. He nodded and sat down to read, ever watchful, as the girl swept or dusted. At ten Sparrow unlocked the door, stationed herself nearby and greeted customers as they trickled in. When there were questions she couldn't answer, she walked to the table and asked Dave, her voice no more than a whisper. Their language was gestures and brief staccato sentences, limited to what was to be done and how to do it. At noon, Sparrow went upstairs to have lunch while Dave ate a can of tuna or Campbell's soup at the table. If the bell jangled, Sparrow ran down the stairs to wait on the customer. Dave gave Sparrow a small stipend and drove her to Kroger weekly to buy groceries.

As she had always done, Sparrow survived her days by living in her fantasies, while her body, separate from her inner self, performed the required tasks. She longed for the late afternoons, when Dave locked the door and limped out to his pickup, leaving her with a wealth of books, stories that filled the space in her desolate being. Within the month she had completed Jane Austen's novels and started on Willa Cather's.

Saturdays, if Mary had gas in her car, she drove to Adrian and the two friends ate lunch at A&W. Mouth dripping with catsup, using dramatic gestures, Mary tried to amuse Sparrow with the happenings at Milan High. Sparrow nibbled on a burger and feigned interest. It was difficult for her to wrap her mind around the words; nevertheless, it was reassuring sitting next to Mary, watching her smile and gesture. Sometimes Mary would clap Sparrow on the shoulder, and the touch felt warm. When Mary tried to hug her goodbye, Sparrow turned away, not because she didn't want to be hugged, but because the touch was gone too quickly and left her feeling more empty and alone.

Sundays Sparrow did her laundry in the bathtub and hung the clothes on a rope across the kitchen area. If it was a nice day, not too cold, she walked three blocks to Comstock Park, a small square with grass and trees. She sat on a bench and tried to read, but instead watched the neighborhood children play. Her heart ached to be with Robin and Jay, but her mother would not allow them to visit.

Dave had been unable to part with Emily's belongings. Her citrus cologne still stood on the dresser next to his keys. When he was bereft, he would creep into the bedroom, caress her cashmere sweater, the one she did not send to the cleaners often, bury his face in it, and inhale her lingering woodsy scent. Having her clothes in the closet, her bathrobe on the hook, and her slippers under the bed consoled him. He felt her presence, as though any moment she might come walking out of the bathroom in her robe. The thought of purging the house of her was wrenching. He could not bear the thought of some bargain-hunting woman walking into Booknook wearing one of Emily's sweaters.

Clare complained that Dave's house was filthy, that he needed to pack up and dispose of Emily's belongings. She knew it was hard for him, but Sparrow could help. He grumbled that he didn't want *anyone* messing with his stuff, but Clare persisted.

With trepidation disguised as bad humor, Dave allowed the girl to clean his house and, finally, to empty Emily's closet. He watched as Sparrow stroked the fox collar of his wife's good black coat, folded it, and put it into a garbage bag for the Goodwill. He knew Sparrow needed clothes, a coat, but he didn't think he could bear to see Emily's belongings on her. But through his pain Dave could hear his wife cajoling him. *You're just being silly. I'm dead. Let me go. You give that girl anything she needs. Put my clothes to some good use. You know how I hate to waste anything.*

Dave said, "Okay, you win."
Sparrow looked up. "What?"

"Nothing." Dave took the coat out of the bag. "Can you use this…? Might as well go through this stuff and see if there's anything you need. I think you're about her size."

Sparrow hesitated. She had few clothes and they were getting snug. Although she ate little, she thought she was gaining weight, especially around her middle. "Oh, thank you. I can alter them if they don't fit." Smiling, she reached into the bag.

"Take your time." Dave left the room.

The clock ticked out the minutes as Sparrow sorted through the garments, laying them out, touching them. She took only the most necessary items—a couple of skirts, several blouses, a dress, a sweater, jacket, and the coat. She carefully folded and replaced the remaining clothes in the bag.

That night Dave took the bottle of cologne and buried it in the back of his drawer behind the underwear. He closed the closet door, went into the living room, and sat in the dark. When the clock struck eleven, he dragged himself to bed. In the morning he wakened thinking of Sparrow. Although he wondered which of Emily's outfits she might be wearing, he told himself it did not matter. They were just clothes. On arriving at the store, he was puzzled to see her in a tailored blue shirt over an ankle-length brown skirt, the shirt looking vaguely familiar. When he commented on it, Sparrow responded that it must be one of his discarded dress shirts.

She smiled. "I used the old Singer to even the hem and shorten the sleeves. Do you like it?"

Dave was stabbed with a memory, a memory from his youth long kept under wraps. "*No, not that shirt!*" Sparrow was wearing *his* shirt, the one that Emily had worn to cover *her* tiny bump. She had not yet needed such a shirt, and they had joked about her wearing it. She had worn it the night he took her to the hospital. Afterwards she washed it. And it hung useless in the closet for many years.

Sparrow stood riveted to the spot, tears welling in her eyes.

Dave heard Emily's voice. *Calm down. She doesn't know. It was thirty-seven years ago.*

Christmas Surprise

*T*he days grew colder. Wind blew leaves down Maumee Street, piling them against doors. The snow came. There was no talk of Sparrow's leaving. She was like a ragged old slipper, useful, demanding nothing. Thus, Dave managed to tolerate her presence. Alone at home in the ease of his stuffed chair with his leg resting on the hassock, Dave thought that if Emily were still alive she would be pleased with his tolerance toward the girl.

One day early in December, it snowed six inches. Dave, irritated with his crutches, had tossed them prematurely. Now he dreaded shoveling the walk. He was concerned that he couldn't support himself on his good leg and still have enough leverage to lift the heavy snow and toss it to the side of the street. When he arrived at Booknook, he was relieved to see that the walk was free of snow and wondered which of Emily's friends had cleared it. Inside the store, cheeks and hands crimson with cold, Sparrow was unbuttoning Emily's coat.

Dave's pleasure vanished. He pulled off his gloves and waved them at her. "You can't be shoveling in your condition."

Sparrow stood her ground. "I can! I just did. You can't be shoveling in your condition. You can barely walk."

Dave's face turned as bright as Sparrow's. "I am not a doddering old man. I'm not helpless."

Sparrow straightened her shoulders. "And I am not helpless! I'm just trying to earn my keep."

Dave raised his arms in surrender. "Okay, okay, you're right," he mumbled. And then more clearly, "You're one spunky girl."

Sparrow giggled, a sound as clear as a tinkling bell. The two laughed, Dave steadying himself on the shovel, Sparrow secure in Emily's warm coat.

Christmas dawned crisp and white. The tree outside Booknook glistened; snow dusted the sidewalk. Sparrow had anticipated dinner at Mrs. Washington's for weeks. She'd sewn herself a new black skirt with an over-blouse that camouflaged the bulge of her tummy. Still, it had been difficult for her to dress; her hands were all fumbles and her hair had a mind of its own. Sitting next to Mr. Stanley in the pickup, her hands and feet icy cold, she could feel her heart beating. Milan seemed a different life, a distant country.

A memory pierced through the cloud of Sparrow's mind. She was in her yard, her meager belongings strewn around her feet. Elvira barring the door, screaming "You will not bring shame on this family. You're no daughter of mine. Don't you ever come back!"

Digging her thumbnail into her palm until she could feel pain, Sparrow attempted to dispel the memory. Her mother would not know she was in Milan; she was safe with Mr. Stanley and Mrs. Washington. Although she longed to see her brother and sister, she would never risk an encounter with her mother. Tears in her eyes, she could not see the deserted road, the cloud-white fields, or the farmhouses with sparkling Christmas lights.

Dave glanced at Sparrow. His voice was gruff. "Be just the three of us today. It's different since Sam's been gone." He couldn't mention Emily's absence.

"Sam?"

"Samuel, Clare's husband, dead five years."

"Oh?"

"Heart attack—no warning, just driving down the road."

"Really?" Sparrow studied Dave's veined hands resting on the wheel.

"He was forty-five, hardly middle-aged. Good thing they didn't have kids. Clare would be raising them alone. It's a hard thing to raise a kid by yourself."

Sparrow stared out the window.

Clare greeted Dave and Sparrow in a low-cut, full-length black velvet dress with heavy silver chains enhancing the neckline. Silver hoops dangled from her ears. The tree, its angel reaching for the ceiling, glittered with lights; the fire blazed warmth. Hot cider, a cheese ball and crackers sat on the counter. The rich smell of roasted turkey permeated the air. The table was set with china and crystal. Hungry-eyed, the girl devoured the room. After Clare took her coat, Sparrow remained immobile, eyes transfixed by the fire.

At dinner Sparrow sat erect, taking one sliver of turkey, a dainty scoop of potatoes with a smidgen of gravy and a small helping of stuffing. She forked a tiny bite of turkey, then put it back on her plate. Her hand trembled when she raised her glass; she set it back on the table. Attempting to put the girl at ease, Clare chattered softly. Oblivious to Sparrow's unease, Dave heaped his plate to overflowing and dug in.

Finally, Clare could stand it no longer. "You don't like the food, Sparrow?"

The girl looked guiltily at her untouched plate. "Oh, yes!"

"Are you feeling ill, nauseous?"

"Oh, no! It's just so elegant, with all the china and crystal, and the food is so pretty. It's like in the movies." She pointed to the casserole covered with melted marshmallows. "That must be sweet potatoes. I can tell by the smell. At home we just have them in their jackets."

Clare patted her arm. "Hmm, okay. Well, you're a part of this movie, so let me help you to some." Clare put a big dollop of the casserole on Sparrow's plate.

Sparrow managed a few bites. Although the sweet potatoes slid down her throat, they seemed candy-sweet and her stomach rebelled. She tried the turkey but it stuck in her throat. She thought that if she could be alone, in the privacy of her apartment, perhaps she could relax and eat.

After Clare and Dave had finished, Sparrow helped clear the table, reluctantly scraping delicious morsels from her plate into the garbage. Now that the opportunity to eat was gone, she was famished.

When the kitchen was in order, Clare announced it was time to open gifts. Dave went out to the pickup and returned with a finely knit black woolen cap and matching mittens, tags dangling. He thrust them at Sparrow.

"They're so soft," she said, holding them to her cheek.

Dave turned away. "Need something warm when you shovel."

Sparrow had made Dave handkerchiefs out of old white shirts and Clare a scarf from some of the calico in the box from under the stairs. Clare gave Sparrow a gift certificate to Klein's and a very small box.

Careful not to tear the paper, Sparrow removed the scotch tape. "Oh, the box is so pretty."

Clare chuckled. "Why don't you open it?"

Sparrow snapped the lid open and took out a delicate pendent on a sterling silver chain.

"Do you like it?" asked Clare. "We can exchange it if you don't."

Sparrow smiled. "It's like the stone you wear."

"Yes, it's onyx."

Sparrow's eyes shone. "Thank you…I never thought…."The bell rang.

"I wonder who that could be?" asked Clare, as she went to open the door.

Robin and Jay rushed in. Robin lunged for Sparrow, knocking her backward. Jay caught her, and the three clung together.

"How…how did you get here? Did Mom let you come?" asked Sparrow.

"No way," said Robin. "Mrs. Washington told Jay you'd be here, and we begged Mom to let us go for a walk."

"Oh," said Sparrow, "I don't want you to get into trouble."

"We'll be careful. We just had to see you."

Clare ushered the siblings into the den, where they could visit undisturbed. Their voices and laughter reverberated through the house. Later they feasted on cookies and milk in the living room. Robin and Jay were fascinated with the white-haired man who said little, but matched them cookie for cookie. Sparrow settled back onto the couch, her face open, eyes shining. She too ate cookies—biting off the snowman's head, dusting the crumbs from her dress onto a napkin, careful not to get them on the cream-colored carpet.

Intrusion
February 1960

*F*or Sparrow, Christmas day had been a fantasy. She had been transported to a storybook world, filled with beautiful things, delicious food, gifts and laughter. She had seen her siblings! Her body had been aquiver, threatening to betray her with uncontrollable giggles and tears. The experience depleted her. Exhausted, she returned to the solace of Booknook.

The winter passed with Dave and Sparrow sharing the work and the shoveling. Dave continued with physical therapy and his knee grew stronger. Sparrow's stomach spread little; her cheeks were hollow; her arms and legs sticks. She seldom saw Mary. The heater in Mary's convertible did not work well, and her father only allowed her to come to Adrian when the temperature was above thirty and the roads clear. Sparrow was left with quiet days and endless nights. She kept reality at bay by living in books. When she was not reading, the stories continued to play out in her mind. She was in awe of Daisy Miller, Henry James's heroine. Daisy, although innocent, lived her life as she wanted, with no social constraints. But in the end, it was this lack of regard for rules that caused Daisy's death.

Visits from Clare brought energy and dissent to the bookstore. She breezed in with brownies or cookies. The three sat at the table, Dave and Clare enjoying the dessert, Clare urging Sparrow to eat. The girl would take a few nibbles, then discreetly wrap the treat in a napkin and put it in her lap, telling herself she'd have it later when she was alone in the apartment. Clare would ask Sparrow how she was feeling. Sparrow would say "Fine." When Clare asked what her plans were after the delivery, Sparrow seemed not to understand. It was as though Clare was speaking a foreign language that could not be translated.

Late February, Clare declared that something had to be done. "You are due in April. You've got to decide what to do about this baby. I'm calling Catholic Social Services."

Sparrow's chair scraped across the floor. Her cookie fell from her lap and crumbled on the floor. Rigid, she turned and walked up the stairs to the apartment.

Clare threw up her arms in exasperation. "What is the matter with that girl?" She glared at Dave, and stalked out of the store.

Dave picked up the cookie and threw it into the wastebasket.

Upstairs, Sparrow lay on the bed, holding her swollen belly. She had tried to make it go away. She had eaten little and worn tight jeans to hold it in, but it just gurgled and thumped and got bigger. Now Clare was angry with her.

In March, the social worker, Miss Dunston, came to interview Sparrow. The two retired to the privacy of the apartment. Dave found himself standing at the bottom of the stairs, wondering what they were saying, but he heard nothing, not even the rise and fall of voices. When the woman left, Sparrow was pale and withdrawn. She did not speak, and Dave could not ask.

The snow gave way to the warmth of spring. Daffodils passed their bloom and tulips poked through the earth. Robins came to mate and rear their young. Dave's knee, although tender, was much better and he walked to Booknook, enjoying the budding of the trees, the birds' chirping — all the signs of new life. It reminded him that Sparrow's time was near, that although her stomach was round as a melon, a very small melon, and her step heavy, she did not acknowledge her approaching delivery.

At the door Sparrow greeted him with her forced, turned-up-lip smile. "Good morning, Mr. Stanley."

"Sparrow, it's beautiful out there. You've got to get out, get some exercise, build up your strength." Dave took a deep breath. "You've just got a couple of weeks left."

Sparrow gasped.

Dave forged ahead. "Is your mom coming?"

Sparrow looked at him numbly.

"The social worker from Catholic Social Services — is she going to take the baby from the hospital?"

The words found their mark, but not in the way Dave had intended. Sparrow heard the accusing voice of her mother and flushed with shame.

Dave touched her shoulder; she flinched.

He stepped back. "Well, you have to make some plans."

Sparrow shook her head.

Dave made his voice softer. "Will you call me if something happens?"

Birth Day
April 15, 1960

Sparrow's stomach had ached the entire day, the cramps coming and going at random. Now her back was sore. As she struggled into Emily's oversized nightgown, she glimpsed her swollen belly in the mirror. She eased into the bed, pulled the quilt under her chin and fell into an uneasy sleep. Awakened by throbbing in her abdomen, she wondered if she was constipated. Grasping the handrail, she made her way downstairs. On the toilet, pain exploded in her stomach and surged up her back. She groaned and pushed, but could not rid herself of the foulness. At last the pain abated. She sat panting for several minutes. Nauseous, she gulped for air and retched into the sink. Water streamed down her legs. She stumbled to the phone and dialed.

Dave shook himself from sleep and reached for the ringing phone. "Yeah."

"Mr. Stanley....I think I'm sick," Sparrow whispered.

Dave snatched up his trousers and put them on over his pajamas. His slippers were next to the bed, jacket on the doorknob. He grabbed the keys from the dresser. Disregarding the residual tenderness in his knee, he ran to the pickup and sped to Booknook.

Sparrow, in her nightgown, hair tangled from sleep, leaned against the door clutching her bulging stomach. Dave stripped off his jacket, put it around her shoulders, and half carried her to the pickup, her bare feet stumbling over the cement.

At Bixby Hospital, a white-coated young man appeared with a wheelchair and whisked Sparrow through the emergency room to the maternity ward. Dave's hands shook as he filled out the paperwork. Promptly escorted into the labor room, he was both relieved and anxious. He needed to know that she was being cared for, but did not know if he could bear to see her pain and fright. She lay mute and ashen on the white sheet. Tentatively, he reached for her small, cold hand and held it in his warm one.

When the contractions came, Sparrow closed her eyes and gripped his hand. Dave mopped her forehead with a damp rag and gave her ice to suck. She looked at him with her pleading puppy eyes, as if to ask, What's happening to me? But because she could not speak, he could not answer.

Through a mist of pain and confusion, Sparrow could see white-uniformed people. Someone pressed on her stomach and put his hands between her legs. Mr. Stanley sat beside her, his wavy white hair tousled, pajama collar turned in, deep circles under his eyes.

"I'm sorry. I peed myself."

Dave wiped the perspiration from her face. "No, your water broke. That's what happens when you have a baby."

The nurse's voice rang out. "She's fully dilated. Get her to delivery. Get the doctor!"

Although she struggled against it, Sparrow's legs were opened and shoved into stirrups. Light blazed down on her, the pain excruciating. A whitecoat yelled, "Push! Now! That's right—more. That's good. It's crowning."

Sparrow pushed with her entire strength, pushed until she felt her insides explode and break apart. A burst, a gush, a boulder between her legs. A baby cried. A whitecoat hurried from the room; an infant's crying echoed in the hall. Sparrow was freezing, her body in spasms.

The nurse returned and covered her with a warm blanket. "It's over. You did fine. You had a healthy baby girl."

Sitting alone in the waiting room, Dave heard the baby cry. Tears trickled down his face. After Emily died, he hadn't wanted to live, didn't think he could. Then Sparrow, deposited on his doorstep, had intruded into his despondency. With disbelief, he had stood by and watched her settle in. He had deluded himself that she would leave next week, next month. But as the weeks passed, he found himself waking in the morning thinking of her. It was he who had insisted that she go to the doctor. When she would not or could not make the phone call, he had made the appointment and taken her. Now she had had her baby. His job was finished.

When Dave returned home, he sat slumped in his stuffed chair, trying to catnap, but his mind was whirling. He could not understand Sparrow. She had not talked about the baby or what she would do after. Last night she had acted as if she didn't know she was having a baby. The lack of acknowledgement had been as distressing to him as the fearful birthing process.

But at least, now she would go away, and he would be free of the worry of her.

He glared at Emily's empty chair. "Damn it, Emily. Why aren't you here?"

From deep within him, he heard her reassuring voice. *She's young, Dave, scared, needs your help. You can do this.*

As it had been when she was by his side, he was soothed. He closed his eyes and slept.

Awakening

*T*he evening dusk filled the hospital room. Sparrow stirred from a deep sleep; thoughts began to shape themselves in her head. She whispered, "I had a baby girl. I have a baby girl." Hearing the words made it real.

Mary had told Sparrow that she was pregnant when she found her vomiting in the school restroom. But Sparrow did not comprehend it. She had floated over the scene, watching Mary fuss and fume. She had thought that her friend looked strange—all mouth and eyes. And then her mother's accusation, "You haven't had a period in months." Only then did Sparrow know there was something terribly wrong, not the flu, not an upset stomach. But it had not seemed real. She thought she would wake one morning and everything would be the same, as it used to be. For months Sparrow had been in a dream-like state. When someone mentioned the baby, she felt dazed, removed, as though she were watching events unfold in someone else's life.

Now, thinking made her tired. She had to rest, get some sleep. Mr. Stanley would come and help her figure this out. She slept again. When she awoke, it was dark and she was ravenous. She devoured a turkey sandwich that the nurses' aide brought her. She felt her hollow, Jell-O tummy. Although she ached all over, her mind was clear, like the alcoholics she had read about who, after drying out, were suddenly lucid. She had had a baby; she was a mother. She recalled how tiny and cuddly Robin and Jay had been when they were first born, like newborn kittens. She wanted to see her baby. She put her light on, but no one came. Clasping her stomach, she slid out of bed and made her way to the nursery.

There were four babies in bassinets. All had name tags, three with names, the fourth reading GIRL BABY. The door was unlocked. Sparrow looked up and down the hall, then snuck in and picked up the infant. Back in her room, she eased herself onto the bed and studied the sleeping baby. She was pink, with a chubby face, dark hair, and long, skinny arms and legs. Sparrow unwrapped the bunting, inspected the little body, and kissed her belly. The infant opened her eyes and looked up at her. This minute being had miraculously appeared out of nowhere. No—from her own body. It belonged to her. The young mother held her baby and slept.

A white uniform floated above her. A face appeared, stern and exacting. "You can't just go into the nursery and get the baby. It's better not to see her."

Sparrow tightened her grip. "But she's my baby!"

The nurse scooped the baby from Sparrow, whose empty arms dropped onto the white sheets. She could hear the mewling of her infant as she was carried down the hall. Hungry, Sparrow thought. Her own stomach rumbled in empathy with her child; she touched her breasts, which were beginning to swell with mother's milk. She had to think, make a plan, but she was exhausted. Uneasy sleep rescued her from her thoughts.

The glass on the untouched breakfast tray reflected the sun's rays. Sparrow lay curled in a fetal position, the sheet covering her head. Miss Dunston, the social worker, dressed in a powder-blue spring suit, carrying a leather briefcase, tiptoed into the room.

She touched the sheet. "Good morning, Sparrow. How are you doing?"

Sparrow stirred, uncovered her head. She did not recognize this person. Then she recalled a blurry woman in a dark skirt and sweater talking about babies. Sparrow's thoughts became clearer. The woman had stressed how important it was for a child to have a two-parent family. She had said that life is very hard for a single mother and her baby, that she, Sparrow, could never give her child the advantages of a stable couple, that sometimes the most loving thing a mother can do is to let her baby go.

"Remember me?" Although the woman smiled, her eyes did not.

"Yes." Sparrow's heart pounded.

"You had a healthy baby. You did well." She smiled that dead-eyed smile again. "Remember what we talked about?"

The social worker continued. "The important thing is to give the baby a good home. Then you can get on with your life. I've brought the form." She pulled a document out of her briefcase and handed it to Sparrow. "This is where you sign."

"I don't know. I'm not so sure." Sparrow let the paper fall from her hand.

Miss Dunston picked it up. "What do you mean? You said you would give up the baby." The woman's mouth seemed gigantic, her tone accusatory.

"I don't remember."

"But you did. You said you would do what was best."

"No."

"It's not unusual to have these little twinges, but it's best to get it over with, get on with your life. This is where you sign." The social worker held out the paper.

A voice in Sparrow, an unfamiliar one, cried out, "Not now!"

"But I have a good home for her. A family who can give her so much."

Dave, standing in the doorway, spoke. "She said 'Not now.'"

Miss Dunston turned to him. "But it's so much better for the mother and the baby to do it quickly."

"She said, '*Not now!*' Come back tomorrow."

The social worker shrugged, put the paper in her briefcase and handed Sparrow a card. "If you change your mind, just call this number." She closed the door behind her.

Dave crossed the room. "How are you feeling?"

"Like I just lost my insides. Tired, and…and weird."

"Well, you had a baby."

"Did you see her?"

"Sure did. She's a cute little mite. Did you?"

"Yeah, I stole her from the nursery. I held her. She was so sweet…and mine…. I feel like I just woke up from a long sleep."

"You're having second thoughts?"

"I guess I'm finally thinking. It all seemed like a dream, like I was watching it happen to someone else. I haven't thought about anything 'til now. I don't know what I'm going to do."

"It'd be pretty rough bringing up a baby on your own."

"But I took care of Robin and Jay when they were little. I'm good with kids."

"Sure, but raising one by yourself is different." Dave cleared his throat. "How are you going to earn a living?" He turned away, his voice a mumble. "You haven't even graduated from high school yet." He sat down in the chair next to the bed.

Sparrow's eyes met his. "Couldn't we just stay at the bookstore and work for you?"

An Intervention

Sprawled out in his overstuffed chair, stocking feet on the hassock, unopened paper lying on the floor, Dave sat staring at the smaller, empty chair across the room. "Okay, Emily, why aren't you here where you belong? You always had all the common sense. I can't let Sparrow bring that baby home. We never had kids. I wouldn't know how to help. And I don't want to! I'm too old. If you were only here...." Dave's eyes closed; his breathing grew slow and heavy. He snored. Startled, he jerked awake, eyes riveted on the vacant chair. He listened.

The next morning harsh wind whipped through the forsythia bushes, giving flight to yellow petals. Tulips stood naked, with their adornments strewn about. Holding his jacket closed, Dave limped toward the hospital. The building was cool, the corridors empty. Nodding to the aide at the nurses' station, he continued to Sparrow's room. Hearing muffled voices through the door, he paused.

"No!" It was Sparrow's voice.

Dave yanked the door open. Miss Dunston stood over the bed, holding a form on a clipboard, pushing a pen at Sparrow, who, wide eyed, held her knees tight to her body as though protecting herself against invisible blows.

"I won't sign that paper!"

"But Sparrow, you agreed. Don't you remember how we talked about giving the baby a good home, parents who can give it all the advantages, stability and material security that you can't provide?

"That was before she was born, before she was real. She's *mine*. You can't have her!"

Miss Dunston waved the pen at her. "But you're just a child. You have no education. How are you going to support her?"

Sparrow sprang out of bed, grabbed the pen and flung it across the room. "Go away! Go away, now!"

"You'd better go," said Dave.

Open mouthed, the social worker stared at Dave, then nodded. "Call if she changes her mind." She left the room, leaving the pen on the floor.

Sobbing, Sparrow flung herself into Dave's arms. He patted her back, then led her to the bed, where she sat on the edge, gasping for breath.

Dave had never seen the girl in such a state. She had never raised her voice; indeed, she seldom talked. She had seemed half alive, going through the motions, a chameleon merging with the woodwork. Now that the baby had wrested itself from her body, emotions came pouring out. Perhaps she had always hidden her feelings, learned to suppress them when she was a child. After all, she had been abused, hadn't she?

Sparrow blew her nose. Her words came in spurts. "Mr. Stanley, I've been thinking. I want to keep my baby. I have to keep her. I didn't realize. I didn't know…. Can't we stay in your apartment? I can work for you. You need me. You know you do. Babies sleep a lot, don't eat much." She grabbed his wrist. "Please, *let us stay!*"

Dave took her hand and held it. "Could you go home to your mother?"

Sparrow's face clouded.

Of course, he thought. She's been abused. She can't go home.

Sparrow's imploring eyes met his. "Mr. Stanley, I'm a hard worker. We won't be any trouble. Please, help us!"

Dave felt his heart near to bursting. Oh, Emily, he thought. What do I do now? He felt her presence. Emily smiled. *Why, Dave, you know exactly what to do.* Her face faded, and was replaced by that of the child mother. He shook his head in disbelief.

"No, don't say 'no'!" Sparrow pleaded.

Her panic ripped through his heart. "No, I don't mean 'no.' I just don't know."

Puppy eyes beseeched him; she reached for his hand. His chest felt as if it would implode, explode, that his heart would burst.

"Okay…you can stay—for a while."

"Oh, thank you, Mr. Stanley." Sparrow lunged into his arms. "Thank you!"

As if she were a breakable china doll, Dave held her tenderly until her trembling ceased. Gently, he pushed her away. "On one condition."

Sparrow held her breath.

Dave smiled. "You'll have to quit calling me Mr. Stanley."

Gathering

"Why did you name the baby Finch?" asked Dave.

When Dave came to take them home, Sparrow had been waiting at the hospital entrance, the baby bundled as though it were winter. Now they were in the pickup, Finch on her mother's lap. To Dave's relief, Sparrow had pulled back the blanket so the little one could breathe.

"Don't know. Guess it's a family tradition?"

"Tradition?"

"Sparrow, Jay, Robin." She smoothed the baby's hair. "Mom likes birds."

"For your mom?"

Sparrow snorted. "Hardly. She'll never see this baby. She's not the forgiving type."

"She'll come around."

"I think she was pregnant with me when she married Dad. She hates me."

Dave tried to concentrate on the road. "You don't know that."

"Sure felt like it, growing up. She named me Sparrow. Ugly. Jay and Robin got nice names. She wouldn't let me do anything that other kids did. No friends, no movies, home right after school. I was her slave. Maybe that's why I named the baby Finch…to spite Mom."

"Maybe she was frightened for you?"

"No, she was just plain mean."

Dave patted her hand. "Finch is a pretty name."

Sparrow smiled at the baby. "Finches are beautiful, bright and yellow. When it's cold and nasty, they fly south where it's warm and sunny and then come back in the spring."

"Not all. Some hardy finches can handle the cold."

"Yeah, like sparrows."

Dave had not heard Sparrow say so much at any one time, and she'd never talked about her feelings. He cleared his throat. "I like your name just fine."

At Booknook, Dave opened the pickup door and helped Sparrow out. She carried the baby into the store, but found it difficult to navigate the stairs. When Dave tried to help her, Sparrow offered him Finch. He looked up the long, narrow staircase, took the infant in his open palms, and carried her up. With a sigh, he laid her on the bed. A bassinet stood in the corner of the bedroom, filled with boxes.

Sparrow spied the bassinet loaded with packages. She laughed. "Wow! For the baby?"

Dave nodded.

Sparrow tore the boxes open and pulled out tiny shirts, sleepers, and diapers.

"Oh, Mr. Stanley…Dave, I didn't know what I was going to do. Thank you. I remember the day I tried to clean out the storeroom. I wondered what was in those boxes." Sparrow's eyes were questioning. "Why…?"

Dave ran his hand through his hair. "Thought we'd need them once.... Didn't. Been stored here a long time. Good to get some use out of them."

He remembered Emily, pale and wan, lying in the hospital bed. The doctor had said, "No more pregnancies. If you want children, you'll have to adopt." In spite of this, Emily had wanted to try again. There was little he would deny his wife, but he would not risk losing her. Then, when she pleaded with him to adopt a baby, he could not. He was frightened that it would not work out, that they were too old, or there would be something wrong with it. He did not know that Emily could take another disappointment, but it was not clear in his mind, and he could not find the words to express his fears. Instead, he said that he was afraid he could not love a child that was not a part of her or him. Now, he smiled at that thought. Here he was, a grumpy old man with a child mother and her baby.

The first week passed with Sparrow and Finch sequestered in the apartment. Dave spent extra hours at Booknook and made frequent trips up the stairs, checking on them. He bought groceries and heated soup for Sparrow. The infant slept, cried, ate, and slept again. It seemed the two were doing well, but he didn't trust his judgment and waited anxiously for Clare to come and pronounce everything okay.

On Sunday, an unusually warm spring day, Mary's convertible screeched to a stop in front of Booknook. Robin and Jay, laughing, with wind-blown hair, clambered out of the back seat. Baseball cap holding her hair in place, Mary hopped out of the driver's seat. Clare emerged, straightened her shoulders and untied the plaid scarf covering her hair. The car was filled with packages. Watching from her window, Sparrow was reminded of Christmas at Clare's. However, this time the gifts were wrapped in pink and yellow and they were all for her.

Sparrow skipped down a stair, felt a pain, slowed, and used the handrail. She flung open the door, and Robin burst into her arms.

"Sparrow, Sparrow, I've missed you so much. Momma said we couldn't come, but Mrs. Washington made her let us. We rode in the convertible with the top down. It wasn't a bit cold. Where's the baby?"

All arms and legs, Jay stood by. Sparrow pulled him into the circle. The siblings had not been together since the holiday.

"Where's the baby?" said Robin. "I want to see the baby."

The words reminded Sparrow. She had forgotten her baby, left her alone in the bassinet. Forgetting her discomfort, she rushed upstairs to the sleeping infant.

Mary and Jay lugged the bulkier gifts up to the apartment; Robin and Clare carried the lighter ones. They gathered around the bassinet.

"She's so little," said Robin, touching Finch's face.

"Got quite a head of black hair," said Mary.

"She's perfect," declared Clare.

Jay took the sleeping infant's hand. Sparrow watched little fingers curl around his bigger one and was reminded of the thrilling first touch of her baby.

Packages were strewn about the floor. Robin sat at the table with Clare, attempting to look ladylike at a grown-up party. The girl crossed her legs in an imitation of Clare and rested her heart-shaped face on her hand. Mary sprawled on the couch, and Jay lingered by the bassinet. Sparrow tried to untangle a denim seat with straps and wires.

"I'll do it," said Mary. "It's a bouncy swing. When Finch gets bigger and wants to boogie, you can put her in there and she can bounce away." Mary took the swing, shook it loose and hung it over the door.

"Open mine, open mine! I made them myself," cried Robin, forgetting her resolve to act like a lady.

The package was wrapped in several pieces of notebook paper, colored pink and taped together. Sparrow carefully removed the masking tape and held up three pieces of gingham, each the size of a large napkin. She looked quizzically at Robin.

"Don't you know? They're burp rags. I made them out of Daddy's old shirts, and I hemmed them by hand myself."

"Oh, yes, of course, and look at the nice stitching."

"Yeah, just like you taught me."

Sparrow hugged Robin.

"I knew you'd like 'em," whispered Robin.

"Here," said Jay, thrusting a soft package at Sparrow.

"Such pretty paper. I love the babies floating on the clouds," said Sparrow.

"Mrs. Washington wrapped it for me."

"I see that."

Sparrow pulled out a well-worn blanket with patches of blue, green, pink, and yellow. She pressed it to her face. "The quilt! You got Mom to give me our quilt?"

"Not exactly. But we all used it when we were babies, and I thought the new baby should have it."

"You snitched the quilt?"

Jay shrugged.

The gifts were unwrapped. Baby clothes, blankets, diapers, diaper bag, bottles, stuffed animals, and toys lay across the bed; a stroller was propped against the dresser.

"Gees, how can one baby use all this stuff?" asked Sparrow.

"You'd be surprised," said Clare. "I asked Dave what you had, but he wasn't sure. I had to guess. Not everything's new, but it's all in good shape and things I think you'll need."

Conversation dwindled. Jay shifted in his chair. "Hey, what about lunch?"

"Oh, I almost forgot," said Clare. She nodded to Sparrow. "I promised Jay and Robin that we could have carry-out from the Grasshopper." She opened her purse, pulled out a list and several bills and handed them to Mary. "You take the kids over and get it."

"Can we get a coke while we wait?" asked Jay.

Clare nodded. After the little group left, Sparrow and Clare worked in silence, picking up boxes and folding clothes.

When the job was finished, Clare said, "So, you're keeping the baby."

"Yes, ma'am."

"Well, what are your plans?"

"What do you mean?" Sparrow shifted her weight from leg to leg.

"Taking care of a baby and rearing a child are two different things. How are you going to manage?"

Sparrow sucked in a breath. "I don't know...but I love her, and she loves me. She's the first thing of my own that I've ever had."

"But you don't have her. She's not a possession. She's a human being. She'll grow up."

"I know that."

"But it's going to be hard. You'll need money. Will her father help?"

Color drained from Sparrow's face. "I don't know where he is."

"Well, maybe you should find out."

The shop door slammed and laughter came pounding up the stairs. Mary, Jay and Robin crowded in, carrying brown bags filled with nachos, cheese enchiladas and burritos. Oil shone wet on the bags; spicy fragrance filled the room. The Grasshopper was owned and run by Mexicans and noted for its ethnic comfort food. Sparrow had watched patrons amble in and come out with brown bags or plates of food wrapped in foil. She had been curious but had never eaten there. Neither she nor Robin nor Jay had ever eaten Mexican food. Their mom cooked meat and potatoes with vegetables fresh from the garden, or canned in the winter. They never ate out.

Clare organized the dinette table, took the aluminum foil off the plates and explained what each dish was. Mary dug in, filling her plate to the brim. Jay helped himself to nachos. Clare put a taste of everything on Robin's plate.

"These nachos are dee-licious," said Jay, cramming one into his mouth.

"Help yourself, Sparrow," said Clare. "The baby's sleeping, and you should eat while you can. You'll need your strength."

Stinging from the earlier conversation with Clare, Sparrow sat erect in the rocker, tears pooling in her eyes. But the confrontation had not erased gratitude that Clare supported and cared for her, that Clare had gathered her family and brought her gifts.

Robin folded herself into her big sister's arms and asked, "What's the matter?"

Sparrow sniffed. "It's like a party. I've never had a party."

Later, after the paper plates and plastic forks were discarded and the gifts put away, Sparrow watched the convertible zip away. She rubbed her stomach. Although she had eaten more than she had in months, she somehow felt empty. Exhausted, she lay down on the bed to rest and fell into a deep sleep. In what seemed like moments to her, she was wakened by the crying of a baby.

Reality

*D*ave was restless. He'd forgotten to bring Hemingway's *The Old Man and the Sea* home, and nothing else appealed. The moon was full and inviting. He decided to walk to Booknook, retrieve the novel, and check on Sparrow and the baby. Finch was a month old, alert and growing, but Sparrow looked tired and drawn. The three had settled into a routine, with Sparrow tidying the store before he arrived in the morning and working a good part of the day, while Finch slept in her bassinet at the back of the store. Although wary of the infant, Dave was getting used to having her around. He'd moved the bassinet close to him and kept an eye on her while he did accounts or read the paper. When she fussed, he rocked the bassinet. If this did not calm her, Sparrow took her upstairs.

Unlocking the door, Dave heard squalls coming from the apartment. He went to the stairwell and yelled, "Sparrow, are you all right?"

Sparrow's reply was muffled. "I can't get her to quit crying."

"I'll be right up."

"What the hell!" exclaimed Dave when he opened the door. A rope crisscrossed the room wall to wall, with diapers, nightshirts and infant blankets flung over it. Sparrow, cradling a screaming Finch, paced the floor, weaving in and out amongst the laundry, tears streaming down her face.

"She does this every night. She cries and cries…. I don't know what to do."

Dave watched Sparrow wander through the maze. How he missed Emily. She'd know what to do. She'd know how to comfort the baby. Still, he placed his hand on Sparrow's shoulder, turned her around, and took the infant. He held her against his chest, rocking her and rubbing her back. She burped. As Dave walked in and out amongst the canopy of diapers, Finch closed her eyes.

"She's like this every night?"

"Almost. I usually carry her in the huggie, but when I put her down, she cries. I can't get her to stop."

Dave had never questioned how Sparrow managed alone at night or how she did the laundry. "You wash diapers every night?"

"Yes."

"Ever been to the laundromat?"

"No."

"Adrian Laundromat is just down the street."

Sparrow fingered a diaper hanging on the line. "I know."

Dave laid the sleeping baby in the bassinet. "Well, something has to be done about that." He pivoted on his heel and headed down the stairs.

Sparrow stared after him. What did he mean, something has to be done?

Unaware of the effect he'd had on Sparrow, oblivious of the fresh spring air or the smell of blooming lilacs, Dave shuffled home deep in thought.

"Damn, damn the laundry, damn the baby, damn Finch, and damn Emily for dying. What am I supposed to do, take the laundry to the Laundromat? Sparrow can take care of her own dirty clothes."

Like the breeze in the trees, gentle on his ear, he heard Emily. *Dave, Dave, settle down. Sparrow can't drag all that laundry and carry Finch. You'll have to take her. Can you imagine her in a room filled with whirring washing machines, water flowing in and out, dryers rotating, zippers clanging against metal, all those people? She'd be overwhelmed.*

"She can wash her clothes any damn way she wants," muttered Dave. "I'm not responsible!"

A car sped around the corner, windows rolled down. A boy and a girl laughed and waved at the lone old man walking in the moonlight. Dave was struck by the girl's resemblance to Sparrow. That's what she should be doing. She's just a kid, he thought.

Yes, and she needs your help. Look at how you quieted the baby.

As if Emily's lips were there, Dave touched his ear.

It was almost ten, late for Dave to be arriving at work. He hollered from the entrance. "Sparrow, come hold this door open."

Sparrow ran to the door and watched Dave pull a wooden rocking chair from the back of his pickup.

"It was in the basement getting no use, never did get any. You need it for Finch. Need to rock that baby."

Sparrow put her hand to her cheek. "Oh! You shouldn't have."

"You should have told me you were having trouble getting that baby to sleep."

Sparrow nodded, then turned her attention to the chair. She ran her hand over the smooth wood. "It's oak, and look, the north wind is engraved on the back. It's beautiful, a real antique. Thank you....You're so good."

Dave's face reddened. "Did you get some sleep last night?"

"Yeah. After you left, Finch slept all night."

The breeze came again. Dave heard Emily whisper. *Told you so.*

The rest of the morning Dave scarcely worked on his crossword puzzle. He would walk to the front of the store, gaze out the window, return to his chair, and then repeat the process.

"Is something the matter?" asked Sparrow.

"No." Dave continued his pacing.

Finch was fussy, and Sparrow found it difficult to focus on any one task. "Is Finch bothering you?"

"No." Dave continued his pacing.

At noon, as Sparrow was going up for lunch, a pickup pulled up in front of the shop.

Dave rushed to the entrance and greeted two burly fellows. "Did you have any trouble getting them out of the basement?"

"No, not at all," said the older man. "Been doing this for years."

Under Dave's watchful eye, the men made quick work of hauling a washer and dryer out of the pickup and into the store. They placed them in an alcove behind the bathroom.

Sparrow watched in amazement. "What have you done?"

Dave shrugged. "Well, they're just our old Maytags. Couldn't get downstairs when I tore my meniscus, so I got a little stack in the kitchen. You can't be washing diapers in the sink."

"Oh, Mr. Stan—...Dave, you're so good to us." Sparrow burst into tears and fled upstairs.

That afternoon the plumber came and hooked up the washer and dryer. The following day the electrician finished the job.

A Working Mother
1961–1962

*I*t was a slow Saturday. Sparrow and Dave relaxed at the table, Dave drinking coffee, Sparrow tea.

Sparrow blew steam from her cup. "Mr. Stanley?"

Dave shook his head. "What's my name?"

Sparrow cleared her throat. "Dave…how did you name Booknook?"

"Emily named it."

"Why 'Booknook'?"

"Oh…she wanted a cozy shop where people could browse, not feel compelled to buy a book. Be at home, keep coming back." Finch stirred and Dave gently pushed the bassinet with his foot.

"A cozy store?"

"Yeah, she perked coffee, baked cookies. We had a couch and a couple of easy chairs. Customers sat and read and drank coffee. It'd be like she invited them into her home. She visited with everyone. People we scarcely knew told her when there'd been a birth or death or even when someone was sick. They bought books for their kids, for birthdays and Christmas. Business was good."

"Not so good now."

"Nope, guess not. When she got sick, I didn't want to talk. Everybody sitting around like they were waiting for Emily to serve coffee. Just wanted to be left alone. One day I got so mad, I dragged the couch and chairs out to the curb."

Dave took a drink of coffee and wiped his lips. "Guess that wasn't such a good solution. But one good thing did come of it." He grinned. "That afternoon a young couple pulled up in a beat-up pickup and hauled that furniture away. They needed it a sight more than I did. So customers got the message, bought their books and left. Some just quit coming. Over the years we lost shoppers to that huge Borders in Ann Arbor, to the library. I don't begrudge them the library. That's a good way to get educated, get some use out of our taxes. Don't see why they have to run off to the city." Dave paused. "What are you getting at?"

Sparrow rocked the bassinet. "Well, perhaps we could do something, make it more attractive." Finch whimpered. Sparrow rocked harder.

Dave sighed. "Are you going to wake that baby up or tell me what's on your mind?"

Sparrow put her hands in her lap and began the speech that she'd practiced the previous evening. "We can do like Emily. There's plenty of space. We could get a couple of area rugs, a couch and some chairs, make a couple of reading areas. I could clean up that big coffee pot. Coffee's cheap. Maybe on Saturdays I could do a children's story hour like they do in kindergarten. I used to love that, and I read to Robin and Jay all the time. And I could make bookmarks and put one in each book we sell. I'd type up flyers. It wouldn't cost anything to advertise."

Dave held up his hand. "Wait a minute, young lady. I'm not going to be railroaded into a lot of extra work."

"I'm sorry. I thought with the baby and all the extra expenses...and the store isn't doing so well." Sparrow squared her shoulders. "But it wouldn't be a lot of extra work for you. I'd do it!"

Dave stood up. "You do plenty, and then you apologize. I'm sick and tired of your apologizing!"

Finch let out a wail. Both reached for her, but her mother was quicker. Dave's arms dropped to his sides.

Sparrow glared at Dave. "See what you did! You scared Finch with your hollering."

"Sorry, didn't know I was so loud."

"Oh! So *you* can say you're sorry."

Dave grinned. "You think you got the market on it?"

They laughed. Sparrow gently patted Finch until her cries subsided.

Dave sat down. "And where would we get the money for rugs and furniture?"

Sparrow's eyes met his. "It doesn't have to cost much. I've saved a little from my pay, and we could go to the Goodwill for furniture. If you keep looking, sometimes they have nice stuff."

"You're not spending your money to spruce up this place."

"If you're going to make money, you've got to invest in the business. And I want to do my share."

"Humph." Dave studied Sparrow. "And what's your notion about arranging this stuff?"

Sparrow juggled Finch on her lap. "There's space by the window where we could put a big rug, with a couple of chairs. The kids could sit on the rug, and people would see it from the outside. It'd be inviting, like with Emily. And there are a couple of empty corners where we could put chairs. Oh, Mr. Stanley, I think it would help."

"Humph." Dave plunked his cup on the table and strode to the other side of the shop.

That evening, as Dave nodded off in his chair, Emily appeared.

Dave, she's right. You know it. You are so stubborn, always have to be right. But if you're going to keep the shop open, you have to make some changes. How are you going to pay Sparrow if you don't bring in more revenue?

"Who says I want to keep the shop open?"

Well, it looks like you've made a commitment to that girl and her child. Besides, what would you do if you closed Booknook?

"Oh, Emily, she looks like a twelve-year-old, with that peaked face and her hair pulled back in a ponytail. She doesn't know about running a business."

That's just looks, David. It's got nothing to do with what's inside. She's showing determination, enthusiasm. She'll learn—just like we did.

On his walk the next morning, Dave wandered into Hammerman's furniture store, his feet leading him to the clearance department. He was surprised to find some inexpensive and useable items, an eight-by-ten Oriental rug with a crimson and gold leaf pattern, and a couple of wing-back velvet chairs in a similar red.

Later that week, Dave, Sparrow and the baby made a trip to the Goodwill store. The massive warehouse was filled with clothing, dishes and other household items, with furniture crowded to one side. Dave stood uncertain, overwhelmed by the array of cast-offs. Sparrow headed toward the furniture section.

"There, there it is!" she cried.

Dave could see a muddle of lamps, scarred tables, worn and dirty sofas and chairs. "Where?"

"There!"

Indeed, as though it was too classy to associate with the beaten and battered, apart from the rest sat an antique love seat upholstered in a dark print.

"It just has a small stain, right there. See? Just a little one. I think I can get it out." Sparrow settled into the cushions and stroked the fabric. "It's soft and comfortable. Oh, there's a lamp. It would work. I know where there's an outlet. Can we get them?"

A sign in Booknook's window read, CHILDREN'S STORY HOUR SATURDAY 10:00 A.M. Throughout the previous week, Sparrow had slipped a handmade bookmark advertising the event into each book she sold. Dressed in her best, she combed her hair into a French roll, imitating Mrs. Washington's. However, unlike Mrs. Washington's, resistant strands of Sparrow's hair curled around her face, giving her an impish look. In the back of the store, Dave watched as Finch bounced in her swing. Two six-year-old girls sat cross-legged on the Oriental rug, staring at Sparrow in rapt attention as she read *The Velveteen Rabbit*.

Magic Fairy was speaking to the bedraggled and discarded toy rabbit: "'I take care of all the playthings that the children have loved. When they are old and worn out and the children don't need them anymore, then I come and take them away with me and turn them into Real.'

"'Wasn't I Real before?' asked the little Rabbit.

"'You were Real to the Boy,' the Fairy said, 'because he loved you. Now you shall be Real to everyone.'"

Sparrow closed the book and stretched her legs.

"Oh," said the cherub-faced blonde girl. "I have a bi-i-g fuzzy teddy bear. Can love make him real?"

"Isn't he real to you?" asked her mother.

"Can I have the book? Mommy, can I?"

The mother stroked the girl's shiny blonde hair. "How can I refuse?"

Sparrow rang up the sale of two books and invited the girls to next Saturday's reading. "And bring your friends," she called, as they walked out.

Sparrow heaved a sigh and turned to Dave.

He nodded. "You did just fine."

Sparrow picked Finch up and swung her around.

As a child Sparrow had been humiliated and smacked into submission. With the birth of her baby, feelings awakened. Her body was a-tingle, filled with contradictions and longings. Days were a whirl of purpose, but nights were dark and alien. In the sparsely furnished apartment, with Finch asleep, she sat at the table with an open book, watching couples stroll into the Grasshopper. Later, they emerged— women in the arms of their men, kissing under the street lamp. Nights when Finch's howls pierced her dream-thoughts, Sparrow paced the floor with her, suppressing the urge to slap or shake the baby into submission. Once in the wee hours of morning, when the young mother was unable to calm Finch, she threw the baby into the crib. Exhausted and filled with guilt, Sparrow lay on the bed, her sobs mingling with those of the infant.

Months passed. Finch was no longer content in the huggie close to her mother's chest. She needed even more space than the playpen and would pull herself up and bang on the slats to be let out. Sparrow feared for her baby's safety, but Finch's persistence left her no choice. By the child's first birthday she toddled about the store, weaving around and under tables. Her mother filled a laundry basket with toys and placed it in a corner near the story rug, where Finch played with her blocks observant of the goings-on about her. Later Dave would build her a bookcase in the back of the store, which Sparrow kept stocked with books, paper, colors and paints.

By the time Finch was two, customers knew her well, brought her treats, and teased that they would take her home with them. Thriving on the attention, Finch seemed to need her mother less. As the child grew more independent, Sparrow turned away, busying herself with cleaning or customers. Slim and lithe, skirt swirling, she darted from book to book as a bird might search for worms, or string to build a nest.

As a toddler, when frustrated or tired, Finch longed to be wrapped in the soft fabric of her mother. She would reach for the elusive dark cloth floating above her. Stretching her arms she'd touch it with tiny hands as it swirled by; she hurried after it, clutching it, swaying with it. Sometimes Sparrow would flit too quickly, and Finch would collapse under one of the tables. There she sucked her thumb and watched her mother's loafers move about the shop, followed by others' polished shoes or dirty sneakers. On days when Booknook was not busy, and her mother did not dart about, Finch could attach herself to the black flannel skirt and sneak a suck off the bottom edge. In summer, Sparrow wore polyester or cotton. To Finch's tiny mouth, polyester was slick, temporary. Cotton was substantial and salty, like crackers.

The Circle Broadens
1964

*I*n 1964 Finch was four, Sparrow twenty-one, and Dave had turned seventy. They were a family of sorts, mother, daughter and "uncle." At two, Finch had called Mr. Stanley "Dave." To Sparrow this seemed disrespectful, but "Mr. Stanley" was too formal, and "Grandpa" untrue. Sparrow decided on "Uncle Dave."

Between Dave's Social Security and the proceeds from Booknook, the little family managed. Sparrow's innovations and hard work made the shop more inviting; sales rose. Patrons sipped coffee while perusing a book. Saturday morning story hours attracted young mothers with children. Encircled by five to ten preschoolers, Sparrow came alive as she read.

Early one morning Sparrow and Dave sat at the table, Sparrow working on a book order, Dave a crossword puzzle. In her favorite red shirt and pink shorts, Finch bounded down the stairs. Hands on skinny hips, tummy meeting Sparrow's knees, she leaned into her mother.

Sparrow smoothed her daughter's tangled hair. "Finch, go back up and brush your hair. And change your shirt. Red doesn't go with pink."

Finch stepped away and continued an argument that had begun the previous evening. Thrusting her chin out, she said, "I want to see *101 Dalmatians*. I'm a big girl. Four-year-olds go to movies."

Sparrow's face clouded. She picked up her pencil and bent over the paperwork.

Finch stamped her feet. "Mommy, I want to go!"

"I guess four is too young to be running off to the movies by yourself," Dave said.

"But I'm not going alone! Angie's mom is taking us."

Dave winked at Finch. "Well, in that case it sounds like a fine idea."

"Please, Mommy! Uncle Dave says it's okay."

Sparrow gave Dave a withering look. Then to Finch, rearranging her face, words heavy on her tongue, she said, "Well...I'll think about it."

Finch did a pirouette. "Thank you, Mommy!" She hugged Sparrow and danced outside to her sand pile.

Dave had seen this coming. Finch rode with him in the pickup when he ran errands; her mother took her to the grocery store. Occasionally the three of them picnicked in the park. Although Finch could watch the street scene out front, she could not play there. Other than the sand box behind Booknook, there was no yard. The child needed more space, new experiences.

Dave set his cup on the table. "You don't want her to go?"

Sparrow pursed her lips. "Well, I've heard the movie is violent."

"It's a kids' movie."

Sparrow tapped her pencil. "But they want to kill those puppies. They want to murder them for their hides."

"But they don't. You read her stories that are more frightening."

"That's different!"

"Millions of kids are going to that movie. Do you think they'll all be scared?"

"Finch is vulnerable."

"How so? She's a plucky little rascal. You're the one who's afraid to go anywhere. You're getting the two of you mixed up."

Sparrow folded the order form and stuck it in an envelope, licked the flap and pressed it shut so tightly that the tips of her fingers turned white.

Dave waited.

She put the envelope on the counter. "I just want to protect her."

"The way your mom protected you?"

Sparrow thumped her pencil on the table. "That's not fair! My mom just needed me to take care of the other kids, to help with the cooking, the washing, and the cleaning. She kept me home to be there for her! I want Finch to have a life."

Dave spoke gently. "I know you want the best for her. But you can't keep her home. Do you want her dangling from your skirt at eighteen? Booknook can't be her world. It's not a life for a little girl." Dave's eyes met Sparrow's teary ones. "And it can't be your world either. It's time you got out and did something—get your GED, take some college courses."

Sparrow paled.

Dave pushed back his chair. "Guess I'd better go pick up that book order from the post office."

Sparrow watched as Dave, holding himself erect, trudged out of the shop. The nerve of him! He didn't know anything about raising a child. But what would she do without him? If he hadn't taken her in, she would have lost her baby.

She had difficulty calling up the father's face, but sometimes she would wake feeling empty, a void without a bottom. She could feel his body pressing into her, his arms around her, his face warm against hers. She'd wanted to be part of him, for her body to merge with his. Instead, a baby grew inside her. After Finch's birth, she had felt as though she'd been blown apart and was trying to tape herself together. Waiting for a letter that never came, Sparrow had isolated herself in the bookstore. She lived in her fantasies, caring for Finch and comforting herself with books. At night she clambered into bed, pulled her child next to her, spoon-style, and hoped that sleep would come before Finch became restless and moved away.

Sparrow rested her head on the hard, cold surface of the table, closed her eyes and let her mind drift. She was twelve years old, standing at the kitchen sink peeling carrots, pleading with her mother.

"Mom, please let me go see *The Wizard of Oz*."

"You will not go to the movie." Her mother's voice reverberated in her ears.

"Pleeease! Everyone else goes."

"You and your high-falutin ideas!" Whack!

Sparrow reeled from the slap. Finger marks showed on her cheeks. Holding back tears, she methodically stripped away the skin of the carrots and washed them under the faucet. She cut them into small hunks and placed them on a plate, vowing never again to ask her mother for anything.

When Finch came back into Booknook, banging the back door shut, Sparrow did not stir but continued to sit, face in her hands, still lost in memory.

Finch tiptoed up to her mother. "What's the matter, Mommy? What's wrong?"

Sparrow put her chin on Finch's tousled hair and caught a whiff of Breck shampoo. "I'm okay, Precious. I was just thinking…about the movie."

"Can I go?"

"Yeah…yeah. I guess so."

Finch could go to the movie. But she had a nagging doubt that something wasn't right. "I can stay home with you, Mommy."

"Don't be silly. Of course you'll go. It'll be fun."

Finch studied her mother's face.

It was a simple seashell necklace that had thrust Maria and Angie Garcia into Finch and Sparrow's lives. One Saturday morning Sparrow was reading to a group of six children. With the exception of her daughter, all of them were mesmerized by the story and the melody of Sparrow's voice. The bell chimed, and a bronzed-skinned woman entered with a chubby little girl sucking her thumb. Wavy dark hair with a vibrant copper cast covered the girl's shoulders. Sparrow motioned the child to join the group. The mother nodded reassurance, and the girl sat down beside Finch on the fringe of the circle.

Sparrow resumed her reading, and the mother sat on the love seat. The child wore a bright red cotton dress with a ruffle on the bottom, black patent leather shoes, and a seashell necklace. Finch touched the ruffle, and the girl grinned. Throughout the reading of the story, Finch gazed curiously at the necklace. As

Sparrow closed the book, Finch grasped a shell. The thread broke. Pieces scattered.

The red-dress girl's eyes opened wide.

Sparrow gasped. "Oh, Finch, look what you did!"

The other children scuttled away. Finch teared up.

Sparrow gathered up the shells. "I'm so sorry. We can fix them."

"It's okay," said the bronze-skinned mother. "The string wasn't heavy enough."

"I didn't mean to," said Finch.

"I know you didn't. But sometimes you get too excited. You shouldn't be handling other people's things." Sparrow sighed. "I've got some twine. We can restring them."

The girl's mother patted Finch's hand. "The shells come from the beach in my home town in Mexico. I found them when I was a little girl just like you."

Thus began the friendship of mothers and daughters. Maria brought Angie to the Saturday-morning book readings and sat on the loveseat, paying careful attention to the reading. Without fail, she bought a book. On Wednesdays, Maria and Angie came to the shop just as Sparrow opened for business and Sparrow offered her tea. After several visits, Maria confided that, although she had spoken English as a child, she was just learning to read it. Sparrow began helping Maria with her reading, while the girls played. During cold weather, Finch and Angie sat on the front window seat, hosting pretend tea parties for their dolls. When it was warm, they played "going to Mexico" in Finch's sand box.

Sparrow looked forward to Maria's weekly visits, but was still lonely. Mary was a senior at Berkeley, and her letters were few and far between. Jay, in his junior year of high school, no longer wrote his cryptic notes.

Other than Clare's occasional visits, Sparrow's only news of home was from her thirteen-year-old sister.

One slow day, Dave sat at the table, working on a crossword puzzle, a captive audience, while Sparrow read him Robin's letter.

Dear Sparrow,

I have good news and bad news. First the good. Mom is working cleaning houses. She says she doesn't like cleaning up other people's dirt. The first few weeks she was awful mean but she isn't home when I get out of school so I can walk down to Mr. Jensen's drug store with my friends. Jay gives me free Cokes. Or maybe he pays for them. He doesn't say. That's the other good news. Jay is working at the drug store just like you did. Maybe I can work there too when I get older. He's trying to save some money to buy a car, then we will drive down and see you. But he will probably bring his girlfriend and that won't be as much fun.

Now the bad news. But in a way it isn't so bad. Dad hurt his back at the factory and is off on sick or comp or something. Anyway he is not too bad. (That's why mom went to work.) So, dad and I make supper together. I am learning to cook good stuff. Last night I made biscuits.

So I got to study. Write me back. Kiss Finch for me. XXXX I miss you.

Love, Robin

P.S. I am doing what you told me. I'm doing good in school. I'm doing better than Jay. He gets Bs, and I get mostly As. But then he is working, so maybe it's not that I'm smarter. Maybe I just study more.

P.P.S. Mom still won't talk about you or Finch. It's weird. It's like you died. But I still think of you all the time.

Sparrow folded the letter and put it back in the envelope.

"Ah ha," said Dave, as he filled in the *h* of *telegraph*. He looked at Sparrow. "You miss them, don't you?"

"I wish they could come visit, at least Robin. She'd want to come."

"You could go see them. If you got your license, you could take the pickup and go."

"I…I couldn't drive your pickup."

Dave filled in *pole*. "Why not?"

"Oh, you just don't understand!"

Dave sighed. "No, guess I don't…. If you really want to go, I guess I could take you."

"I can't go back there!" Sparrow fled up the stairs.

Dave folded the paper and put his hands on the table. His fingers tapped the rhythm of a song he'd thought forgotten. He didn't know how to help her. Okay, so she was too embarrassed to go back to Milan. She could still learn to drive. Or could she? Sparrow seemed perfectly fine in the store. She worked, took care of Finch, was helpful with customers. But when she walked outside that front door onto Maumee Street, she became a nervous Nellie.

First Overnight
1968

*D*ays had faded into weeks, months, and years with Sparrow entrenched in Booknook—her fortress. To her, Adrian remained a frightening, alien place. With Dave's urging, Sparrow would take a walk with him and Finch or go for ice cream. Once he persuaded her to picnic at Wamplers Lake where, overwhelmed with memories of her family's vacations, she scarcely spoke. When Finch entered kindergarten, it was Dave who walked her to school. He taught her how to cross the street, to watch for red lights, to look both ways for cars. It was Dave who attended Finch's teacher conferences.

Now Finch was eight years old and having her first overnight with Angie. She'd begged her mom for months, but only after Uncle Dave's eyes got really big, and he stuck his lips together and marched out of Booknook, had her mom given permission.

Finch felt as if she was going to pop right out of her skin. Her grocery bag was stuffed with her toothbrush, underpants, shortie pajamas, clean T-shirt and favorite doll, Suzie. She'd unpacked and repacked.

She asked if she could take toothpaste, but her mom said no, that it might come open and end up all over the clothes. Sparrow assured her that Angie would have toothpaste.

"Bye, Mom," Finch called as she raced out the door and into the Garcia's waiting car. Her mom stood in the open doorway, waving and smiling, but her face had that wrinkled look she got when she smelled something bad.

Angie's house was filled with the scent of fried tortillas. The table was set with a red tablecloth and bright yellow dishes. Maria had bowls of shredded beef, cheese, lettuce and little green things. There were spoons in each container and the girls were allowed to fill their own tacos.

"Ooh, a real Mexican supper," said Finch.

"Not exactly," Maria said with a smile. "I'm making an American-Mexican supper for you."

Finch carefully spooned the beef and cheese into her taco shell. It cracked when she bit into it, and the cheese melted in her mouth.

Angie's father loomed over Finch. "You're only having one? You won't grow up to be big and strong if you don't eat more. You need some meat on your bones!"

Anton, a barrel-chested man with huge hands, had a voice that filled the room. Finch found him both fascinating and frightening. When he was around, she was all eyes and ears. Tonight, under the bright kitchen light, her stomach churned, refusing more of the delicious food. Her right side ached, and his remarks worried her. She wondered if she might be a skinny midget. Her lips quivered.

"It's okay," Anton said. "I was just teasing. You're a perfect size."

Later, while Angie's parents watched TV, the girls went to Angie's room. They stretched out on her bed and played with paper dolls. Finch colored a ruffled dress for her doll, Suzie.

"We'll make her a princess and give her a crown," Finch said.

"My mom has a crown," bragged Angie.

"No, she doesn't. Only princesses and queens have crowns."

Angie put her hands on her hips. "My mom has a crown!"

"No!" Finch shook her head.

"She does too, and it's got diamonds."

"Diamonds?"

"Come on. I'll show you." Angie took Finch's hand and led her into Maria's bedroom.

"Maybe we should ask," said Finch.

"Mom lets me look in her jewelry box all the time."

The last rays of the sun peeked through the window and settled on a polished mahogany box sitting on Maria's intricate crocheted doily. The bedroom seemed a private place, the box forbidden.

Angie raised the lid. Jewels: gold and silver bracelets, earrings, and necklaces were jumbled together in the box. She touched her finger to her lips and then carefully opened a drawer. A delicate crown sparkled on a blue velvet cloth.

Finch gasped. "Wow!"

"Told ya."

Finch fingered the crown. "How do you know its diamonds?"

"'Cause it's so shiny."

"Are your folks rich?"

"Nah, but my grandparents must be. They live in Mexico and have a maid."

"You're lying."

"Ask my mom."

"Really?"

"Grandma gave the crown to Mom."

"But they can't be real."

"I can prove it. My folks watched a TV program on diamonds. It said they're real strong and won't break. They can cut glass."

Angie picked up the tiara and placed it on Finch's head. The girls gazed at their reflections in the mirror. Two eight-year-olds holding hands: Angie in her ruffled nightie, a mop of curly dark, copper hair framing her plump face; Finch in homemade shortie pj's, the lopsided tiara dwarfing her elfin face.

"You're the fairy princess and I'm your lady-in-waiting," declared Angie.

Finch placed her right hand on her hip and pranced about the room, arching her head from side to side to see the gems glisten in the mirror. "Fetch me my slippers, my lady," she commanded.

Angie scurried to get Finch her socks. Finch demanded necklaces and bracelets, until she was well adorned.

Angie grew tired of fetching and clasping. "Okay, let's test 'em."

"Test 'em?"

"Yeah, I'll prove they don't break." She took the tiara from Finch's head.

"But do we have to cut a window or something?" Finch fingered the tiara nervously.

"No, that'd make Mom mad. Let's try to break 'em."

"How?" Finch looked around the room, and her eyes settled on Maria's collection of ceramic dancing dolls on their shelf.

Angie followed her gaze. "Na, let's bite 'em."

"Are you sure?"

"Yeah. You do it."

Finch shook her head.

Angie put her hands on her hips. "Well, do it!"

"No, you do it. They're your mom's."

"Yeah, and I'm the boss."

Finch held the crown in both hands and studied the brilliant stones. "Are you sure we won't hurt them?"

"Course not, silly. They can cut glass. You can't break 'em. Bite 'em!"

"Where?" asked Finch.

"Anywhere."

Finch put the two end stones in her mouth and held them between her teeth.

"Do it!"

Ordinarily, Finch was the leader, but tonight was different. It was her first time away from home. Angie's house, Angie's toys, Angie's ideas. There was an ache in Finch's side and a grumbly feeling in her tummy. She put the end of the crown in her mouth and bit down hard.

She gagged and spit bloody saliva and tiny flakes of glass into her hand.

Angie grabbed the crown and popped it into the box. They raced to the bathroom, leaving the jewelry drawer open. Angie filled a glass with water and thrust it at Finch, who swirled the water in her mouth and spat red-water droplets into the sink.

Tears welled in Finch's eyes. "You lied! It wasn't diamonds."

"I'm sorry." Angie sniffled.

"I've ruined it, and I've swallowed glass. I'll die. And your mom will hate me. And I'll never be able to stay all night again."

"Mom never wears it. She won't notice. Do you think you swallowed any? We did rinse it out pretty quick."

"I don't know, but I don't feel so good."

The remorseful girls scuttled into bed and pulled the covers over their heads. When Maria came in a few minutes later, they were curled up on their tummies as though asleep. She pulled back the cover and kissed their cheeks. She wandered into her room, noticed the open drawer of her jewelry box, and closed it.

Back at Booknook, Sparrow thought it wasn't worth cooking something just for herself. After an unsatisfying supper of leftover spaghetti, she curled up in the worn recliner, bare feet snuggled under her cotton nightie. She picked up a book, opened it, and then tossed it on the floor. She told herself that it was natural to be concerned about Finch. Sometimes the girl had nightmares. But it was good to have some solitude, time to think. Light faded, streetlights shone through the dusk, the Grasshopper sign flashed and beckoned. It began to rain, drops splattering on the window. Uneasy, she wandered around the apartment. Perhaps some herbal tea would calm her. After making it, she held the cup in both hands while it grew cold. Outside, cars sloshed past in the rain.

When Sparrow had been pregnant, she had been sleepwalking. She had functioned, but denied herself thoughts, feelings, even food. Now, she shuddered to think how she had put Finch's health at risk. Before Finch was born, Sparrow had been nothing. With a baby, she had an identity. She was a mother. She had resolved that Finch would be loved, cherished and protected. At the time, the adolescent could not imagine that her doll baby would grow into a spirited little girl who would want to explore the world outside the safety of Booknook.

On this night, with Finch gone, Sparrow remembered the difficulty her tyrannical mother had letting her children out of her clutches. Like mother, like daughter, she thought. She poured the tea down the sink and crept into bed. Filling empty arms with the frayed soft blue blanket, she buried her face in it.

From a deep sleep, Sparrow heard the banging on the door. She shook herself awake, grabbed her flannel robe, and ran down the stairs. Something had happened to Finch.

"Finch, is that you?"

"Mommy!"

Sparrow flung open the door. Anton held the pajama-clad child in his arms.

"Mommy, my tummy hurts."

Sparrow scooped up her daughter, said a hasty thank you and hurried upstairs, leaving a bewildered Anton with an explanation still on his lips. Finch whimpered as her mother laid her on the bed. Pressing lips to Finch's feverish forehead, Sparrow cursed herself for not keeping her daughter home.

"It hurts real bad."

Sparrow felt her forehead. "What did you eat?"

"Tacos." Finch did not tell her about the glass.

"I should have kept you home."

Sparrow felt the presence of her own mother, saw the fire in her eyes and the belt in her gnarled hands, her voice matching the blows of the belt: "Always crying to go, to walk to town, to the library, somewhere—always somewhere. You gotta learn to stay home, where you belong!"

Sparrow stroked Finch's arms and whispered, "It's okay. I'm here."

Too miserable and ashamed to confess, Finch did not respond. She was certain she was dying, that her stomach was being cut into shreds by bits of glass. When Finch had cuts on the outside, she could put Band-Aids on them, and if a cut was really bad, the doctor could sew it up. But she couldn't Band-Aid an inside cut, or sew it shut; there was no way to see it or get to it. Maybe she would bleed to death. Her mother would be so sad if she died; then maybe her mother would die, too. And she would never get to stay all night with Angie again. With these thoughts swirling in her brain, the child lapsed into a feverish sleep.

Children's aspirin did not break the fever, and Tums did not relieve Finch's pain. Dripping with sweat, dark hair matted around her pale face, she moaned and clutched her stomach. She needed a doctor. Sparrow had no car and could not afford an ambulance. Panicked that she might not be able to wake Dave, terrified that she would, Sparrow dialed the number.

On the seventh ring there was a groggy "Hello?"

"Dave. I'm sorry to bother you. But Finch is sick. I can't get her fever down. She's in terrible pain!"

A pause. "I'll be right there."

Sparrow dropped the phone and grabbed her clothes. By the time she was dressed, she heard Dave's heavy feet on the stairs. Throwing open the door, he stood panting, hair rumpled, plaid pajama top over a pair of torn jeans, slippers on his feet. She giggled through sobs, "You're not quite dressed."

He laid a hand on her shoulder. "You don't look so great yourself." He turned her toward the bedroom. "Let's see what's wrong with Finch."

Finch opened her eyes and murmured, "Oh, Uncle Dave, I knew you'd come."

"There, there, little bird. We are taking you to the doctor, and he's going to make you right again."

He wrapped the sweat-drenched girl in the blue blanket, took the bundle in his arms and made his way down the stairs.

Bixby Hospital's ER was well lit. Finch blinked in the light and clasped Dave's pajama top.

"Where is everybody?" whispered Sparrow, peering around the empty waiting room.

"I've got a little girl who needs to be seen," boomed Dave.

There was a pop. A young receptionist looked up from behind the counter, a ring of bubble gum plastered across her nose and cheeks. "Oh, you startled me!" In one swoop, she tore the gum away. All business, she pressed a button and a nurse appeared. When Sparrow turned to follow Dave and the child, the young woman cautioned her to stay and register.

"No," Dave said, more forcefully than he intended. "She should be with the child. I'll come back out and register."

"But the mother must sign the forms."

Dave's eyes blazed, but his voice was calm. "I'll give you the information, then you take the forms to her and she can sign."

The receptionist shrugged. "Sure."

Dave followed the nurse to the examining room and laid Finch on the table. Sparrow stood by the table, holding her daughter's hand.

Back in the reception area, Dave answered the obligatory questions. When asked for the father's name, he replied, "None."

The young woman typed "not available" on the form.

When asked about health insurance, he replied curtly, "None. But don't you worry. I'll see that the bill is paid!"

The young woman nodded and continued typing.

The doctor, awakened from his late-night nap, became alert as he examined Finch. When he prodded her burning right side, she screamed.

Three hours later Sparrow and Dave sat waiting on a well-worn vinyl couch. Dave slumped forward, his head nodding on his chest. Sparrow, fingers digging into her palms, replayed the preceding days and weeks. What had she missed? Was this some sort of delayed punishment for her sins? "Oh God," she prayed. "Let her live. I will be a better mother."

The door swung open; the surgeon, head still covered, mask around his neck, walked to them. Towering above them, he cleared his throat. Dave roused from his sleep.

"You got here in time. It wasn't ruptured." He smiled. "She's going to be fine."

When Finch awoke, her mom was holding her hand. "I didn't die."

"Of course not, silly. You just had your appendix out."

"Pendix?"

"Yes, it's a part of you that you don't need, and it was sick. So the doctor cut you open, and took it out, and sewed you up. You will be as good as new."

So that's what the glass did, thought Finch. It cut up my pendix.

Peacocks and Witches

While Finch was recovering from her appendectomy, Angie came to visit. The girls were lounging on Sparrow's bed, eating Maria's famous chocolate chip cookies.

"Be careful, don't get any crumbs on the cover," said Finch, rescuing a chocolate chip from the white spread. She leaned toward Angie and whispered, "Did you look at your mom's crown?"

"She never wears it. She won't know. Do you think it caused your operation? Did you tell your mom?" She popped a half cookie into her mouth.

"No!" Crumbs spattered from Finch's mouth. "I can't tell my mom. She'd never let me go anywhere again."

"I heard my folks talking. My mom says your mom is protective because you don't have a father." The words tumbled out. Angie had spoken the unspeakable. She fixed her gaze on the wall.

Finch busied herself swishing crumbs off the bed. Did she have a dad? Her mom was always there, although sometimes she would sit really still at the table for a very long time, reminding Finch of a department-store dummy. At those times Finch had to talk really loud or touch her mom to get her attention. Uncle Dave said Sparrow was a daydreamer. There were other kids in her class who lived with their mothers. Eddy brought a duffle bag with him to school on Fridays when he spent weekends with his dad. One day Susie cried at recess and said her dad was going to live in an apartment. These kids didn't live with their dads. But she was the only one who didn't have a daddy at all. Finch watched the last of the crumbs fall to the floor.

"I do too have a father," said Finch.

"Well, where is he?"

"Mom won't say. Says she'll tell me when I'm older and can understand. She gets all funny when I ask." Finch sighed. "But I make up stories about him."

"You do? I love your stories. Tell me."

Finch shook her head. "No, you'll laugh."

Angie got on her knees and clasped her hands. "Pleeease!"

"Hmm, well, I made up a fairy tale."

"Tell me."

"You've got to promise not to laugh."

"I promise." Angie set her glass on the floor, propped herself up on a pillow and shut her eyes.

Finch crossed her legs and cleared her throat. "Okay." She whispered, "Once upon a time, in a land far away, there lived a bunch of beautiful peacocks with real bright blue-and-green wings. They had a language, just like people, and could fly wherever they wanted. Now, one guy was the most handsome of all the peacocks. All the girl peacocks wanted him… *but he was already married*. Now, there was a *very ugly girl peacock* with dull, droopy wings who looked more like a vulture than a peacock." Finch screwed up her face and dropped her arms to her sides.

Angie giggled.

"Now this ugly peacock wanted this guy for herself. So, she went to the local witch and asked to be made beautiful, so that the peacock would love her."

"Was the witch like a person or a bird?"

"A witch. Witches are witches. You know that! Now, the witch was a *very bad* witch and was jealous of all the peacocks flying around so easy when she had to work so hard to make her broom catch the wind. And on days when there wasn't any wind, she couldn't even fly." Finch took a deep breath and made her voice shrill. "She said, 'I can't make you beautiful but, if you will forfeit the ability to fly, not just for you, but for all peacocks, I'll send the handsome peacock's wife away!'"

"Why couldn't the witch make the ugly peacock pretty?"

"'Cause she didn't have pretty powers, stupid. She just had change powers. So, the ugly peacock wanted the handsome peacock more than she wanted to fly, so, she said, 'Okay.'"

"Ooh, that was real mean, making a promise like that!"

"Do you want to hear the story or not?"

"Yeah, sure, sorry." Angie stretched out on the bed.

Finch whispered, "Well, one dark and evil night there was a huge, gigantic wind…. And the witch swatted her broomstick and rode that terrible wind up into the tree where the birds slept…. A twig snapped and they stirred…." Finch stopped.

"Then what happened?"

"The witch sprinkled magic dust in their eyes to make them sleep, and twirled her magic wand and said the magic words, 'Alakazam! Carry this bride away from this land.'" Finch spread her arms wide. "Swoosh, swoosh, swoosh. The wind blew harder and harder. It blew so hard that it snatched up the pretty peacock and threw her in a dark hole in the sky!"

"How is there a hole in the sky?"

"Do you want to hear the end?" Angie nodded. "Well, she was thrown down to earth. And she lost all her feathers." Finch's voice reached a crescendo. "The bird became a woman! She was set down in this very spot, and you know what?"

"What?"

"She was still holding the egg that she was hatching."

"She'd laid an egg?"

"Yeah. Now, the handsome peacock was so mad he tried to kill the witch, but of course, you can't kill a witch. So, she threw him out of peacock land! He turned into a person, too. But the witch was mean and nasty. *She sent him clear to China!*"

"Ooh!"

"So this is the way the story ends. The egg hatched and became a beautiful baby girl. To this day the daddy is searching the world to find his wife and his baby. And," Finch spoke with authority, "that's why peacocks can't fly."

"Oh, that's real sad."

"No, it's not." Finch sat up. "My daddy's real smart. He'll find us. And right now we have Uncle Dave. He's like a grandpa. And if my daddy doesn't find us, when I grow up, I'll find him."

The Bully
Winter 1969

*I*n the fourth grade, Gurnsey Oltman started calling Finch "Bastard Girl." She looked up bastard in the dictionary: "an offensive or disagreeable person...an illegitimate person." The words stung. She looked up illegitimate: "born of unmarried parents, illegal, not recognized by law as lawful offspring." She was illegal? She didn't belong to her mother? However, a synonym for bastard was "love child." Her mom loved her, and her dad would, too, if she could find him. But each time Gurnsey said the word, it felt like she'd been punched in the stomach.

One snowy January day Finch and Angie were hurrying home from school when Gurnsey and a couple of boys caught up with them. "Look here!" Gurnsey yelled, as he chucked a snowball and hit Finch in the back. Finch scooped up snow and threw it with all her might, hitting Gurnsey in the face. Gurnsey hollered, "We'll get you for that! Come on, guys!" The three boys each packed a snowball. Finch and Angie ran, but a snowball struck Angie in the back. She fell face down in the snow, crying.

The other boys ran off, but Gurnsey threw more snowballs. He taunted, "What's the matter, Stubby? Bastard Girl can't protect you?"

"Don't you call us names!" Finch threw herself on Gurnsey's back. He threw her off and made another snowball.

Three stores away Sparrow, sweeping the entry to Booknook, saw Finch fighting with Gurnsey. Leaving the door agape, brandishing her broom, hair and skirt billowing, she raced toward the three, yelling, "What's going on here? You leave those girls alone!"

Gurnsey flung his snowball and fled.

"So that's the bully you've been telling me about," said Sparrow, surveying the white-powdered girls.

Finch leapt up and stomped her feet. "He's the meanest kid in school. Everyone's afraid of him. He makes me so mad!"

Sparrow helped Angie to her feet and brushed snow from her coat. "Are you okay, Angie?"

"Yeees, I guess so."

"He's dead meat!" muttered Finch.

"Let's make some cocoa and get you warm." Sparrow put an arm around each girl and ushered them into Booknook. "He looks a little out of your league. Perhaps I should go to the principal."

Sparrow's words were different than her thoughts. She dreaded the idea of going to the school. With the teachers, most old enough to be her mother, she would feel like a child called down for some imagined infraction. Confronting the principal would be excruciating. Finch was resilient. Surely she could work it out on her own. She walked to the back of the shop, put water on to boil and heaped tablespoons of cocoa into mugs.

Their wet coats and mittens piled on a chair, the girls sat at the table drinking cocoa. Finch dropped a third marshmallow into her cup, splashing cocoa onto the table.

"Look what you're doing, Finch!" said Sparrow. "What're you thinking?"

"Mom, you were awesome. You had this big broom and your hair was wild, and your skirt was flapping. You looked like you were going to scoop Gurnsey right up and sweep him into the street."

"Yeah," said Angie. "You were real mean looking, like a witch getting ready to fly at him."

"Or cast an evil spell, turn him into a frog," chimed in Finch.

Sparrow laughed. "And wouldn't he have looked funny hopping down the street in the snow?"

"That was real brave, Mom, coming out like that in the snow and all."

"Why…what do you mean, Finch? You girls were in trouble."

That night Finch lay in bed staring at the ceiling, thinking. She couldn't bear the thought of talking to the principal. She would have to *tell*. How could she say Gurnsey was calling her Bastard Girl? She'd be telling a secret—a secret about her dad—a secret her mom never talked about. Uncle Dave said that telling secrets was like airing dirty underwear. And she wasn't going to do that.

Somehow she'd make Gurnsey pay. He was tons stronger than her, but she was smarter. Finch remembered being little and pretending that she had magical powers. She had often thought of making crotchety customers disappear, and sometimes even her mom, when she was stern with her. It had helped her feel better. But pretending now wasn't going to help. This was real. Gurnsey was just a big, dumb, mean kid who wore Sears Husky jeans with the pants legs rolled up. The kids called him "cow" behind his back. He was a bully and a coward who picked on her because she was small and he didn't think she could fight back.

What could she, a puny seventy-five-pounder, do to the biggest bully in the school? This had to be what Mom called mind over matter. She had to outwit Gurnsey. But how? She was a good storyteller; on a dark night she could scare Angie with her witch stories. Maybe she could think of a way to scare Gurnsey. Maybe she could make up a terrifying tale of something bad happening to him and somehow make it seem real.

Sunday evening Finch took a piece of paper and printed in huge letters:

> BEWARE IF YOU CALL NAMES.
> SOMETHING GHOSTLY WILL HAPPEN TO
> YOU! SINCERELY, THE GOOD WITCH.

When Finch entered the classroom, she slipped the note under the lid of Gurnsey's desk. She slid into her desk and opened the book *Matilda*. Finch admired Matilda, whose magical powers helped her foil the evil people that she encountered. But this morning Finch could only stare at the pages. At 8:58 Gurnsey plodded in, went to his desk, opened it, took the note out and read it. Finch watched as he looked warily around the room.

At recess Gurnsey showed the note to the other boys. His voice a sing-song, he chanted, "The witch is going to get me, the witch is going to get me." Then he wheeled on Finch and yelled, "Hey, Bastard Child, are you the witch? Like your mom's a witch with her big old broom. Does she fly around at night? Hey, everybody, Finch's mom's an old witch. I saw her flying down the street on her broom. Finch, the witch's daughter, the little witch!"

Finch bit down on her tongue until she could taste blood. She gave him an Are-you-crazy? look and continued playing hopscotch.

On Tuesday Finch wrote another note:

YOU WILL BE SORRY IF YOU
DO NOT CHANGE YOUR WAYS!
SINCERELY, THE GOOD WITCH.

On the playground during recess, Gurnsey targeted Angie. "Angie is a Tubby, Tubby, Tubby!" He spoke low enough so that Mrs. Molly, the elderly playground supervisor with a scarf wrapped around her head, couldn't hear him. He menaced Angie, dancing around her, waving his arms above her, until she ran to the girls' bathroom.

There was a note each day that week, and each day Gurnsey shared his notes with the boys.

Friday's note:

THIS IS YOUR LAST WARNING. IF YOU
DO NOT CHANGE YOUR WAYS, YOUR
TRUE NATURE WILL BE REVEALED, AND
SOMETHING TERRIBLE WILL HAPPEN TO
YOU! SINCERELY, THE GOOD WITCH

Gurnsey pranced around waving the note as though he'd won some honor, but when he called out, "Bastard Child," his voice cracked.

The notes were making things worse. Gurnsey's behavior had escalated. Finch was distressed. She had to do something else—but what?

That day when she went to gym, she noticed Gurnsey's dirty shorts on the bleachers. As he often did, he had forgotten to take them home to wash. He would drop them while he got a drink from the fountain and forget to pick them up. The next Monday he would find them where he had left them. After weeks of this, the shorts would give off an offensive odor, and the kids would call him "stinky cow" behind his back. Eventually he would take the shorts home to wash. Finch thought of stealing his shorts, but he'd probably just think he had lost them. She would have to take more drastic action.

After school, heart galloping, she loitered in the gym until everyone had left. She was in luck; Gurnsey's shorts were on the bleachers. She rolled them in a tight ball and stuck them in her backpack.

After supper, Finch announced that she was going to make her doll a dress and went to work in the back of the store. Carefully, she cut the shorts away from the waistband and sewed band and shorts back together with a single thread, making half-inch stitches. She gave the shorts a tug to make sure that they held. In the bathroom, she emptied a can of citrus-scented spray on them and wrapped her smelly creation in a plastic bag.

Monday Finch woke feeling queasy. She thought she was sick, but then remembered what she'd planned. She'd never been in serious trouble at school. She considered staying home, but rolled out of bed and dressed. At breakfast, bites of pancake stuck in her throat, and the milk tasted sour. She folded the remainder of the pancake into her napkin and dropped it in the wastebasket.

Moments before the last bell, she darted into the deserted gym, tore open her backpack, pulled out the plastic bag, and tossed its repugnant contents onto the bleachers.

Gurnsey was late for gym. When he huffed in, the kids were occupied with kick ball. In the locker room, he shed his jeans and pulled the smelly shorts over his bare bottom. Gurnsey ambled onto the gym floor, a fruity scent emanating from his shorts.

Tom, a boy nearly as big as Gurnsey, sniffed the air. "Gurnsey, you stink. You got perfume on!"

"Naaa!"

"Yeah." Tom cavorted down the court. "Hey guys, Gurnsey's got perfume on!"

"I don't!" Gurnsey ran after him.

Tom stood his ground. "You smell like rotten oranges."

"Oooh!" Gurnsey pushed Tom.

They dropped to the floor, arms and legs flying. Mr. Krause, the teacher, blew his whistle and pulled them apart. The boys stood up.

Gurnsey's shorts dropped to his ankles.

On Sunday Finch wrote her last note, but could not sign it. On Monday she put the note in Gurnsey's desk:

> NOW YOU KNOW WHAT
> THE GOOD WITCH CAN DO.

"Good morning, class!" said Mr. Rice. "You all look bright and cheery this morning."

"Good morning, Mr. Rice!" All of the fourth graders, even those who hated school, liked Mr. Rice. He was funny and treated them as if they were real people. It was rumored that he had never flunked anyone. If a student couldn't get it, Mr. R. would work with him until he did.

"Let's get started. Open your books to page sixty-seven…."

The door opened and Gurnsey, eyes downcast, shuffled to his seat.

"Good morning. We're on page sixty-seven," said Mr. Rice.

Gurnsey, hand covering his right eye, pulled out his math book and opened it.

"Did you see that shiner?" Finch whispered to Angie.

"Yeah. I wonder who he got in a fight with this time."

There was a rustle of whispers around the room. The teacher cleared his throat and began. Finch could not think of math. She had to know what had happened to Gurnsey. She watched as he sat attempting to cover his black eye. When he laid his head on the desk, Mr. Rice went over to him, put his arm on his shoulder and spoke softly. The boy nodded.

"Gurnsey isn't feeling well. I'm taking him down to the nurse. Do your homework, and keep it down. You're on the honor system."

For two days Gurnsey's desk sat empty. On the third day, Mr. Rice told them that Gurnsey had had an accident that had caused him some internal injuries. He was in the hospital in Ann Arbor. Tom asked what kind of accident. The teacher replied that he didn't know, but it was serious. Then Mr. Rice suggested they each write a get-well card, and he would take them to Gurnsey.

Finch had wanted to embarrass Gurnsey, to make him sorry, and now he had had this accident, and it had happened right after she sabotaged his gym shorts. She could keep her secret no longer. At recess she told Angie.

"You did that?" Angie giggled. "You cut his shorts apart! It was you? Wow!"

Finch moaned. "But look what happened."

"Why didn't you tell me?"

"Didn't want to get you in trouble. Besides, it turned out lots worse than I thought it would."

"Oh, it's not your fault. That had nothing to do with his getting hurt."

"But he felt so bad. Maybe he just picked a fight, maybe with someone bigger."

"Nah."

It turned out that it was Gurnsey's dad who had beaten him, and it wasn't the first time. Belinda, the doctor's daughter, had heard her dad telling her mom. He'd treated the boy, and Finch thought it must be true. Gurnsey was getting out of the hospital and going to live with another family: foster care, it was called.

Before Gurnsey returned to school, Mr. Rice made an announcement. "Gurnsey has been very ill. And because of some difficult family circumstances, he's living in a different home." Mr. Rice cleared his throat. "Imagine how hard it would be for you to leave your family, to go to a strange home. Gurnsey is no different. I know that Gurnsey acts pretty tough, mean at times. But this is an opportunity for you to help him and welcome him back to class."

When Gurnsey walked into the room, he looked different, pale and caved-in. Head down, he slipped into his seat. Joe reached across the aisle and play-punched him on the shoulder.

"Hi, Gurns," he said.

Gurnsey stared straight ahead.

Mr. Rice stepped out of the room. Kids began to whisper. Gurnsey appeared to be engrossed in his math book. Finch, sick with guilt, tore out a piece of notebook paper and printed:

THE GOOD WITCH WAS NOT
GOOD. THE GOOD WITCH DID NOT
MEAN TO HURT YOU. I AM SORRY!

She wadded it into a ball and tossed it to Gurnsey's desk. He unrolled it, glanced at it, and squashed it back into a ball.

Mr. Rice rounded the door just as Gurnsey made a perfect shot into the wastebasket.

"Great basket, fellow," said Mr. Rice with a wink.

Gurnsey didn't look up to see the wink.

After class Mr. Rice detained Gurnsey. "You have good aim. You should work on it. I'm going to be coaching middle-school basketball next year. I'm working out on Saturdays, getting in shape, can't expect those kids to do anything I can't do. I know you'll still be too young to play, but why don't you come down and practice with me, bring some of your friends?"

Gurnsey looked up. "Practice with you?"

"Yes."

Gurnsey nodded and shuffled out of the room.

Mr. Rice stuck his hand in his pocket and felt for his pipe. It was too bad about the boy. Although he didn't show it, he was a smart kid, but he didn't have a chance with a father like his. It was no wonder he was a bully. The big one beats on the little one, and the little one beats on the littler. Now that Gurnsey wasn't living at home, maybe he'd do better. The teacher took a puff off his dry pipe. "There's something about that boy," he said to himself. "Maybe I could make a basketball player out of him."

On the Court
Spring 1971

*A*ngie's tongue swirled around her cone, making the cool white mound into a perfect column. Finch's Mudslide was melting, and pecans oozed off the spoon before she could get them to her mouth. The girls had walked to Frosty Boy on the way home from school to celebrate the last day of fifth grade. Next year they would go to Dragger Middle School.

"I've got to stop and finish this. My backpack keeps slipping," said Finch.

"It was your big idea to eat on the way home. We could've sat at a picnic table."

"You know your mom told you to get home early." Finch pointed toward a fenced-in area. "Look, the guys are playing basketball with Mr. R."

"Let's watch just for a minute," said Angie.

"You're the one who'll get in trouble." Finch took a huge bite and tossed the dish into a trash container.

The girls tossed off their backpacks and sat cross-legged under the sycamore tree, watching the boys do lay-ups. Mr. Rice stood at the sideline, giving pointers. "Take your time, take your time," he called.

A sturdy kid with an unruly shock of dark hair was all over the court, tossing the ball in each time it was his turn. "That-a-way to go," hollered Mr. Rice.

"Would you believe that's Gurnsey?" asked Angie.

"Never."

It had been more than a year since Gurnsey's "accident." Last summer Belinda had spread the word that Mr. R. had got something called a foster-care license and Gurnsey was living with him. The change in Gurnsey had been so gradual that they had not noticed. For months after "the accident" he had kept to himself and done his homework. When Finch spoke to him, he turned away. She thought he must know that she had written the notes.

Gurnsey made a slam dunk.

"Cool," said Angie.

Finch shook her head.

"He really is," said Angie.

"What?"

"Cool."

"He's pretty good at basketball," admitted Finch.

"Duh!" Angie flicked Finch's arm.

John, the half-pint, ran under the basket and tossed the ball. It danced on the rim and then went in. "Yeah!" the boys hollered. Gurnsey clapped him on the back.

Mr. Rice walked across the court toward the girls. "Want to shoot a few?"

"Me?" asked Angie. "No way. Besides, I have to go home, but Finch is good at basketball."

Finch shrugged.

"Want to?"

Finch demurred. "Oh…"

Gurnsey caught her eye. "Come on, Finch. You're not bad for a girl."

"Not bad!" Finch wiped her hands on her jeans, leapt to her feet and found herself on the court.

"Don't be too hard on them, Finch," called Angie. She picked up her backpack, slung it over her shoulders, and started walking. She looked back just as Finch missed a basket.

Found Out
Spring 1972

*F*inch prodded Angie to hurry as they walked to catch the bus. They arrived just as the sixth graders were lining up and the yellow bus belched to a stop. Finch grabbed Angie's hand and ran to the front of the line. When the door opened, she shoved Angie into the bus and pulled her down on the front seat. Angie bounced up; Finch jerked her back.

"What's with you?" asked Angie, flinging off Finch's hand. "We're just going to an old art museum. Let's sit in the back, away from the teachers."

"No."

"Why not?"

"It's just that I've never been to Ann Arbor, and I wanna see exactly where I'm going."

"No! Everybody's been to Ann Arbor."

"Shh, someone will hear you."

Gurnsey—now called Gurns—jumped up the steps and entered the bus. His eyes lit on Finch.

"Hi, Gurns," said Finch. Then she whispered to Angie, "I must have been there when I was little, just

125

don't remember. You know my mom doesn't have a car."

"Mom calls her a recluse. Says your mom is so smart, and she just sits in that drafty old bookstore and wastes her life away."

Finch burned with the slap of the words. "She's not a recluse! She works all day, and she talks to people all the time. She's tired at night."

For the remainder of the ride, the two sat with a wall of silence between them. Gazing intently out the window, Finch counted red cars. By the time the bus groaned to a stop in front of the museum, she had counted 197. Inside, the girls walked stiffly through the exhibits, together but apart. Once their hands touched, and Finch jerked hers away.

Gurns and his friend Sam fell in behind them. Gurns stepped on the back of Finch's loafer. "Sorry," he said.

Finch glared at him and adjusted her shoe.

At lunch Gurns and Sam rushed to sit across from the girls. The boys ran rivers of ketchup over French fries and devoured hamburgers. Their voices boomed above the racket in the cafeteria as they talked about the upcoming football game with Chelsea. Angie, head bent over burger and fries, ate in mincing bites. Finch's lunch sat untouched as she sipped her Coke and looked off into the distance.

Angie peered over her sandwich and held out fries. "Want some?"

Finch shrugged, turned her lips up in a fake smile and took one. Angie sighed. Gurns, stuffing his mouth, spat out, "What's with you girls?"

After school, Maria parked behind the bus and watched the girls tumble out into the wind. By the time she dropped Finch at Booknook, the wind was ferocious. Sparrow, hair billowing about her face, waited on the sidewalk, gripping her full-length skirt.

"How was it?" Sparrow asked, as she smoothed Finch's hair with her free hand.

"Fine," Finch replied, pulling away. She ran into Booknook and stomped up the stairs. She went into her makeshift bedroom, separated from her mother's by curtains, and plunked onto the narrow bed, leaving her shoes on. She thought that if she dirtied the spread it would serve her mother right. Finch had thought that Sparrow was capable and smart, running the bookstore and reading all the books. She would wake at night and see her mother curled in the armchair, a book in her lap. But Sparrow seldom left Booknook. And each time Finch wanted to go somewhere different, someplace she had never been, she had to beg and plead. Sometimes she worried when she left her mother home. She had known that something was amiss, something unspeakable, but now Angie had given it words. Her mother was a recluse. And at that moment Finch despised her.

Finch sulked through supper. She played with her goulash, scooping it into a mountain and stabbing it with her fork. Food splattered onto her lap.

Sparrow looked up. "What's the matter with you?"

Finch picked the macaroni from her lap and tossed it onto her plate. "Nothin'."

"You haven't told me anything about the class trip, and you've been irritable all night. Did something happen?"

"No."

Sparrow made her voice light and touched Finch's arm. "Ah, come on. Something's bothering you."

"No, nothing's bothering me!"

Sparrow drummed her fingers on the table. "What is wrong, Finch?"

Something broke inside of Finch. "Yes! *Something's wrong with you!* You're not like other mothers. You never go anywhere. You never do anything. You just sit in that rickety old chair and read." She paused, and then yelled, "You don't even drive!"

"We…don't…have…a car."

"Uncle Dave has offered to teach you to drive, and we could get a car."

"Finch, we don't have a lot of money."

Finch wished her mother would scream at her. Then Finch could pull the pieces together and fight her. "Angie's mom says you're a recluse!"

"Oh." As if traveling from a long distance, Sparrow's voice was barely audible. "Well… I do like to be alone."

Finch stood, her chair screeching across the linoleum. "And what about my dad! Where's my dad?"

Sparrow averted her eyes. "I've told you. He came to town one summer to work. I don't know where he is."

Silence. Sparrow sat. Finch stood listening to the kitchen clock, counting the ticks. When she reached sixty, she threw up her arms and ran down the stairs. Sparrow watched, elbows on the table, face in her hands, as the remainder of Finch's goulash mountain sank and spread across the plate.

Determination

*T*hat night Sparrow could not lose herself in a book. In bed, her self-recriminations kept her awake. Finally she cocooned herself in the well-worn blue blanket and waited for daylight. In the morning, her body stiff with tension, she readied the shop for business and then sat down at the table.

About nine-thirty Dave arrived, carrying two stuffed Kroger bags. He fumbled for his keys. "Damn, why can't she at least unlock the door?"

Sparrow rushed from the back of the shop and let him in. "Why didn't you honk?"

"Couldn't hear me if I did," Dave grumbled.

Sparrow took a sack and climbed the stairs.

Dave, panting, stumbled after her. "Don't know why you don't go yourself." He paused and leaned against the rail.

Sparrow put her bag on the counter and hurried back to take his. "Someone has to mind the store."

"Booknook open twenty-four hours a day?" Dave eased himself onto a chair.

Sparrow rummaged through a bag. "Dave, I don't have a car."

"And you don't drive. And you won't learn." Dave thumped his fingers on the table.

Sparrow poured him a cup of coffee. "Is it getting to be too much?"

"Damn it, Sparrow. I'm not doddering, at least not yet. But this is no life for you. Getting you out of here is like taking a crowbar to a piece of wood. What's the matter with you?"

Sparrow set the pot on the stove. "I don't know."

Dave cradled the cup in both hands and plunged ahead. "I think you need help."

"Help?"

"There's that new counseling place by Bixby Hospital that I've been reading about in the *Telegram*. They've got counselors, doesn't cost much. You go and talk to them about things. They straighten you out."

"Counseling? You want me to go to counseling? . . . I couldn't talk to strangers."

"Just an idea."

Sparrow's head felt heavy, her hands disconnected. She lifted a can of peas, but set it down. The antiquated refrigerator seemed to taunt her: "No frozen food for you." The tiny freezer compartment was useless; ice-cubes were cold-crusted water. It would be nice to have a new refrigerator—frozen vegetables, ice cream. Strange, she had not thought of that before; she had not known she wanted anything.

She shook her head to clear her thoughts. "Remember when I got my GED?"

Dave nodded.

"You kept at me that first year when Finch went to school." Sparrow got up and put a box of saltines in the cupboard."Remember how you got me to do it?"

"I told you I wasn't going to have a high-school dropout working in my shop."

"You threatened me." Sparrow folded a paper bag and put it in the drawer. "It had been so long since I'd been in school. I didn't think I'd pass. I was going to prove that I couldn't do it."

"So, what's this all about?"

"Finch called me a recluse." Sparrow forced her lips into a tight smile. "I'm afraid she might threaten to fire me, too. She's like you, thinks there's something wrong with me.... And there is. I'm always scared, afraid to do anything. I've thought about going to school, getting a driver's license. But it's almost as though my mother is outside the door, shaking her finger at me, telling me that I'll make a mess of it. The only way I've been able to survive, be half a mother to Finch, is, is because you took us in."

Dave held his mug in both hands. He did not have words to tell her how she and Finch had given him a reason for living.

"But you're both right. I can't hide any longer. I can't live through Finch. I have to make a life of my own." Tears trickled down her cheeks. She brushed them away and then studied her hands, as though to find some answer in their damp lines. Sparrow lifted her face. "I'm not ready to learn to drive yet, not yet, but I'll do something."

Dave nodded.

Sparrow spoke with an assurance that she did not feel. "Siena Heights. It's close. I could walk there. I'll take a college course, like you've been saying."

As though to call time out, the shop bell rang.

Help Comes in Many Forms
Late Spring 1972

Sparrow was determined to keep her promise. Although her stomach ached and she felt a headache coming on, she got out of bed, washed her face, brushed her teeth and dressed. She put a piece of bread in the toaster and paced the length of the kitchenette and living room while it toasted. She buttered it, took a bite and set it on the plate. Then she walked down the stairs and out the door to wait for Dave.

"Good morning," whispered Sparrow as she slid into the pickup.

"You're looking real pert this morning," Dave said.

It wasn't like him to give compliments, and certainly not to lie, but today he was desperate to boost her confidence. She was dressed neatly in a gray gored skirt with a fresh white blouse. Although her hair was pulled back, curly wisps had escaped and framed her pale face. Deep circles under her eyes offset the hint of lipstick on thin lips.

"The pansies are about done for," said Dave.

Sparrow did not reply, nor did she look at the drooping flowers. She sat rigidly, head forward, alert for unknown danger.

Dave continued, "The lawns are real green from all the rain, and the petunias are getting a good start."

Sparrow clasped her arms together. She could not bring herself to gaze at the pansies, or the lush lawns. They drove on in silence. Dave stopped the pickup in front of a group of well-cared-for brick buildings. A sign read Siena Heights College. Sparrow did not move.

Dave spoke softly. "Want me to go in with you?"

Sparrow willed herself to push the door handle down and step out of the car.

"I'll…walk home." She stumbled, caught herself, and started toward the buildings.

Dave watched as Sparrow trudged up the walk in her dated clothes. She reminded him of a doomed prisoner. But she was just registering for one summer course—a small thing. Why the hell did she have to act like every new thing might be the end of her? He put the gearshift in low, pushed on the gas pedal and pulled away faster than he intended.

Sparrow saw the campus in a blur. She had an appointment with Sister Mary at eight-thirty; it was now eight-twenty-five. A boy and girl walked across the lawn, talking and giggling. As they passed, she tried to ask where the Admissions Office was but could not make her lips form the words.

When she was able to locate a sign, the letters seemed to run together as though the paint had dripped, and she could not make them out. Her heart raced; the ground beneath her swayed. Through a haze, she saw a bench and, like a sailor on a rolling ship, made her way toward it. Grasping the back of the bench, she lowered herself onto it and clung to its slats while the ocean roared in her head. She had had this feeling on the first day of school, at the drug store, when coming to the bookstore. But she had not felt it in a long time.

After a while, she made out shapes crossing the campus. Girls in sandals, with painted toenails, dangling earrings, colorful shirts and skirts, were laughing and talking as they strolled to their classes. She looked at her own drab skirt and black flats. Always out of step, a misfit. It was a mistake thinking she could come here, that she could be a part of this. She rose, the ground feeling more solid. She walked across the lawn, to the sidewalk, and away from campus. The sun blazed its way through the clouds. Oblivious to the heat, she put one foot in front of the other. Perspiration dripped from her face; her hair loosened itself and clung to her neck. A memory floated, unreachable in the back of her head. Something she had thought about, something that had been said. An image formed in her mind. She had been crying; Clare was there, her face one large mouth, lecturing her. "You need to do this. If not for you, for Finch."

Instead of turning left at Main Street toward home, Sparrow continued on along Siena Heights Drive, right on Bent Oak, then left on Riverside Avenue. Her feet seemed to lead her—over a bridge, up a hill, past the lake. Breathing heavily, she stopped in front of a new brick building. The sign read PROFESSIONAL BUILDING, BIXBY COMMUNITY MENTAL HEALTH. As though pulled by a magnet, she made her way to the entrance.

The glass door was heavy. A blast of freezing air made her clutch the wall for support. She stood frozen as the hall spun around her. Rubber legs no longer held her; her back slid down the wall until she slumped onto the floor.

From a distance she heard a voice. "Are you ill? Can I help you?"

Sparrow opened her eyes and saw two identical portly women swaying above her. Twins, she thought. As the women bent toward her, they became one. "I don't know. I don't think so. I get this way sometimes, but it hasn't happened for a long time. I saw the sign and…."

"Sit here for a minute, and I'll get you a drink of water." The woman disappeared through an office door.

Had she been able, Sparrow would have stood up and left, but she could only lean back against the wall and listen to the breathing of the alien person inhabiting her body. When the woman returned with a paper cup filled with water, Sparrow swallowed it in greedy gulps. The woman brought her a second cup.

Sparrow whispered, "I was going to register for college. I was scared…I felt sick…. Clare said… and Dave too…they said I should come.

Dr. Nickels, director of the fledgling mental health clinic, was well acquainted with the symptoms of panic attack. She put her hand on Sparrow's shoulder and said, "I'm going to the clinic. I think you should talk with someone. I'll show you the way."

"Well, I'm not sure. I should get back…." Sparrow's words trailed off.

Dr. Nickel's voice was quiet, reassuring. "Just come and see where the clinic is. You've had a fright. We'll see if someone is available to see you. If you want to talk, you can. Or you might want to make an appointment. At any rate, you should sit a few minutes and make certain that you're okay."

She guided Sparrow down a flight of stairs, through a door and into a room lined with blue upholstered chairs. She led her to one of the soft chairs, and Sparrow sank into it.

The doctor peered into the receptionist's window. "Joan, we have a walk-in. Is there a therapist available?"

Joan came out of the windowed office and invited Sparrow in. She asked for name, address, phone number, age and finally income. She explained that the clinic had a sliding fee scale and Sparrow's fee would be five dollars.

Sparrow nodded.

When asked why she had come, Sparrow replied, "I don't know, I'm not certain, but I think something happened to my mind this morning."

Ms. Sparks had soft dishwater-blonde hair and spoke with a hint of a southern drawl. She introduced herself as a social worker, said they would talk for a while and try to figure out what had been so distressing. Could Sparrow tell Ms. Sparks about herself?

An hour later, her face tear-stained, Sparrow emerged from the office. She took an appointment card from the receptionist and asked to use the phone. When Dave answered, she asked, "Can you come and get me? I'm at the Bixby Outpatient Mental Health Clinic on Riverside."

Enchiladas
Fall 1972

Several months later, in the therapist's office, Sparrow sat on the edge of her chair, black skirt covering her legs. Thrusting a strand of errant hair behind her ear, she inadvertently knocked out several of the hairpins that held her hair in place. Hair tumbled about her shoulders; she shook her head and swished strands from her face. Ms. Sparks sat relaxed in her chair, skirt just reaching her knees, soft, wavy hair accenting her gentle face.

"She's always at Angie's. When she is at home, she's in her room reading or listening to music. She finds time to play chess with Dave but doesn't have the time of day for me. She treats me like a non-person." Sparrow glared at Ms. Sparks. "You haven't said hardly anything. What can I do? I feel like I'm losing Finch!"

"First of all, it's natural for a young adolescent to pull away from her mother, to need some space. Remember how it was?"

Sparrow flung herself back in her chair. "But this is not the same. I *want* Finch to have friends, to have a life."

"Yes, but what about you?"

"What do mean, what about me?"

Ms. Sparks inclined her head. "When you first walked in here, you were talking about the things you needed to do. You said you wanted to go to school, learn to drive, make friends. You didn't want to be like your mother. You wanted to conquer your fears."

Sparrow bristled. "Well, I do have a job. My mother didn't. And I will be learning to drive, and I do intend to register for classes...." She ran her hand through her hair. "But I guess I haven't done anything much different...yet."

Ms. Sparks waited.

"Oh, I get up in the morning, and I think of all the things I have to do, and I say, Oh, I'll drive tomorrow, or I'll call the college tomorrow.... I don't feel anything. But if I try to do something new, something out of my routine, I'm terrified. I dread to go somewhere I've never been, and I worry about Finch when she does. Sometimes it even bothers me to go to the grocery store!"

Sparrow leaned forward. "The other day I found this picture of my mother. She must have been about my age. She was holding Jay, and I was standing next to her holding on to her long skirt. Her hair was in a bun, sort of like mine, and it occurred to me—I look just like her, my clothes and the way I wear my hair. How can that be? It's like I'm becoming my mother. And I hate her!" Stunned by her confession, she gripped the arms of her chair.

Ms. Sparks opened her hands. "Sparrow, that is the only life you knew. Your mom was afraid, and you learned that fear from her. You never had the opportunity as an adolescent to experiment, to move away, and when you did, it was with disastrous consequences. You lost your family! So for you, to take action is frightening."

"But I want my life to be different. I want to be independent."

"If you truly want to be more independent, more your own person, you need to begin to try new things."

"Like what?" Sparrow's eyes blazed. Her anger was palpable. But the anger masked helplessness. She was stuck and demanding suggestions that she could not act on.

Ms. Sparks spoke tenderly. "Something you'd like to do. Go to a movie; go out with Maria. So, you feel vulnerable and you're afraid of doing something wrong, of being embarrassed. But these are little steps, not too risky, and you might actually enjoy them." She smiled. "Have you ever asked Maria up to your apartment?"

A vinegar decanter with three yellow daisies adorned the sky-blue tablecloth set with white Corelle and paper napkins. Sparrow sighed as she took the mismatched silverware out of the drawer. Wrapping place settings in triangular napkins, she put them on the counter next to Finch's Betty Crocker brownies. The tossed salad was in the refrigerator; enchiladas, a recipe from an Old El Paso sauce mix, were bubbling in the oven. Milk and ice tea were poured and on the table. Six o'clock: time for them to come.

Sparrow went downstairs to make certain the door was unlocked. Back upstairs, she took the enchiladas out of the oven and rested them on a scorched hot pad. Back down to the bathroom, she washed her face, brushed her hair, put a rubber band around it and pinned it off her neck. Back in the kitchen, she covered the casserole with a towel and took the salad and French dressing from the refrigerator. Then she sat, hands clasped, studying the cracks in the yellow and blue linoleum, listening to the refrigerator's deathly rasp, the clock ticking in the background.

Ten minutes. She rose and paced the length of the apartment, peered out the window. Six twenty-one. Maybe something had happened to them. It was raining. They could have had a wreck. She should call, but if they were en route they wouldn't be home. Still, if they were confused about the day or time, they might be there. She picked up the phone and then returned it to its cradle. She walked to the easy chair and sat down.

They were not coming. Damn that Ms. Sparks and her big ideas! She jumped from the chair and hollered. "Finch, Finch, they're not coming! We're going to eat, come on now, get your head out of that book and get up here!"

She went to the kitchen, wrested an enchilada from the pan and plopped it on a plate. Red sauce spread across the dish, matching her mood. The doorbell pierced her rage. Sparrow dropped the spatula and ran to the stairs. There the two women met, Maria's plump body filling the staircase, Angie bringing up the rear.

"I'm so sorry to be late," Maria apologized. "Anton called just as we were walking out the door. I complain about that man not talking, and then the one time I'm in a hurry he can't shut up, and then I couldn't find my keys, and there was this fender-bender on Beecher

Street. You know how slick it is out there. And I was sandwiched in between two cars."

Sparrow backed up the stairs in front of the panting Maria. "It's okay, no problem. It's fine."

Maria, Angie, Finch and Sparrow filled the kitchen area, the sloping ceiling confining them in a tight circle. "How cute," said Maria.

Finch looked at Angie and grunted. The girls sat on chairs at the empty place settings and waited.

Holding her purse, Maria stood by the table. "Is there anything I can do?"

"Oh, no." Sparrow turned toward the stove, then the table, uncertain where to begin.

Maria put her purse on the counter and sat in a chair by the wall.

"We're just having enchiladas. Finch says you like them." Sparrow's hand shook as she filled the remaining plates and placed them on the table. She eased into her chair.

"Mom, we don't have any silverware," said Finch.

"Oh!" Sparrow extricated herself from the chair and jerked the napkins off the counter. One unfurled and a fork and knife fell onto the cracked linoleum.

"Mom!" scolded Finch.

"I'm always dropping things," Maria said.

Sparrow grabbed the fork and knife from the floor, rinsed and dried them and thrust them toward Finch.

Finch did not pick up her fork, but sat staring at Sparrow.

"What?" asked her mother.

"Where's the chips?"

"What do you mean?" Sparrow felt the red rising in her cheeks.

"You know—the taco chips and salsa and hot sauce. We always have them at—"

"Oh, no," Maria interrupted, "not true. I don't always have them."

"That's right," piped in Angie. "Sometimes we just have beans and rice with enchiladas."

"Have some salad, girls," said Maria.

"You know I don't like tomatoes, Mom," Angie pouted.

Sparrow's cheeks were scarlet. "Oh, I didn't know."

"Pick them out," said Maria through clenched teeth.

Finch popped up, took out a tray of crusty ice cubes and banged them on the table. Water sloshed onto the silverware.

Sparrow sponged it with her napkin.

Oblivious, Finch plunked a cube in her milk. "Want one, Angie?"

"Sure,"

"Want some, Mrs. Gonzalez, Mom?"

"No, thank you." Maria took a drink of tepid tea.

Eyes riveted on her daughter, Sparrow said nothing.

"Gee, Mom, what did I do?" sputtered Finch, as she crammed a huge bite into her mouth.

"These aren't enchiladas. They're made out of flour tortillas." declared Angie.

In therapy the following week, Sparrow sat with her head down, avoiding Ms. Sparks's benevolent eyes. "It was awful! The enchiladas were cold, made out of a mix. I can't even get it right with a mix. The milk and tea were warm. The girls were nasty, and I was a nervous wreck. I invited Mexicans over for what *I* think is a Mexican meal. How stupid can that be? But what really bothers me is that I sort of froze up. I couldn't think. I was terrified that they wouldn't want to come. And when they were late, I thought they weren't coming."

"What made you think they wouldn't want to come?"

"I don't know. I guess it's how I felt as a kid, that we didn't have anything nice. We lived in a dilapidated house and no one ever came to visit. I wore homemade, patched clothes to school. Once I had a favorite red-checked dress that got worn out. It was faded and ripped. Mom cut out pockets from an old pair of jeans and sewed them on the dress. I could put all sorts of things in those pockets. I loved it. Then I went to school and the kids called me Patches.

"That must have been very hurtful."

Sparrow nodded. "I was so humiliated. I'd never thought much about how I dressed and all of a sudden I knew my clothes were raggedy. Nobody liked me… and I wanted to disappear!"

"So you were concerned you would be humiliated like you were when you were a child, that Maria wouldn't want to come and the dinner wouldn't be good enough. But…." Ms. Sparks paused. "But she did come."

"But the food wasn't right and the apartment is shabby."

"So you were embarrassed. It was your first dinner party, and it didn't go as you'd planned."

"No." Sparrow rubbed her hands over her skirt.

"Was it all that bad?" asked Ms. Sparks.

Sparrow pursed her lips. "Well, they ate it. But I know they didn't like it. The girls started talking and giggling about the terrible school lunches, and I thought they were making fun of my food, and I was hurt. I don't know what came over me. I told them it wasn't right to make fun of me like that!"

Ms. Sparks smiled.

Sparrow did not notice the smile. "Then they all felt bad and said they didn't mean anything by it. Then Maria said that everyone gets nervous when they cook for company…. We did play Monopoly, but I was just tied up in knots. I feel embarrassed even talking to you about it." Sparrow folded her hands and studied the wall.

"Oh, yeah, Maria did invite us over for enchiladas the Mexican way."

Romance Awry
Spring 1973

*O*n a beautiful spring morning, Dave dallied on his way to Booknook. It was after ten when he arrived. As he reached for the door it swung open and Sparrow emerged.

"I wondered what happened to you."

"What do you mean?"

"I'm taking the morning off."

Dave shook his head. "You didn't tell me."

Sparrow grinned. "I just decided."

"So, you just decided, and I should know?"

"I'll be back about noon. Think you can handle it yourself?" She started down the walk.

"Where are you going?"

"I have to do some stuff."

Dave leaned against the door and watched Sparrow saunter down the street wearing faded jeans and T-shirt, her hair pulled back in a rubber band. It was unlike her to spontaneously leave the shop, and when she did leave she was always immaculately groomed. He wondered what she was up to. It had been almost a year since he'd dropped her at Siena

Heights. He'd been irritated, angry even, that she'd not started college. But she had gone to counseling, was still going. He wasn't sure how it worked, talking about things instead of doing them, but she did seem different, wound less tight. He couldn't quite put his finger on it, but she was easier. She and Finch were getting on better, which was no small feat, as Finch was finishing sixth grade and had a mind of her own. Life was good, Dave thought. He opened the door and walked into the store.

Sparrow marched down the street. The snow was long gone. Tulips bloomed in sidewalk containers, and the sun felt welcoming. She was delighted at Dave's bewilderment and chuckled to think of what his reaction might be when she returned. It was a short walk to Adrian Beauty Academy. Sparrow flung open the door and was greeted by a honeysuckle scent. Then she caught a sour whiff of activator. A teenager with bleached hair sat behind the desk, reading a textbook.

Sparrow whipped the rubber band off her hair, tossed her head and said, "Cut it off—all of it."

"Cool! I can do that. Step right over to my chair."

Within the hour, Sparrow left the school sporting an Audrey Hepburn pixie haircut, although unlike the star's well-behaved hair, Sparrow's was a mass of soft curls, each going its own way. She ran her fingers through her hair and opened her arms to the sun. Feeling lighter, she proceeded up Maumee Street and entered Klein's Department Store.

In the jeans department, she picked up a pair of size eight Levi's and a red-and-blue T-shirt. Then she made her way to the dresses, where a gray-haired clerk asked if she could be of assistance. The peach dress Sparrow tried on accented her small waist and came just below her knees. She twirled in front of the mirror, the flared skirt billowing around her.

The motherly clerk smiled. "You look so pretty."

"I do?"

"Oh, yes. The dress is just right, and I love your hair."

When Booknook's bell rang, Sparrow looked up from her dusting chores. A young man stood in the doorway—not tall or fat, but his broad body seemed to fill the space. His bulky plaid shirt hung loosely around him. Ebony hair fell on his forehead, and his smooth square jaw was nicked from shaving.

Still holding the rag, Sparrow moved toward him. Something about him made her regret that she was wearing Dave's old white shirt as a coverall and had neglected to put on lipstick.

"Is there a clerk around?"

"I'm in charge."

"Oh, I thought maybe you were the cleaning girl." He pointed to the rag in her hand.

Sparrow thrust it behind her back. "I do everything."

"Really!"

Sparrow felt the color rise in her cheeks.

"No offense. I'm Ted." He paused, looked around the store. "What's your name?"

Sparrow shifted on her feet.

"Should I call you girl-who-does-everything?"

"No, I mean, yes. I'm Sparrow."

"Sparrow, like a bird—nice."

Sparrow was backed against the table. She thought, if she were a bird, she could fly up to the highest bookshelf and peer at him from a safe perch.

Ted stepped back. "I'm looking for a book for my niece. She'll be five."

"Oh, she'd like *Goodnight Moon*, or perhaps one of Dr. Seuss's books."

"She lives in Nebraska, where I'm from, little town of Imperial. Maybe you've heard about it on the weather channel?"

Sparrow shook her head.

"Always the hottest or the coldest." He leaned toward her. "I'll be in Imperial for her birthday."

Sparrow picked up a book and held it to her chest. The man moved closer;

Sparrow smelled his after-shave—Aqua Velva. She stepped back. It felt like a dance where they couldn't find the beat.

He was looking at her as if she should say something. She asked, "Have you read Willa Cather?"

"Who?"

"Willa Cather, a famous Nebraska writer. She wrote about the prairie, classics: *O Pioneers!*, *My Antonia*." She gulped for air. "But, of course, it would be way too old for your niece. I just thought since you're from Nebraska...."

A half step toward her. Sparrow was engulfed in his sweet scent. Words blurred; time stood still.

"...New here...don't know anyone...."

She stepped out of his space.

"...Really great book shop."

As she handed him the book, his large hand touched her small one.

"See you next time."

She saw him stride out of the shop, as if in slow motion.

Every day that week when he came in, Sparrow was swept into a dizzying dance—two steps forward, one back. Ted bought another children's book, asked for an engineering text that she didn't have; finally, the day he purchased *O Pioneers!*, she agreed to go out with him.

Finch was staying all night with Angie; the girls were planning to eat sandwiches at Millers, and Anton would drop them at a movie. Sparrow told her daughter that she was going out, but not with whom or where.

Finch answered, "Oh, good, you never go anywhere."

Sparrow was disappointed that her daughter was too self-absorbed to ask where she was going, but relieved that she did not have to explain. She wondered what Ms. Sparks would say. Dave, Ms. Sparks, Finch, Maria, they all said that she should have a social life. After all, she was almost thirty—practically middle-aged. Other than Rob Roye, she had never had a date. In retrospect, her experience with Rob Roye did not seem like what she would call dating. Her idea of dating came from romance novels; it was courting, with dinners, concerts, movies, and long walks in the park. The hero was masculine, yet gentle and protective, and never would he take advantage of the heroine. She hoped that Ted would be that way. And she wished they had talked about where they were going, what they would do. She felt caught up in the vortex of something that she hoped would not spin out of control.

She wore the new peach dress, brushed her short hair until it shone and applied a little makeup. She liberally sprayed Finch's lilac cologne on her neck and wrists. But tonight the odor seemed too strong. She rubbed her wrists to rid herself of it, but some fragrance lingered. Ready ahead of time, stomach churning, she waited by the door. At seven a 1970 Thunderbird pulled to the curb in front of the store. Locking the door behind her, she joined Ted on the street.

"Hi." He put his arm around her shoulders and guided her to the car. "It's going to be a great sunset."

Indeed, the sky was vibrant with reds and yellows, but Sparrow could only nod as she settled herself on the leather seat. They had not talked about where they were going, and she was terribly anxious. "*Guess Who's Coming to Dinner* is playing, with Sidney Poitier." She paused and gulped for air. "I hear it's real good."

"I thought we'd go over to the Holiday Inn, have a few drinks and listen to some music. Rick Evans, this guy who wrote "In the Year 2525," is entertaining there. You've heard it." Ted sang, "'In the year 2525, if man is still alive.'" He grinned. "And he grew up in Imperial, my home town. I'd like to hear him."

"But, but," Sparrow's mouth went dry. "I don't drink."

"You don't drink? That's okay. I think they have Coke." He reached across the car and drew her near him.

They drove to the Holiday Inn in silence, Aqua Velva mingling with a trace of lilac.

The lounge was dark and small, Rick not yet playing. Ted ushered Sparrow to a corner not far from the stage. A barmaid came over.

"Screwdriver and a Coke and whiskey," he said.

"But," Sparrow protested.

"Try it, you'll like it."

She did like it. The whiskey made the Coca-Cola taste sweet, yet pungent. It eased the lump in her throat and the dryness of her mouth. Between swigs Ted rotated the glass in his hand, ice clinking, a few drips spilling onto the table. He talked about his work as an engineer, how he missed his family and the farm, but didn't think he'd go back. He emptied his glass; Sparrow's was still half full. He called the waitress over and ordered another round of drinks. He was thirty-three, he said, had been in the Marines, was still in the reserves, worked full time at GM, and attended Siena Heights College. He didn't have much free time. Sparrow nodded, took small sips and dabbed at the moisture on the table until the tiny napkin was soaked.

With his story out of the way, he looked at Sparrow expectantly. When she did not speak, he took her hand and one by one stroked her fingers. Rick Evans crooned, "In the year 2525 if man is still alive, if woman can survive…."

A tingle started at the tip of Sparrow's fingers, traveled up her arm and down her spine. She jerked her sweaty hand away and wiped it on her dress. Ted reached into her lap, retrieved it. His thumb circled her palm. The tingling again—up her arm, down her spine.

The music was mellow. Sparrow floated on a white-hot cloud. Ted ordered her a third drink, but she did not touch it. He gulped his, and they left the bar, Sparrow fitting snugly into the crook of his arm.

"Want to see my apartment?"

"Oh, no, I've got to get home." She paused, trying to think. "To Finch," she lied. But her body defied her, and she snuggled into his warmth.

When Ted turned off Maumee Street, Sparrow roused from a trance. "You're going the wrong way."

He held her more tightly, but did not reply. She opened her mouth, but nothing came out. He pulled into his apartment complex and parked next to the trash container.

When Sparrow's door opened, she found her voice. "I said I needed to go home!"

"It's all right. I just want to show you my apartment. Come in for a while."

She did not have words to insist that he take her home. As though she was incapacitated, he took her arm and helped her out. He propelled her up the wooden staircase to his apartment and held her tightly as he unlocked the door.

The living room was dark and spartan, furnished with a couch, easy chair and end tables with lamps. A large photo album lay open on the coffee table. A mirror over the couch and a picture of a brilliant sunset on the opposite wall completed the decorations. The apartment smelled of lemon Pledge, and Sparrow could see vacuum tracks in the shag rug. He motioned toward the couch.

"The picture's a Nebraska sunset," he said. "Nebraska has the most brilliant sunsets. It's flat, and you can see for miles. The colors fill the sky."

Her hand on the couch, Sparrow traced the smooth cool texture of the leather.

"I'm really enjoying the book." He gestured to *O Pioneers!* on the end table. "The description of the prairie before the land was settled. The hunting must have been terrific. It's still good, but every year there are fewer pheasants. When I was in my teens, I'd go out with my dad and we'd come home with four or five birds. Mom fried them like chicken, then simmered them in cream. So good! I always go back during hunting season. Here, look at these pictures." He placed the bulging album on Sparrow's lap.

Sparrow ran her fingers over the slick vinyl of the book. Ted turned on the stereo. Soft music filled the room. He came to her, eased her back on the couch and opened the album. His life lay before her: a weathered two-story farmhouse, an unpainted barn, and fields of wheat and corn. Then a serious, dark-haired boy, sitting on a tractor, gazed up at her.

"That's me. Cute kid, huh?" He laughed.

Sparrow had been tremulous all day. At supper she'd left a half-eaten baloney sandwich on her plate. The alcohol had eased her anxiety. Limp with exhaustion, she rested her head on Ted's shoulder.

"Let's dance." He took her hand and held her against his chest.

As they danced, Sparrow melted against his warm, rugged body. At the bedroom door, she opened her eyes and pulled her arms from his neck. He clasped her more tightly and kissed her. She could not breathe. She struggled, tried to push him away, but he held her, forcing her forward. Then the bed was at the back of her knees, the weight of his body pressing her onto the bed.

His kisses were hot and wet, her "no" muted. She pummeled his back. He reached for her panties. She resisted, pushing her bottom into the mattress. As though she was weightless, he lifted her and pulled off her pants. One hand holding her arm, he reached into the bedside table drawer and took out a condom.

"No," Sparrow moaned.

"It's okay."

"No," she moaned again. He opened her legs. Touched her. She was split, struggling against his strong hands, yet in a heat she could not comprehend. A cat screeched from the parking lot.

155

Afterwards, holding her close, he lay spent. "I'm sorry," he said. "I was so excited. Next time it will be better for you. Spend the night with me. Let me make it up to you."

"*No!*" Sparrow leapt out of bed and dressed quickly, hiding herself as best she could. "*I've got to get home!*" She headed for the front door and waited, hand on the knob, until Ted came out of the bedroom.

At Booknook, Sparrow allowed Ted to tilt her head and kiss her. As though in apology, he kissed her gently, his lips barely brushing hers.

"I'll call," he said.

The bell clanged as Sparrow entered the shop. Finch would not be home until after church in the morning, and Sparrow was alone. She dropped her wrinkled dress on the floor, ran a steaming bath, scrubbed herself, then soaked until the water grew tepid. She crawled into bed and fell into a deep sleep.

In her dream, she was running from a huge ball of fire. She bolted upright, heart palpitating, and stared into the bright morning sun. Head aching, mouth like sandpaper, she made her way to the bathroom and gulped a glass of water. The mirror reflected a pale-faced woman with wild hair and dark circles under her eyes.

In spite of her confusion, Sparrow recognized her anger. She had been raped! Or had she? She had said no, and she had struggled. But she hadn't fought. And in the end she had felt the most intense release. He'd asked her to stay, to spend the night, but he had not argued with her. With Rob it had been different, two kids discovering each other, exploring. She'd wanted to crawl into his body, to become a part of him. She had dreamed of him all these years, held him close in her heart. Still, he had deserted her. And he had left her pregnant!

She didn't think Ted meant her any real harm. And he had worn a condom. How could he know about this shame that rose like bile in her throat? And how could she feel so humiliated and yet have so much desire? It was as though she had discovered an empty room within her that cried out to be filled. She splashed cold water on her face and covered her toothbrush with mountains of toothpaste. Although she brushed her teeth ferociously, she could not rid herself of the dry, sandpapery taste.

Endings and Beginnings
Late Summer 1973

*S*parrow's unseeing eyes were fixed on the picture of a sailboat floating across Ms. Spark's blue wall. Sparrow was certain that she could not tell her therapist what had happened. A simple question, "Sparrow, what is the matter?" brought a flood of tears.

The story tumbled out. Then accusations. "Something's wrong with me. My mind tells me one thing, my body another. Why didn't he listen to me, take me to a movie? He forced me. But I let him.. I can't stand myself. My mom was right. I'm no good!" She put her head in her hands.

Ms. Sparks's eyes mirrored the sadness of the young woman. She waited.

Sparrow raised her head. "But why does he keep calling?"

Ted had kept his word and called. With little help from Sparrow, he made small talk. He asked her out. She made excuses—she had to work, or Finch was ill. She could not bring herself to tell him not to phone. Ted persisted. When he stopped at Booknook, there were other customers in the shop and Sparrow managed a business facade. The phone calls were a different matter. Sitting on the kitchen floor, clutching the phone, she found herself crossing her legs, right hand on left shoulder creeping toward her breast. After several weeks, she agreed to another date. As before, in spite of her resolve, it ended in his apartment.

In her weekly therapy sessions, Sparrow spewed humiliation, anger, sadness and—yes—excitement. She admitted to Ms. Sparks and, more importantly, to herself that those forbidden, nasty body feelings were indeed pleasurable. As the unspeakable was shared with someone who seemed to care, the shame that enveloped her in its tight snake's skin began to fray.

One sweltering August Sunday morning, when Finch had gone to church with Angie, Sparrow found herself knocking at Ted's apartment. Dressed in briefs, with liquid sleepy eyes, he opened the door, held out his hand, and took her into his arms. Only after they had made love did she tell him they had to talk, do ordinary things, get to know each other. There must be more to their relationship than falling into bed.

Unlike on the first night, Ted heard her. He said that he hadn't known she felt this way. And then, smiling, said, "Oh, you'd like to be courted." They agreed to meet for lunch at Mr. Ed's.

At lunch the conversation was formal, stilted. After he'd finished his meal, Ted wiped his mouth and folded his napkin. "Well, Sparrow, exactly what is it that you would like to do?"

Sparrow put down her half-eaten burger. "I, I'm not sure. I've been so busy with Finch, working at the bookstore. I guess I'm a little envious of all those girls who have regular dates, go to the movies, out to dinner, on walks, or just lie on a blanket at the park and talk."

Ted picked up the check; he winked. "Okay, I'd like to do those things, especially the part about lying on a blanket with you at the park."

Thus followed a series of proper dates. Sparrow confided that she was enamored with Rod McKuen's poetry. "Who's Rod McKuen?" he asked. When the poet came to Ann Arbor, Ted invited Sparrow to the performance, where he stifled his yawns with good humor. Rod's songs of love and loss lived in Sparrow's head. She longed to share her thoughts with Ted, but did not know how. He put his arm around her and drove home, west on Highway 12 and south on 52.

As they passed the McDonalds on the north edge of Adrian, he held her close. "Want to come over for a while?"

Sparrow pulled away. "No, that's not what we agreed."

"Just for a while?" He put his hand on her knee.

She removed it.

He delivered her to Booknook and kissed her goodnight, his body pinning her against the door.

Sparrow eased away. "Thanks. I really liked the concert. Goodnight." She unlocked the door and crept up the stairs.

When she entered the apartment, Finch sat up in bed. "Why are you so late?"

Ted and Sparrow's relationship changed in subtle ways. She risked asking for assistance, and Ted responded, screwing in a light bulb over the stairs, fixing the leaky kitchen faucet, or driving her on an errand. When she knew what she wanted and needed and was able to make it clear, he was willing to accommodate. Thus, she again allowed her passions full rein, with most dates ending in frantic coupling in Ted's bed, where afterward they would lie sated and silent.

On dates he told her stories of the Marines or about people at work, but he didn't talk about his feelings and didn't seem interested in hers. When she told him about an argument with Finch, or a happening at Booknook, he had nothing to add. No comment. Sparrow longed to have a dialogue with him, to have him listen to her.

With Finch, Ted was polite, even friendly, but again not communicative. The adolescent was cool to Ted, withdrawn and resentful. She was sullen when Sparrow went on dates. "Him again!" she'd say. He'd become a wedge between mother and daughter. Sparrow became determined not to let her physical needs rule.

The evening she told him, Finch was at a movie with Angie. Ted had brought a bottle of wine to her apartment; they were sitting silent on the sofa, sipping it from juice glasses.

She began, "I really like you."

He replied, "I more than like you."

He looked at her with unsuspecting eyes. The realization thundered in her head. This man was vulnerable. He cared about her. But she did not, could not love him. For once she was in control, the one in charge. From somewhere in the depths of her she spoke. "I don't love you. I can't see you anymore."

Without a word, he set his half-filled glass on the table and left the apartment.

Sparrow heard the door slam and watched him through the window. Head down, hands in his pocket, he walked to his car and sped away. She sighed, picked up the bottle, and poured herself another glass.

An hour later Finch came home from the movie and sprinted up the stairs. Sparrow sat in the same chair holding a glass, the empty bottle on the table.

"What are you doing, Mom?"

"Thinking. Just thinking."

The next Monday Sparrow walked to Siena Heights and registered for English 101.

Freshmen Don't Dance
Fall 1974

*I*t was a crisp October day. Finch and Angie had finished decorating for the freshman dance and were strolling home from high school. Angie's blouse, held snug by the straps of her backpack, revealed the curve of her breasts. At five-four she was the taller of the two. With little warning her plump, pubescent body had transformed into that of a woman, firm breasts, small waist and generous hips—a body that she was not yet comfortable in. Her coppery onyx hair curled about her face and neck.

"I can't wait for Friday," said Angie, tiger-eyes sparkling.

"Not me. I don't think I'm going," said Finch, avoiding a crack in the sidewalk. A stranger would have taken Finch for a younger girl. Her baggy black T-shirt hung in gathers from the straps of her backpack, concealing any trace of breasts or hips.

"We've got to go to the dance!" Angie pleaded.

"I don't want to go to any old dance and stand around holding up the wall. Besides, the freshman boys are square."

"You volunteered to decorate. We just spent an hour carving pumpkins. Yours were the best."

Finch trudged ahead, avoiding another crack.

Angie grabbed Finch's shoulder. "Gurns likes you."

Finch flipped her ponytail and quickened her pace. "He likes basketball."

Angie ran to keep up. "No fake. He'll play varsity next year."

"And he hardly talks to me."

"He's always hanging around your locker."

Finch slowed her pace. "Do you think he can dance?"

"Sure. He's got great moves on the basketball court."

The girls walked on in silence.

Angie touched Finch's arm. "Do you think Gary's cool?"

"He's totally awesome. But don't go getting any big ideas. He's Belinda's boyfriend."

"He asked me if I was going to the dance."

"Oh, gees," grumbled Finch. "I thought your dad wouldn't let you go."

"Nope. But mom reamed him out. Said it was a school dance and there would be plenty of chaperons. Asked him if he didn't think I was a good girl. How about your mom?"

"Haven't asked."

They reached Angie's house. Maria opened the door and waved to Finch.

Angie started up the walk, but then turned back. "Come on, Finch. Ask your mom."

As she continued home, Finch thought about Belinda, rich and spoiled. She had to admit Belinda was pretty, with her Florida tan and long blonde hair. In grade school Belinda had teased Angie, called her

Little Orphan Annie. She said Angie had to have been adopted, that Mexicans didn't have red hair.

It was in third grade, on a brilliant spring morning, that Belinda had appeared on the playground. Wearing a powder-blue dress and black patent shoes, she smiled through sparkling blue, rubber-banded braces. A velvet ribbon held her shoulder-length, sun-lit hair away from her face. Twirling a strand around her forefinger, she looked as if she had floated in on the morning mist.

"Let's go talk to her," said Finch.

Angie had hung back, but Finch pushed her way into the group, dragging Angie with her. Belinda looked toward Angie, who was wearing a dress that Maria had made, the red skirt gathered in three tiers, the white bodice drawn up around her shoulders, and the sleeves puffy.

Belinda pointed to Angie. "What's that?

"W—what do you mean?" asked Angie.

"You look weird, like Christmas!"

"W—what?"

Belinda snickered. One by one, the girls giggled. Angie fled, tripping over the edge of a bike stand, ripping the bottom ruffle of her dress.

Belinda, convulsing with laughter, lost her balance and grabbed Finch's shoulder. Finch shoved her, and Belinda fell, pulling Finch to the ground with her. The girls grappled in the dust, attracting the attention of the playground supervisor.

"She pushed me!" cried Belinda. "I didn't do anything. She pushed me!"

"She grabbed me!" shouted Finch, above the din of the students.

"Enough!" said the supervisor. "Finch, you apologize. Belinda is a new student. We need to make her feel welcome."

"Sorry," muttered Finch. She dusted herself off and ran to find Angie.

Princess Belinda, as Finch and Angie nicknamed her, became the trendsetter of the class. In fourth grade, she was the first girl to be sent home to change her skirt because the hem did not touch the floor when she knelt. She was the first to wear culottes. And she lost no opportunity to torment anyone who dressed or acted differently.

A car honked. Finch stepped back onto the curb. Belinda will be at the dance, thought Finch. She will have the perfect dress, the perfect shoes, and the perfect hairdo. And Angie has a crush on Belinda's perfect boyfriend. An empty soda can lay on the sidewalk. Finch kicked it and watched as it rattled down the street.

Maria had cherished the festivals in Mexico when she was a girl. The dresses were pretty, not the plain, skimpy things the girls wore now. Hers had been feminine, with yards of colorful fabric that swirled when she walked. She decided to surprise Angie with a gorgeous, traditional dress for the freshman party.

That week, while Angie was at school, Maria made the dress. Her stitches were even, seams finished. When it was completed, Maria was pleased. A dress like this could not be purchased at JCPenney's. On Friday she displayed the dress on the living room sofa and waited for Angie to come home.

"Angie, I've got a surprise for you!" she called when the girls came in the kitchen door. "I'm in the living room."

The girls hurried into the room where Maria sat on the edge of the overstuffed chair, the dress laid out on the sofa. Angie stood in the doorway.

"You like it?" Maria beamed as she picked up the gown and held it up to herself. "It's a China Poblana, like I had when I was your age."

"A what?" Angie asked.

"It's the kind of dress we wear to fancy balls in Mexico, a national vestido. It's named after Poblana, a legendary princess, who was famous for her generosity and good deeds."

Finch took the dress from Maria. The top was fine white cotton, with a square neck and short puffed sleeves. Maria had embroidered small red flowers with delicate green leaves around the neck. The flared skirt was white with green polka dots, ruffled, with a band of white lace around the bottom.

"Nifty," said Finch. "Did you do the flowers yourself?"

Maria nodded. "It's for the dance."

"Mom-m-m! You—"

Finch put her arm around Angie's waist and gave her a warning squeeze. "We'd better study for that social studies test," said Finch, propelling her out of the room.

In the privacy of Angie's room, Finch turned on her. "You hurt your mom's feelings!" Finch went to the living room, retrieved the dress and thrust it toward Angie. "Try it on."

Angie tossed it on the floor.

"You're a brat," said Finch.

Angie flopped onto the bed. "How could she do this to me? Everyone will think I'm a freak. I won't wear it!"

Finch picked up the Poblana. Her friend was embarrassed about being different. Finch understood that feeling well. Finch did not know who her father was, had never met her grandparents. At least Angie knew where she came from.

"Kids will be wearing skirts and sweaters, and I'll show up in a gaudy formal. I won't go!"

Finch sat down on the bed. "Fat chance." She patted Angie's back. "But we've got to figure out some way not to hurt your Mom's feelings."

The night of the dance, Anton dropped the girls at school. Angie wore Maria's long black coat and carried a bulging grocery bag. They rushed for the girl's room. Angie flung off her coat. Finch unzipped the Poblana. As Angie stepped out of it, the door swung open. Belinda strolled in with an entourage of freshman girls.

Belinda smirked. "Ohhh! Getting ready in the girls' room. I'll bet your mom made your dress."

Angie dropped the Poblana.

Belinda picked it up and held it in front of her. "Why, look at these ruffles! You're wearing *this* to the dance?"

Finch grabbed the dress, but Belinda tightened her hold. Finch jerked. The fabric ripped. A sleeve dangled from Belinda's hand.

"You scum! You moron!" screamed Finch. She seized the sleeve and whacked Belinda across the face.

Miss English stood in the doorway. "What's going on in here?"

"She hit me!" Belinda wailed.

"Yes, I saw that, but what were you doing?"

"Nothing. I just asked to look at her dress."

"She's a liar!" Finch fumed. "She was picking on Angie. She always does. She took her dress."

"You ripped it!" accused Belinda.

"You wouldn't let go!"

"Angie, it seems that this dispute centers on your dress. Can you enlighten me?" asked Miss English.

Clutching the dress, trying to cover herself, Angie said nothing.

Miss English directed her attention to the three bystanders inching toward the door. "What happened here?"

No one answered.

Miss English might have seen Belinda as the innocent victim, had she not been watching the interaction among the three girls in home economics. Now she was losing her patience. "If we don't get to the bottom of this, I am going to kick the whole bunch of you out, and you can all report to the principal's office on Monday."

Silence. Miss English waited.

Anita stepped forward. "Belinda was teasing Angie about her dress. She wouldn't give it back."

With the efficiency of a thirty-year teacher, Miss English extracted reluctant apologies from Finch and Belinda.

"Now, the two of you go home and never, ever let me catch you fighting again!" She sucked in her breath, turned and walked toward the door. "I'll be watching the rest of you. There will be no more trouble tonight." The door slammed.

Belinda glared at Finch and flounced out after the teacher.

"We're out of here," said Anita, as the girls left the restroom.

Finch looked at Angie and shook her head. "Guess I'd better go."

"It's not late. We can walk home," replied Angie.

"She didn't kick you out."

"Everything's all ruined, and it wouldn't be any fun without you. But we'll have to figure out a story about the rip, and why we're getting home so early.

"Your mom doesn't have to know. I can mend the dress. Besides, the dance would have been dorky."

Angie sighed, "Yeah, sure."

Monday morning, as Angie and Finch approached the school, Anita, Melody and Darlene were hanging out at the front door.

Angie stopped well short of the entrance. "Oh, no, there they are." She bent her head as though studying something on the sidewalk.

Finch gave her a shove. "Remember Anita told the truth. Just act like nothing happened."

Angie glared at her. "Whatever."

The group of girls fell silent and turned toward them. Finch put her hand on Angie's rigid back to push her through the threesome.

Melody blocked their passing. "That was some smack you gave Belinda. I've never seen anyone stand up to her like that."

"And the dance wasn't all that great," Anita joined in. "The music was lousy and the boys didn't dance, just stood around making jokes."

"And your dress? Can your mom fix your dress?" Darlene asked.

Finch spoke up. "Sure, Angie's mom can fix it. She can do anything."

Inside the building, Belinda, standing by her locker, turned and stared as the five girls walked down the hall, chatting and laughing.

Designing Girls
Spring 1979

Senior prom fantasies warmed the winter air. Girls flirted and hinted to be asked. Angie longed to go to the dance with Gary; however, he was going steady with Belinda. Still, they were frequently on the outs and at those times Gary flirted with Angie, giving her hope that one day he would ask her for a date.

Sparrow was at class and Finch was staffing Booknook. She and Angie were drinking sodas and thumbing through fashion magazines, discussing dresses for the prom.

"I'm dying to go with Gary," said Angie.

Finch flipped a page. "No way. Belinda has that all sewed up. *But* there are other neat senior guys who'd go with you."

Angie set her soda down. "I *want* to go with Gary!"

Finch groaned.

"But what about you? Who do you want to go with?" asked Angie.

Finch stood and swept her hands down her body. "Look at me. I'm a stick. Nobody's interested in me."

"That's not so. You're cute and the guys like you. You act like a, a…snob."

"Snob!"

"Stuck-up. You avoid the guys."

Finch plopped down and stretched out her legs. "Okay. So, who likes me?"

"Gurns?"

"He doesn't even talk to me."

"How can he? You're always running away."

Finch sighed. "Okay, so you're holding out for Gary, and I don't want a date." Finch fingered the magazine. "We can still go to the prom. Anita and Darlene won't have dates. A lot of girls won't. We could make stellar dresses, a white and a black, classy. We'll wear our hair up." She grinned. "You could wear your mom's diamond tiara. Maybe we could add a ruffle or two."

Angie thumped her glass onto the table. "Oh, no, you don't. No Poblana, no ruffles. Mom and Dad have been pushing that all my life. Dad still talks Spanish half the time."

"Everybody likes you. No one but Belinda and a few of her groupies ever tease you about being Mexican."

"You should talk! You could be like everybody else, fit in. But no, you wear black, long skirts, boots. You *try* to be different."

"I'm a misfit. I don't know who my dad is, and my mom's weird. I wish I had your parents. But no, I live above a bookstore! If I don't get a scholarship for college, I'll have to stay here, work in Booknook, and be an old maid, just like her."

"Your mom is not an old maid."

Finch could not deny that her mother had changed, was more outgoing. She no longer wore drab, long skirts, and often dressed in jeans. With her short stylish hair and dangling earrings, she looked like a college coed.

"Well, maybe not, but she is in her thirties and not even out of college."

"So! My mom never went. Who says you have to?"

"We're poor. I have to get an education and make money." Finch's voice caught. "And I don't want a boyfriend…I'm not going to end up like my mom!"

That night, Finch sat at the kitchen table, paper littering the floor as she drew and discarded dress designs. Sparrow, curled up in the chair, was reading Steinbeck's *East of Eden* for literature class.

Finch's chair scraped on the linoleum as she jumped up. "I've got it!"

"Oh, nice," said Sparrow, when Finch showed her the picture. "I've got to finish this. Can we talk later?"

Finch shrugged, picked up the papers, went to her room and whipped the curtain shut. She wanted more than anything to be a fashion designer and wished that Sparrow would get more excited about her efforts. Finch could never be certain about her mom. Sometimes she was intensely interested in Finch's projects; at other times she was preoccupied with school and work.

At school the next day, Finch showed the design to Angie. "Look, it has a scoop neck and is fitted past the hips. But it flares before the knees to give you room to dance and it's ruffled at the bottom."

"Not so bad, but I don't like those puffy sleeves."

"Well, it could be sleeveless." Finch covered the sleeve with her finger, demonstrating how it might look. "We'll get sheer fabric and line it. It'll be chic.

You'll have white, and I'll have black. We will be so cool, like twins!"

"Well, maybe, but you're going to make me late for English." Angie turned and hurried toward her classroom.

After school Finch showed the design to Maria.

"Very nice, but black and white? How about red or green, something colorful?" asked Maria.

"It's elegant, Mom, like movie stars," said Angie.

"It'll have a ruffled bottom," said Finch. She danced about the room kicking imaginary ruffles.

Maria's round dark face lit with pleasure. It was agreed. Maria would make Angie's dress and Finch would sew her own.

When Finch returned home, Sparrow offered to help with the dress.

"I can do it, Mom. You're practically running Booknook by yourself and going to college. You don't have time. Besides, it's my project."

Sparrow nodded. She was busy at Booknook, finishing her BA degree and also working for Dr. Stewart, correcting English papers. "Okay. I'll buy the fabric."

Finch made a pattern from newspaper and worked on the formal on quiet afternoons when she was clerking at Booknook. Often, customers were greeted by the whirring of the sewing machine. Finch would walk to the front of the shop, greet them and tell them to ask if they needed help. A few regulars, Miss English among them, came back to chat and see her progress.

One Saturday, Maria stopped by. She made her way past the tables and shelves to the alcove where Finch sat, hunched over the Singer, pushing the delicate fabric past the needle, head darting from the seam to an open book.

Finch was reading aloud, her voice rising above the clatter of the machine. "How could you do this to me?"

Maria cleared her throat. Finch looked up; strands of long hair covered an eye. Glistening satin veiled the black of her jeans and T-shirt.

"I didn't hear you come in. I was learning my lines for the play."

"Yes, you and Angie."

"Yeah, I wasn't going to try out. Angie talked me into it."

"So, you like it?"

"It's okay, but I'm a little busy."

"Yes, you have three projects going, minding the store, sewing, and learning your lines. It's too much. I think I should finish the dress."

"Oh, I can do it."

"I know you can do it. You and your mom always make lemonade out of the lemons. But I will help you make this lemonade. Why, you didn't even hear me come in. Somebody could come in and carry off the store, and you wouldn't know. Your momma is busy with her school, too. I'd like to do this."

Finch shook her head "no." Maria sighed, fingered the chiffon and let it fall. The two watched it drift onto the table.

The school was abuzz with excitement. Contestants for prom king and queen were posted. A king and queen would be chosen from the four finalists. As Finch pushed her way through the crowd, Belinda tapped her on the shoulder.

"Angie's a finalist. Guess she'll be my attendant. But she has to dress right. She can't wear a yucky dress."

Finch turned on her. "Wake up, Belinda. You're a whitewashed face with bleached hair. Angie is pretty and twice the person you are. She will win! You'll be *her* attendant. So *you*'d better dress to suit *her*." Finch strode down the hall.

She was still seething when Angie came out of the music room.

"I can't believe it! They nominated me!"

"For someone so smart, you sure are stupid! You're popular!"

The week before the vote, Belinda avoided Finch and was sweet to everyone else, including Angie. Saturday night Belinda gave a party and invited all the juniors and seniors, with the exception of Angie and Finch.

"She bought votes," Angie lamented.

"Don't be so sure. The Mexican kids boycotted the party. And Anita said it wasn't so great," said Finch.

The day the students voted, Angie and Finch met Belinda in the hall. "Looks like you'll be my attendant, Angie. You should wear something pastel, to go with the blue I'm wearing," said Belinda.

Finch stepped forward. "Didn't you know her mom made her a multicolored gown? Since you'll be *her* attendant, you'll want to wear something more colorful."

"You're not serious," said Belinda

Angie looked at Belinda with innocent eyes. "Yes, it's this special Mexican dress my mom made for me, like the one I would have worn to the freshman dance, only fancier. Remember, the one you ripped?"

"I don't believe you!" Belinda turned on her heel and strode down the hall.

As she rounded the corner, the girls exploded in laughter.

"Radical!" Finch gave Angie a high five.

"Yeah, it's going to be all over school tomorrow that I'm wearing a Raggedy Ann dress to the prom. We'll show up looking sharp, and Belinda will feel like a dork for spreading the story."

The Garcia home was a flurry of activity. Discarded bras and slips littered Angie's bed. The girls giggled in the bathroom as they helped each other with makeup. Marie and Sparrow sat in the kitchen drinking tea, ready to provide assistance.

It was an unusually warm May night, which pleased the girls, as neither had a suitable wrap to wear with her otherwise elegant attire. Angie's shimmering gown accented her rounded breasts and slim waist, her vibrant hair in an upsweep with curls winding down her neck.

Finch stood in front of the mirror, shaking her head. "I look like a stick."

"No you don't. You just need a little help." Sparrow took a couple of foam pads from a Jo-Ann Fabrics bag. "Put these in your bra."

Finch gave her mother a playful shove. "I'm not going to have fake boobs."

"Don't be silly. Just try them." Sparrow thrust the pads at Finch.

She grimaced, but took the pads and popped them into her bra.

"Okay?" asked her mother.

"Not bad," said Angie.

Finch shrugged. "What am I going to do with my hair? It won't stay up."

Indeed, no matter how many bobby pins they stuck into the upsweep, strands would work their way out. "I could wear it down, but then I'd look like a kid."

Maria clapped her hands. "I know, my tiara! That will dress it up."

Angie and Finch exchanged glances.

Their look was misinterpreted. "You don't like the tiara?" asked Maria.

"Oh, yeah," replied Finch. "We sneaked into your bedroom and played princess with it when we were little. We thought the stones were diamonds."

"I wish." Smiling, Maria placed the infamous tiara on Finch's hair.

The girls suppressed sniggers.

"You look like a princess," said Sparrow, who'd never attended a school dance, let alone a prom. To her it seemed like a fairytale. Here was her daughter, gorgeous, looking like Snow White with her pale skin against the black chiffon.

Maria took pictures with an ancient box camera of the girls clowning; Finch held a rose between her teeth. The mothers kissed the girls and wished Angie good luck. They followed the girls to the sparkling-clean station wagon, where Anton waited, dressed as a chauffeur in a navy blue sports coat, with a Detroit Tigers baseball cap. He tucked Finch and Angie into the back seat, careful not to catch their gowns in the doors. Waving his cap, he drove off.

At school, the girls watched Gary and Belinda arrive. Gary opened the car door and held out his hand to Belinda, who was encased in a sea of powder-blue ruffles. She shoved his hand out of the way and flounced out of the car. Gary slammed the door.

Belinda glared at him and swirled around. There was a sound of ripping fabric.

"My dress! You've shut my dress in the door!"

Gary quickly opened the door and yanked the ruffles out.

"You jerk!" Belinda picked up the dangling ruffles and stormed into school.

Gary hurried after her. Passing Angie, he shrugged. The door banged behind him.

Angie squeezed Finch's hand. "Sounds like they're off to a great start. I think they were fighting before they even got here. Poor Gary. Let's wait until the dance begins to go in. We'll make a grand entrance."

Finch, bent over with laughter, shook her head. "If you don't mind, I'd just as soon sneak in."

Heads turned as the two entered arm in arm. A fast dance was playing. With magazine-model smiles, they danced their way to an open space. The juniors had decorated the gym with brilliant colors—orange, red, violet and vibrant blue. Paper lanterns, palm trees, a pond, and a volcano spewing red light transformed the gym from a utilitarian space into an exotic paradise. The mood was electric. Finch and Angie played their roles well and did not lack for dance partners.

Belinda had fled to the women's room, where she had tried to pin her ruffles together. Still her gown hung on the floor and had to be gathered up when she walked. Refusing to dance, she pouted at a table far from the dance floor.

After enduring an hour of Belinda's stony silence, Gary left her and danced with other girls. Although his eyes followed Angie, he did not approach her. Finally, just before the crowning, he cut in.

"You're looking really cool. I've wanted to dance with you all evening, but I didn't want to make her any madder." He nodded toward Belinda.

Angie put her head on his shoulder.

At eleven, Belinda, red-faced, gathered up her ruffles, hobbled onto the dance floor and was crowned queen. Brad, the basketball captain, was king. Head high, clutching her skirt with one hand, she shuffled around the dance floor with her king. The two attendants, Angie and Gary, glided about the room cheek to cheek. When the music ended, he whispered, "Can I call you tomorrow?"

The girls were lying in Angie's bed relishing their victory. "I don't believe it, Finch. I've never had so much fun. It was better than being queen. You and I were totally awesome!"

"*You* were," corrected Finch. "Belinda looked like she was about to puke."

"Oh, Finch, don't be so mean. She dragged her formal around all night and didn't dance till the crowning. I almost felt sorry for her."

"If she hadn't been such a poor sport, you wouldn't have had such a good time with Gary."

"Yeah, and he's going to call tomorrow…or I guess it's today." Angie yawned. "Finch, you should date. Guys do like you. You had plenty of dance partners, and Gurns, you danced with him. He's nuts about you."

"Don't be so sure. Besides, I have things to do—college, a career."

"Is it your dad? Are you afraid of being hurt like your mom?"

"Nah…you think too much. Go to sleep." Tears forming in her eyes, Finch turned toward the wall.

Losers and Winners
Late May 1979

*I*t was ten o'clock. Sparrow in her nightgown and Finch in pajamas were reading on Sparrow's double bed. Light from the street streamed through the living room window and into the bedroom, casting elongated shadows on the wall. The dim lamp provided little light to read by. Sparrow rubbed her eyes. She was tired but did not want to disturb Finch. She had wondered what prompted Finch's cozying up with her. But it was companionable sitting next to her daughter, hearing the cadence of her breathing, occasionally brushing against her arm. We are both so busy, Sparrow thought. Next year, when I'm done with school, we can spend more time together.

Finch sat up. "I've got something to tell you, Mom. You're not going to like it."

"Oh?"

"I'm going to Eastern Michigan University."

The book slipped from Sparrow's hand. "What? You were going to Siena!"

Finch closed her book. "Eastern's not that far, not much more than an hour away."

"You're not serious!"

Finch spoke slowly. "Yes, I am, Mom. Eastern's got a good art program. I can learn design."

Sparrow felt her heart clutch. "Finch, we can't afford it."

"I'm not asking to go to the University of Michigan."

"If you live at home, we can manage college somehow."

"That's exactly it. I don't want to live at home."

"It's a little late now. Why didn't you say something before?"

Finch glared at her mother. "You just don't want me to leave."

"Finch, we don't have the money."

"Uncle Dave will help."

"On social security?"

"He said he'd help."

"You asked him?" Sparrow's shock turned to rage. "*Look around you!* Why do you think we haven't painted in years? We need new furniture, an awning. We're barely making it."

"I've got a job at Frosty Boy for the summer, and I'll help out here."

"Not enough!"

"I'll borrow the money if I have to. Besides, I'm going to try out for the Miss Lenawee Contest. The winner gets a year's tuition to a state college and a thousand dollars."

"Isn't that a beauty contest?"

"You don't think I can win!"

"No, that's not it. I had no idea. It's not like you to enter a beauty contest. I'm just surprised, surprised that you would do so much…to, to leave home."

"That's what kids do. It's not like I'll never be back."

"You don't know that!"

Finch flounced off the bed and pulled shut the curtain to her room. Rather than think about the rift with her mother, she focused on the contest. She was well aware that she was not beautiful. But Miss Lenawee contestants did not have to be gorgeous. They were judged on intelligence, talent and attitude. The winner had to be poised and gracious, not necessarily beautiful. It was most important that she be motivated to do well in college. Participating in this contest was not at the top of Finch's want-to-do list—not even at the bottom. In fact, Finch feared she would be humiliated. But she needed money. Finch got into bed, pounded her pillow and lay flat on her back with her toes pointed upward.

Sparrow listened to her daughter settle herself onto the bed, heard her pummeling the pillow and then the familiar squeak of the springs. Finch was right. Finch would come home. It was she who could never go home. It's sad, she thought; when Finch was little, I couldn't roust myself out of here to take her to the movies or the Crosswell to see a play. Then I was too busy with work and college to spend much time with her.

At school the next day, Finch asked Angie, "Do you think I stand a chance?"

"Oh, yes." Angie's eyes sparkled.

"But I don't have any talent. I can't sing. I don't play an instrument. What could I do?"

Angie put her hand on Finch's shoulder. "You sew. You make things. You're talented!"

Finch was encouraged. Perhaps she could design and sew a dress for the pageant. She remembered first becoming interested in sewing when she had seen the displays at the fair. In grade school the girls had gone to the Lenawee County Fair with Angie's parents. In high school they were allowed to go alone. They had ridden the rides, eaten cotton candy and wandered through the exhibits. Finch dragged Angie through the exhibition barn, where old-fashioned quilts, dresses, suits, even table linens were displayed. When no one was monitoring the exhibits, Finch picked up the garments and examined the workmanship. Angie, impatient to get to the midway, paced the aisles.

"I'll bet I could win a ribbon," Finch had asserted on a hot day as the girls stood sweltering in the barn.

"Go for it! Just get me to the midway," said Angie, turning on her heel.

Finch had thought about this, and the next year had entered a skirt in the competition. She had been disappointed when she did not win a ribbon. However, she persisted, and the following year the dress she entered merited a blue ribbon. Finally, in her junior year she got what she had been aiming for, the grand prize purple ribbon.

Angie had teased, "Gee, you've got a grand champion dress, just like the guys have their 4-H grand champion steers. It's too bad after all the work you put in that you can't get a lot of money for it, like the guys do for their cattle."

"Yeah, it doesn't seem fair. But someday I'll be a famous designer and make gobs of money." The words had rolled of Finch's tongue. She had never thought of herself in such a way before, but found the thought intriguing.

Now, Finch would graduate from high school, and she realized that if she were to succeed, she would have to do it on her own. Dave could help some, but he was not wealthy like Belinda's father. Finch had no illusions about her looks—skinny, with straight hair. But she was determined. She would pocket her pride and enter the Miss Lenawee Contest.

Angie went with Finch to register for the pageant. As they entered the office, Belinda sauntered toward them. She wore a sleeveless yellow shirt with matching shorts, which showed her curves and suntanned skin. Finch was dressed in faded jeans and a T-shirt, her skin paper white.

"Oh, hi. Are *you* signing up?" Belinda asked Angie.

"I thought *I* might give it a try," retorted Finch.

Belinda put her hand on her hip. "You? What can *you* do?"

"I'll think of something."

"You know darn well that Finch is a designer," said Angie.

"You're entering a home-ec project? That *is* different." Belinda fluffed her hair. "I'll be doing something more traditional—a flute solo. I've got to get home now. Mom and I are going to Ann Arbor. Jacobson's is having a great dress sale. Good luck with your stitches." Belinda fluffed her hair again and sauntered off.

"Give me a break," said Finch.

"Yuck," said Angie. "You've *got* to win this contest!"

Angie and Finch sat at the kitchen table, eating Maria's warm sopapillas. Finch licked the sugar from her fingers and looked mournfully at Maria. "What am I going to do? It's August, and I don't even know which design to enter in the talent contest. And even if I had a decent idea, I don't know when I could get it done. It's like summer got away."

"Well, you've been working fifty hours a week. That's where it's gone. I hardly ever get to see you," said Angie.

"I need ideas. Help!" implored Finch.

"That's it!" said Maria. "You needed help on your prom dress, but you wouldn't accept it. You insisted on doing it yourself. For once your stubbornness has paid off. You've already done your project."

"What do you mean?" asked Finch.

"The prom dresses. You designed the prom dresses and you made yours!"

"Oh!" the girls chorused.

"But I hurried with it. I'm not sure it's the best I can do. Will it be good enough?"

"It's a beautiful dress. Enter both dresses for design, and yours for the workmanship. The two of you can model them," said Maria.

"Why didn't I think of that?" asked Finch.

"Perhaps because you do things the hard way," Maria said.

And so it was decided: Finch would enter both gowns in the talent contest. She would explain to the judges that she'd sewn her own dress, but not Angie's. She'd call the project "Black and White."

The three final contestants were dressing for the talent portion of the contest. Finch, Belinda, and a girl named Linda, from Onsted, had made the cut. Angie had joined them to model her prom dress with Finch. Clothes were strewn about the contestant's trailer; the tiny windows were open and a small fan clattered on a dresser.

Finch, still wearing her shorts, pawed through her suitcase, tossing its contents to the floor. "Where can it be? I know I put it in here."

Angie, dressed in bra and slip, wiped sweat from her brow. "Are you sure?"

"I washed it with my panty hose and put them both in the suitcase."

Belinda set her flute down and crossed the room. "Got a problem?"

Angie studied Belinda. "Finch can't find her strapless bra."

"That's too bad. I wonder how that happened."

Finch glared at her. "Got any idea?"

"Not really. You do need one with that dress. I'm not wearing mine. You could borrow it, but it would be too big. Perhaps you could pad it." Belinda winked.

"No thanks, we'll think of something. I'm not letting a *mysteriously* disappearing bra stop me."

"No, of course not," said Belinda. "Besides, you don't really need one. You need padding, but it would be deceptive. A bit like your talent entry." She tossed her head and walked to her corner of the trailer.

Finch clenched her fists and stepped forward. Angie held her back.

"What the hell did she mean by that?" Finch asked.

"I don't know and I don't care. We've got to figure out what to do," whispered Angie. "Belinda's got her flute solo in twenty minutes, then it's Linda's song, and then it's us. We need to put our makeup on. Even if we had a car, we don't have time to go buy a bra."

There was a knock; Finch opened the door a crack. Straw hat shading his wrinkled face and beads of perspiration forming a pattern on his shirt, Dave stood leaning against the trailer. "Oh, I didn't think you'd be dressing. Just stopped to wish you luck. Do you need anything?

The girls spoke in unison. "Do we *need* anything?"

Ten minutes later, Dave was at the mall, hurrying toward the lingerie department at JCPenney's. Shoulders stooped, hands in his pockets, he stood staring at a rack of bras. A young sales clerk, who had frequented his bookstore ever since she was a preschooler, approached.

"Hello, Mr. Stanley. What can I do for you?"

"Julie, you old enough to work here?"

"Yes, Mr. Stanley, I am. May I help you with something?"

Dave held his hand across his mouth and talked through it. "Yeah, thirty-two A, strapless, black."

"I'm sorry. What did you say?"

"A bra! Damn it! A bra!"

"*You* want a bra?" Julie suppressed a laugh.

"No, I don't want one. Wouldn't have come if there was anyone else. It's Finch and that darn pageant. She lost her bra, needs it for the talent. Needs it *now*."

Julie selected a black strapless bra with an overlay of padding and quickly rang up the sale. Smiling, she handed the bag to Dave. "Thanks, come back real soon."

"Rather not."

"Wish Finch luck for me," called Julie.

Dave grunted and hastened toward the door.

When Dave knocked on the trailer door, Finch, oblivious to the fact that Angie was still in her slip, flung it open. She grabbed the bag and pulled out the bra. "It's perfect. You saved my life." She hugged him and closed the door.

Color mounting in his face, Dave strode away.

Belinda, who'd been watching the exchange, jumped from her chair. "Okay, that does it, *I'm telling*. You didn't make Angie's dress, did you?"

Miss English, who was one of the judges, opened the door. "Belinda, it's your turn."

Belinda grabbed her flute and ran from the trailer.

"What was all that about?" asked Angie.

Finch's arms were through the dress, reaching skyward, her face hidden in the bodice. "Help me get this on."

A few minutes later, the trill of the flute floated through the trailer. It was not a difficult piece, and Belinda played it well. Next, the demure Linda crept onto the stage and, after a false start, sang "I Am Woman." As she became caught up in the song, her timidity subsided, and she belted it out in perfect pitch. The spectators burst into applause.

Finch and Angie sat in the trailer, mopping their faces with tissues, dark spots appearing under their arms. Finch shook her head. "I don't know how our dresses can compete with that."

"It's not dresses. It's you. *You* can do it!"

They heard the announcer, "And now welcome Finch Avery and Angela Garcia, modeling gowns designed by Finch."

Angie grabbed Finch's hand and squeezed it. Unsteady in their spike heels, they walked onto the stage. They braced themselves, smiled and managed to saunter up and down the runway without incident. Still, it was difficult for the audience to compare fabric to music; the applause did not equal that of the other contestants.

Back in the trailer, Belinda was changing her clothes. "How was it, girls?"

"Didn't you hear?" asked Finch "We wowed them."

"At least we didn't fall," Angie whispered to Finch.

The pageant ended with individual interviews. Linda spoke softly and seemed uncertain of what to say. Belinda was poised and articulate. When asked why she should be chosen Miss Lenawee, she replied, "Being Miss Lenawee means you represent the county. You set an example for other young women, and I would be the best one to do that."

When Finch was asked why she should be chosen, she felt her knees buckle. She had told herself that she would have to be herself, honest and straightforward, that there was nothing to be ashamed of. She locked her knees and took the microphone in her damp hand.

After a deep breath, in a calm, clear voice, she answered. "I need the money to go to college. But I'm doing it for my mom, too. She's never had much. She's given me everything, and I want her to feel proud of me and of the job she's done raising me. I don't know if I'm the best one to represent the county, but I would do my best. And maybe it could be a message to other kids that you don't have to have everything, or to be the most beautiful, but if you decide what you want and work hard, you can succeed."

The next morning Finch awoke, took a quick shower and threw on jeans and a T-shirt. As she hurried down Maumee Street, the August sun warmed her back. At Lenawee County Bank, she walked to the teller's window, unclasped a small purse, brought out an envelope, and laid it on the counter. "I would like to deposit this check for a thousand dollars."

"Congratulations!" said the teller.

Later, Finch drove to the mall. At Jo Ann Fabrics, Finch walked slowly up and down the aisles, admiring and touching the material. She selected four yards of black wool, twenty-five percent off, soft as cashmere. She then sorted through the remnants, where a piece of brilliant red caught her eye. Thinking that it would be striking with the black, she added it to her pile.

As she left the store, she met Miss English. "Congratulations, Finch! You deserved to win."

Finch lit up. "Thanks."

"The competition was close. We were impressed with all of you." Miss English smiled. "But you clearly were the winner. And I was surprised at Belinda helping you out like that."

"Helping me? What do you mean?"

The lines in the teacher's face deepened. "Didn't you know? She cleared up the confusion about your formal. She said that you'd made yours, but not Angie's. We knew that you designed the gowns, but we hadn't realized you had also sewn yours. Why didn't you tell us?"

"I thought I did."

"I don't remember that, but I do remember you being emphatic that you had not made Angie's. Sewing your gown gave you extra points. Up until then, you and Belinda were very close. The judges liked the idea of your talent being so unusual and that you not only designed the dress, but made it."

"Belinda's telling you *that* made the difference?"

Miss English laughed. "It helped. Wasn't that generous of her?" When Finch did not respond, Miss English continued, "I guess you'll have to thank her. Well, I want to get in on this sale. I'm sewing some new outfits for school. Got to practice what I teach."

"I know—'You can have twice the quality at half the price if you sew your own clothing.'"

Miss English beamed. "I've taught you well."

Finch strode out of the store, remembering Belinda's threat to tell, to tell—what? Unaware of stares of passers-by, she erupted in laughter.

Finch hurried home to call Angie and share the news. Then she cleared the table, gathered her tools, and laid out the cloth. Sparrow watched Finch, absorbed in her project, cutting the red cloth with a sure hand. Sparrow marveled that she had borne and nurtured this confident young woman. She would have liked to stay and chat, bask in the glow of Finch's winning, but, as usual, she was running late.

Sparrow picked up her books. "I'm off to the library." Apologetically, she added, "I need to get an early start with this research project."

Finch was struck by her mother's appearance: Sparrow's short hair framed her face, a striped blue shirt was tucked into fitted Dockers, and Finch's own gold hoops dangled from her ears.

"Gee, Mom, you look like a college kid. Some young stud might ask you out."

Sparrow beamed. "Don't be silly! Got to finish this last quarter. Can't have you getting a diploma before me." Her tone changed to one of concern. "Will you be all right for a couple of hours, watching the store?"

"It's okay, Mom. If people come in, I'll wait on them."

"I know—of course. It's too bad Dave has the flu. It'd be nice for you to have some time for yourself."

"Mom, it's not a big deal."

"But it is. I worry about you."

"Go now!" Finch put her hands on Sparrow's shoulders and marched her to the door.

Outside, as though to wake herself up, Sparrow tapped her face.

For the few remaining weeks before school, Finch did not return to work at Frosty Boy. While Dave was ill, she helped out at Booknook. In her spare time she designed and sewed clothes, among them a black wool pantsuit and brilliant red blouse.

Setting Out
Late August 1979

*T*he day arrived; the girls were off to college. Finch had been unable to sleep. Rising early, she dressed in her signature color—black jeans, T-shirt, and loafers. Bangs covered her eyebrows; straight hair fell on her shoulders. She gazed at her reflection in the mirror and found herself wanting. Let's face it, she thought, I look like a dork. Mom looks more like a college student than I do.

Dave arrived promptly at eight to take Finch and Sparrow to Eastern Michigan University in Ypsilanti, where they were meeting Angie and her parents. By the time Finch had registered for college, the dorms were full; she and Angie had rented an apartment in an old house several blocks from the university.

Wearing his new EMU baseball cap, Dave leaned against the pickup. Still not feeling well, unable to carry things, he compensated by barking orders. Two battered Salvation Army suitcases were wedged against a huge box containing sheets and bedding. Several smaller cartons with miscellaneous items filled the remainder of the space. Finch made room for the old black and white TV that she had found on the curb when she was in middle school. She had been delighted when the rabbit ears picked up the snowy outline of a newscaster.

When the threesome arrived at the apartment, the street was filled with cars and pickups and the Garcias were already unloading their station wagon. Families were hauling clothes and furniture into dilapidated Victorian houses converted into student apartments. The sparse grass of the lawns was trampled down and covered with various objects that had not yet been carried inside: chairs, desks, books, a typewriter, suitcases and sacks of groceries. Trash was strewn about the curb. Sparrow sighed and reached for Finch's hand.

Finch flicked her mother's hand away. "Let's get this stuff in." She grabbed a suitcase and went up the walk.

Anton carried the heavier boxes. The girls ran back and forth with lighter items. Maria and Sparrow attempted to sort out where things should go.

Once they were unloaded, Maria opened a carton of cleaning supplies. "This place is filthy. How can they rent it? We've got to clean it up."

Angie closed the lid. "*No*, Mom, we can do it. It's *our* place."

Finch put her hand on Maria's arm. "Yeah, we've got all day and tomorrow, too. You can come check on us next week."

"I just wanted to help." Maria let go of the box. Teary-eyed, she hugged her daughter.

"Mom, you're *hurting* me," said Angie, pulling away.

Sparrow held Finch and whispered. "I know you want this. You'll do well."

Finch rested her head on her mother's shoulder. Her voice quavered. "Will you be okay, Mom?"

Sparrow nodded and forced a smile. "Take care."

Dave stood apart, hands in his pockets. Finch went to him and gave him a fierce hug. "I'll miss you, Uncle Dave."

"You have a good time, little one," said Dave.

Finch chortled. "I'm going to college to learn, and you tell me to have a good time?"

Dave's eyes twinkled. "Better than not."

"Guess we should go," said Anton as he took Maria by the arm.

"Yeah, it's time," said Dave.

Sparrow, dazed, and Maria, teary-eyed, followed the men from the room. The girls watched from the window as the little group walked to their vehicles and drove away.

Two hours later, the room was still messy, with empty containers and clothing strewn about. Angie sat cross-legged on the bed. The poster Finch was attempting to tack on the wall flopped down onto her head.

"Come on, give me a hand with this," Finch said.

Angie snorted. "Okay! But I'm tired. We should have let our folks stay and help."

"No way. Your mom wanted to clean. Can you imagine what that would be like? Uncle Dave and your dad standing in the hall, not knowing what to do with themselves. Our moms would never get out of here. They'd've made our beds. Your mom would have cried and mine would've been all tight-lipped. It would've been awful."

Angie screwed up her face. "Well. It'd be done, and the place would be a whole lot cleaner."

"You're just too used to your mom waiting on you."

"I am not!"

"Well, when's the last time you changed your own sheets?"

"Today."

"You know darn well that you don't do it at home."

The girls put the apartment together as best they could and headed off to the cafeteria for supper. That night, cartons and suitcases thrust in corners, clothes crammed into the closet, the girls talked in bed.

"The food in the cafeteria isn't half bad. Lots of choices," said Finch.

Angie puffed her pillow. "My mom's food is better."

"Yeah, I know, but we'll be doing our own cooking when we get organized."

"I'd give a lot for one of Mom's tortillas right now."

"You can't be hungry! Are you homesick already?"

"Nah." Angie did not say that it was the first time she would be away from home for more than a week, that she was scared. "Wasn't that Victoria girl something, showing us the way to the cafeteria? She seemed a little bossy, though. I wouldn't want to get on her bad side."

"Remind you of anybody?"

"I'm not thinking of Belinda ever again. She's at U of M. We are rid of her."

The bed felt strange to Finch. She snuggled under the cover, then felt too warm and tossed it off. She wondered what her mother was doing; she must be lonely. Sparrow had never liked Finch being away overnight, and here she was at college. She might not even go home till Thanksgiving. It occurred to Finch that she might miss her mother. She hugged her pillow and waited for sleep.

At that moment Sparrow, propped up in bed with an unused box of Kleenex, sighed and carefully replaced the phone in its cradle. She had just finished talking with her former English professor, Don Stewart. Tomorrow, when she delivered his corrected English papers, they were going to have coffee. This would be their first date. Or was it really a date? They were just going to coffee. When she had become his assistant, it was all business. Sparrow would come into his office, plunk the corrected essays on the desk, and flee. She had told herself that climbing the stairs caused her shortness of breath.

Dr. Stewart was a small, unassuming man, with ordinary features and two distinctive characteristics. First, a cowlick in his dark hair refused to lie down. Gel, mousse or hairspray might tame it for the moment, but by the time he left his apartment, it would spring up. The other was his melodic and soothing voice. He was passionate about the classics, and his lectures were musical and hypnotic. He had traveled extensively, was fond of Shakespeare and had been to England to see his plays. Listening to Dr. Stewart, the door to Sparrow's tight little world had cracked open. She would be transported to England or Rome. She could visualize the Colosseum with its massive stone walls and columns; she could hear the cheering spectators, as terrified Christians tried to flee ravenous lions. She, who lived less than an hour from Toledo, Ohio, an hour from Indiana, two hours from Canada, and yet had never been out of Michigan, fantasized traveling to Italy with Professor Stewart as her guide.

Before Dr. Stewart's call Sparrow had been thinking of Finch. Until recently, Finch had been her chief focus. Sparrow had simply trudged along like a foot soldier, with little mind of her own waiting for the next command. Since she had had no idea of who she was, she could not know what she wanted out of life. Therapy and college had changed that. She was aware of her feelings, which sometimes emerged as delicate flowers, at other times thorny thistles. One day she read the classics, and the next lusted through romance novels. Her eating was askew, her appetite beyond her control; often not hungry, she would fast; at other times she devoured burgers, fries and pints of pecan crunch ice cream. Tonight she'd felt emptied, a kind of emptiness that food could not fill. Donald's call, his voice, had soothed her.

Sparrow had picked at a leftover chicken leg for supper. Now she was starved. She remembered nights when Finch would be hungry and they would get up and make peanut butter sandwiches, Finch slathering peanut butter and jelly on a couple of slices of bread, the filling dripping on the plate, while Sparrow restricted herself to a half sandwich. Tonight she got up and made a whole sandwich, piling on the peanut butter and jelly until it seeped over the edge of the bread.

The huge EMU administration building loomed above Finch, who stood in the cement entryway fingering her checkbook. She had the money. It was before eight. She would be the first one there and wouldn't have to stand in line. Angie's parents were mailing in her tuition, but Finch was using her own money, the money she had won by being crowned Miss Lenawee. How close that had been. Belinda's supposed tattling had assured her the title. She imagined Belinda, so much prettier than her, telling the judges that Finch may have designed the formals, but had *only* sewn her own. Thanks in part to Belinda, the money was Finch's. For the first time she felt compassion for the girl so driven to win, to always be number one. Perhaps it wasn't so easy being a doctor's daughter.

Finch had written few checks and certainly not one for a large amount. She had to get her zeros in the right place. Clutching her checkbook, she entered the building. The door to the Cashier's Office seemed stuck; she banged on it. After some time, it was flung open by a man holding a cup of coffee.

Bob Roland was disturbed from his few minutes of solitude before the business day. Only the insistent banging on the door had pulled him away from his desk and crossword puzzle.

"You're a little early. Girls aren't here yet." Deep blue eyes met hers.

Finch gaped at him. "You're so tall," she blurted.

"So I've been told. What can I do for you?"

"I've come to pay my," her voice cracked, "bill."

The man softened. "Then you're right on time."

She laid her checkbook on the counter and looked at the man inquiringly.

"Make it out to Eastern Michigan University."

Willing her hand not to shake, Finch took the pen he offered.

The door opened and a pudgy girl darted into the office. "Oh, sorry I'm late."

"Not late. Just had a very determined early customer," replied Mr. Roland.

Finch rolled her eyes. She made out the check and handed it to him. He examined the check.

"Finch. Your name is Finch?"

"Yes, like the bird."

"Of course. It's a pretty name, just not common."

"Sorry about coming so early. I didn't realize…."

Mr. Roland smiled, "Guess the early bird gets the worm."

How many times had Finch heard this—hundreds, thousands? She hated it! But somehow when this man said it, it felt okay, as if he didn't really mind her coming early.

The bill was paid. At the door, Finch whirled back. "Do you need any student help?"

Mr. Roland looked her over. "Well, perhaps, when you get settled in your classes, stop by and we'll see. But come after eight."

Finch nodded in affirmation, muttered "Bye" and left the office.

Bob Roland ran his fingers through his dark, gray-streaked hair. At thirty-nine, he was still slim and not bad-looking. He smiled an expansive smile that anchored his broad nose in a slender face. "Guess she'd never be late."

Coffee Date

*D*onald and Sparrow slipped into the only open booth in the Main Street Diner. Sparrow's seat was broken, a spring poking her in the buttocks. Stuck in the cracked vinyl, she thrust herself forward, arms on the table. The morning had been filled with anticipation. She had not wanted to look too dressed up, but would not wear jeans. She had tried on several outfits and discarded them on the bed. Finally, she settled on a denim skirt, put a bit of rouge on her cheeks and carefully applied lipstick

Donald Stewart had also had difficulty choosing an outfit that morning. Somehow his attire seemed important to him in bridging the gap between student and professor. In the end, he selected a pair of khakis and his favorite blue, short-sleeved button shirt.

Sparrow fingered a smudged spoon. "I'll have the English lit essays corrected by tomorrow. I know you like them promptly, and I've had them for a while, but I got sidetracked this week, getting Finch off to college."

"Don't worry. You're the one who likes to get them done quickly. You've been providing instant gratification to my students for two years now. What will I do without you?"

"You're putting me on."

"No, never. You are the most able, responsible teaching assistant I've ever had." He paused and, as was his habit, ran a hand through his hair. For an instant the cowlick lay down, and then sprang up again. "But tell me, what's it like graduating? What are your plans?"

Sparrow shifted in the seat. "I haven't really thought about it. I'll keep Booknook open. Dave is getting older, needs me more. What I've learned in literature and business classes is helpful."

"Sure, you've brought life to that little shop. But you can do more. You should write. You're a natural. Maybe you could do some articles for the Adrian *Telegram*."

An older couple vacated their booth and went to pay.

Donald stood up. "Oh, good, somebody's leaving. Let's get you out of that seat before it swallows you."

Sparrow blushed. "You noticed?"

"I notice everything about you, Sparrow."

"You do?"

They walked down the narrow aisle to the vacant booth. Together they pushed the cups, plates and silverware to the side, and wiped the table with napkins.

Donald ran his fingers through his hair. "Where was I?"

"You were noticing me." Sparrow's eyes twinkled.

"Yes, since the first day you came to class late and dumped your books on the floor."

"I dropped them. It was an accident!"

"You certainly got my attention!"

Sparrow smiled. "You must admit I was never late again."

How well she remembered those first days, slogging across the campus on wooden legs, sitting in back rows trying to make herself invisible. But literature was so fascinating, and she had felt herself pulled in, sitting closer to the front, listening to his words as though they were the notes of a sonnet.

The day the class discussed Jane Austen, Sparrow spoke. "She was amazing. She had no room of her own to work in. She never married, and that's what women had to do back then. Instead, she wrote wonderful books about strong women. Females were like possessions, supposed to be pretty and weak, with the men taking care of them. Austen could see right through it, made fun of it. She had this wonderful gentle humor about society, its norms, its rules."

Dr. Stewart had grinned. "Spoken like a true feminist."

The class laughed. Sparrow felt as if she had burst open. She had come out, not gracefully, more like a bird thrashing out of its shell. But there was no retreating. She began to speak up in class; students learned her name. When others forgot assignments, they relied on Sparrow to help them. She had a peer group of sorts, and her teachers enjoyed her sharp mind.

Students began to ask her out. Sparrow, in her self-conscious way, had said, "Thank you for asking, but I can't go." If the fellow persisted, she would tell him that she was too old for him, that she had a teenage daughter. Although she longed for companionship, after her experience with Ted she was not ready to take the risk. College and the superficial relationships it provided gave her an opportunity to walk on the fringes of a youth she had never had. As Finch marched through life, Sparrow eased into it. Now, she was graduating, and she wanted more.

"I'd like to get to know you better." Donald said, "I've watched you, admired you, but I don't believe in dating students, even exceptional older ones. But now that you're not in any of my classes and about to graduate...."

Donald held out his hand.

Loss
January 1980

"*T*rying to be first, that's what it gets me," Finch grumbled as she unlocked the door to the Cashier's Office. Something had drawn her there; each week she had come to inquire about an opening. Finally in October, when she faced Mr. Roland over the counter, he had said that he had let his morning girl go, that she could not get to work on time. Since Finch was such an early bird, he would give her a try.

The responsibility of opening the Cashier's Office at 8:00 a.m. would not have been difficult had she been living at home. Her mother would have insisted that she get enough sleep. On her own, the late-night parties were nearly irresistible. Evenings when she tried to study, music and laughter from other apartments distracted her. Last night had been no different. She had been reviewing for a physics exam, and the girls next door were partying. Several times, with little success, she'd asked them to hold down the racket. When she finally turned off the light, revenge fantasies competed with equations for space in her mind.

Finch yanked the key from the door, and it clattered to the floor. "Damn!"

Mr. Roland, seated at his desk, looked up from his crossword puzzle. "Good morning, Finch. I see you're in good spirits."

"Oh, I didn't know you were here."

Mr. Roland pushed his reading glasses down on his nose. "'Damn' was a bit out of character."

"It's just this physics class. There's a big test and my neighbors were partying last night." She took off her jacket and tossed it on the coat rack.

Finch had started off well, got to work on time and learned quickly. Still, Bob Roland had an uneasy feeling about her. Plus he was drawn to her in some unexplainable way. To his detriment, he'd been involved with an assistant before. And this one was underage. He folded his glasses and laid them on the desk. "Are you all right, Finch?"

"Sorry, I know it's after eight." Finch walked to the file. Now I'm in for it, she thought. It was not the first time she'd been late, but it was the first time she'd been caught.

Mr. Roland walked to the filing cabinet and turned Finch around to face him. "Are you sure you're okay?"

Caught in the moment, in the fragrance of aftershave, Finch felt the rough texture of his sport coat brushing against her sweater. Old Spice, like Uncle Dave, she thought.

She pointed to the unfinished crossword puzzle. "Uncle Dave does crossword puzzles, too."

Winter brought bitter cold temperatures to Michigan. The previous night's ice storm had transformed the branches of the trees into sparkling jewels. Limbs hung low, like silver swords sheathed in glass, bowing in defeat. Finch battled her way along the icy walk, slipping and sliding toward the Administration Building. She covered her face and bound her scarf more firmly around her neck. In the safety of the building, she ran up the stairs and down the hall to the office. As she reached for her key, the phone rang. She'd overslept again. Good, the door was still locked. Mr. Roland wasn't there. She grabbed for the phone—too late, ten after eight; she hoped it had not been Mr. Roland calling. The phone rang again.

"Cashier's Office, Finch Avery speaking."

"Finch." Her mother sounded as though she'd been the one running up the stairs.

"What, what's the matter?"

"It's Dave."

"Uncle Dave? What happened?"

"There was an accident."

"Is he okay?"

"I have to go to the hospital."

"What happened?"

"Oh, Finch, I don't know. I shouldn't have called. I just needed to know where you were. Stay put, and I'll get back to you as soon as I know anything."

A click and the line went dead.

Finch was struggling to put her coat on when Mr. Roland entered the office. "Are you just getting here?"

Finch stared at him uncomprehending.

"Your face, you're as white as a sheet. What's going on?"

"Uncle Dave—Uncle Dave had an accident. I've got to go home."

"What happened?"

"Mom couldn't tell me. I think it's bad. She's on her way to the hospital. I've got to get there. I have to leave now."

"How are you going to get to Adrian? Do you have anyone to take you?"

"No." Finch started for the door.

Mr. Roland stepped in front of her. "I'll take you."

"But the office?"

"I'll call Alice. She can come in." He made the call, then gently ushered Finch into the hall, locking the door behind them. His hand on her arm, they descended the steps.

Traffic moved slowly on Highway 12; several cars were in the ditch. Mr. Roland maneuvered skillfully over the icy patches. Under different circumstances, Finch would have been pleased to be sitting next to this man, to be having this adventure with him, for she found him mysteriously attractive. Although he seldom talked about himself, she'd heard he was divorced. She'd like to know more. Angie had teased her about having a crush on her boss. But today Finch was preoccupied, slumped in her seat, held together by her seatbelt.

Mr. Roland turned south onto Highway 52. "We'll be there shortly. No use worrying until you know what the problem is."

He glanced at her, but quickly returned his gaze to the icy road. "Tell me about your Uncle Dave."

Finch's mouth was dry. "He's…he's sort of like an uncle or a grandpa. I guess he isn't any real relation, like blood, I mean, but he's always been there. I think Mom went to work for him when I was a baby. He helped raise me. He's always looked after me. He convinced Mom to let me go on my first overnight, have a bike. He's the reason I got to go to Eastern."

"Sounds like quite a fellow…. What about your dad?"

"That's something Mom won't talk about. I used to think I was the only kid in Adrian who didn't have a father. Immaculate Conception." Finch forced a laugh.

"So you never knew your dad, who he was?"

"I'm not sure I would want to know. Mom finally told me it was some guy who came to town one summer. She says she loved him. He just left, no address, no phone, no nothing. She came up pregnant with me, and her mom kicked her out."

Bob Roland gripped the wheel. "I'm sorry, Finch."

"You don't have to be sorry. It's not your fault."

They rode in silence, Finch staring at the few oncoming cars, Mr. Roland concentrating on keeping the car on the road. Finally, they pulled into the emergency entrance of Bixby Hospital.

"Do you want to come in?" Finch was torn between being polite and wanting to leap out of the car.

"No, I don't want to intrude. Let me know if there is anything I can do."

Bob Roland watched as Finch ran through the revolving doors, down the hall and into the arms of a woman.

Celebration of Life

*D*ave had willed the store to Sparrow. The building was paid for, and he had thought she could manage a living, even in these competitive times, until she graduated from college. Then she could decide what she wanted to do. The house was also hers to live in, but if she were to sell it, the proceeds would go to Finch. What little there was in his bank account was also Sparrow's. The funeral was prepaid.

He would have preferred to be cremated and tossed into the Raisin River. But in deference to Emily, he was laid out in a simple pine box at the United Methodist Church and buried next to her in the cemetery. There was one unusual request, though not at all a request, more of an order. In the to-do envelope in Dave's metal box, Sparrow found an open invitation to be placed in the Adrian *Telegram*:

At my passing, I would like to show my appreciation for those who have tolerated and cared for me all these — — years. After my funeral I would like to invite my friends and patrons to a celebration of life at Booknook. Date and time to be determined.

In spite of her pain, Sparrow laughed. Just like Dave, who hated parties as much as she did, to make her throw one at his passing. This would be huge, she imagined, hundreds of guests coming to pay tribute to the crusty old man. Booknook was her safe place. And now, when she needed to be alone and mourn, Dave was demanding that she invite all of Adrian into her space. She would show him. She would do it.

The party became a group effort. Sparrow filled in the blanks in the invitation: eighty-six years, 2:00 p.m., January 19, 1980. She walked the invitation to the *Telegram*.

Clare, her eyes swollen from crying, bustled into Booknook, wrapped Sparrow in her arms, gave Finch a hug and started organizing. She arranged for The Grasshopper to cater and rented chairs, tables and tablecloths. Donald knew students who could set up and clean. The party took on a life of its own.

After the service everyone gathered at Booknook. The Grasshopper provided trays of tacos, burritos and enchiladas, a keg of beer, and bottles of wine, as well as pitchers of soda. The wake took on a party atmosphere. It was impossible to juggle a drink in one hand, a plate in the other, and eat a smothered burrito: a third hand was needed. Some fortunate people found a shelf or a table to set their plates on. The boys from Siena Heights and Adrian College, after furtively observing that no one was checking IDs, gulped down Budweiser in huge plastic glasses and then devoured great quantities of food. Little old ladies and old ladies not so little mingled with college students. Sparrow imagined Dave looking down at her with approval.

One tipsy girl, trying to balance both drink and food, bumped against Clare and spilled her wine on Clare's new black dress. Grimacing, Clare assured her that it was an old dress destined for the Goodwill. It felt to Clare as if Dave was somewhere up there grinning at her. Dave, she thought, even in death you get at fussy Clare. She went to the bar, ordered club soda and a beer, doused her dress with soda and downed the beer.

Sparrow stationed herself at the door, greeting people, thanking them for coming. On an emotional roller coaster, laughing and crying, she listened to anecdotes about Dave. He had been old; he had seen Finch raised. Although Sparrow would miss him terribly, she had her own life now. She also found comfort in the thought of Dave joining his beloved Emily. Standing next to Donald in the crush of warm bodies, Sparrow felt a sense of community and peace. This is what he wanted for me, she thought.

Finch dozed on the apartment steps, black-suit skirt hiked-up above her knees, open jacket revealing a blood-red blouse. She lay wounded. Someone tapped her shoulder. Her aching eyes took in the blurred image of old-lady shoes and plump, black-hosed legs. A glass of beer was thrust toward her.

"Have a drink of this."

Finch looked up into the concerned face of Miss English. "You're offering me beer!"

"Yes, you look like you need it." Miss English grinned. "If it gets around, I'll have an early retirement."

Finch managed a dead-eyed smile. "I didn't know you drank."

"No, you wouldn't."

Finch took a sip, the beer cool and soothing on parched lips.

Miss English sat on the step next to Finch. "You loved your Uncle Dave a lot."

Finch sniffed. "It happened so quick. I didn't get a chance to say goodbye."

Miss English smoothed Finch's skirt. "It's hard when you're young, and you think everyone will always be there. He was a good man. You and your mom were his life."

"And I didn't get a chance to tell him how much I loved him."

"Oh, Finch, he knew." Miss English patted her arm. "A lot of us really cared for him."

"You?" Finch roused from her grief. Miss English cared for Uncle Dave?

The matronly woman shrugged. "I've always admired Dave. Self-educated, knowledgeable, not like other men I've known. When Emily died, he was bereft, angry, unapproachable. I took him a tuna casserole, and he practically slammed the door in my face. He became a recluse. Couldn't be civil to customers. The store was disintegrating around him."

Finch whiffed Miss English's beer and garlic breath and sat back on the step.

"I was relieved when he took your mom in. She gave him something to live for. When you were born, he softened. Walked you around in that little pink stroller, proud as a peacock. I'd come in, and we'd talk about literature, politics, and even social issues. I was interested, but he was older, and too attached to Emily to think about another woman in a romantic way." Miss English smiled. "I thought of him as my special friend."

Finch was touched. This old teacher, held together by her fifties girdle, bad breath and all, was human. "I always wondered why you came in so often, bought so many books when you could get them free from the library."

"Now you know."

Later, Angie found Finch lying face down on her bed. Angie sat and put her arm around her friend.

"Did you know Miss English had a thing for Uncle Dave?" asked Finch.

At eighty-six, Dave had been in good health. He had had aches and pains; his knees slowed him down from time to time, and he had some difficulty urinating, but he had not had prostate cancer, or cancer of any kind, nor had he had heart problems. His blood pressure was low. Other than aspirin or Tylenol he took no medication. Although Sparrow had foisted vitamins for mature adults on him, he often forgot to take them.

In the winter, after a snow, he would walk to work, trudging through drifts in old calf-high buckle overshoes. Arriving at the store, face flushed, he complained to Sparrow about people who did not shovel their walks. Sparrow had worried that he would fall and break a hip. This winter Dave's poor vision had made it more worrisome. For months he had been having difficulty reading. Sparrow had hounded him to go to the doctor. But it was only after Clare came to visit, stationed herself in a chair and declared she would not move until he made a doctor's appointment that he reluctantly complied. Next month he had been due to have the cataracts removed, after which he planned to stay with Clare in Milan for a week. Since her retirement she was busy with church and Senior Citizens, and he had thought that she wouldn't bother him too much. He had planned to sit on her sun porch, watch the birds at the feeder, and listen to books on tape.

The previous week Sparrow and Dave had had a fight. She'd watched him, bent against the storm, making his way up the block. Sparrow had opened the door for him, her words catching on the wind. "You shouldn't be walking back and forth to the store! Your knees have been hurting, and you can't see!"

"What do you expect? Can't drive with these damn eyes. Besides, walking's good for me—reminds me I'm alive." He had clomped into the store.

"It's snowing, and you can hardly see the curb. You just stumbled, nearly fell."

"Did not." He clutched the counter and struggled out of his boots.

Sparrow hovered over him. "I saw you, Dave."

"Well, caught myself, so no big deal." He tossed his boots in the corner.

"Yes, it is. I'll come and get you, take you home. You used to be my driver. Let me be yours."

He had motioned her away. Then he heard Emily. *You're being stubborn, Dave.*

"Damn, it's like having two wives." He stalked to the table and splashed coffee into the EMU coffee cup Finch had given him for Christmas.

Sparrow had grabbed a paper towel and mopped up the spill.

This conversation lived on in Sparrow's head. But unlike in earlier days, when she had tended to blame herself for any problems that befell her little world, she did not take on the responsibility for Dave's death. She explained it to Finch. "It wasn't quite light yet. He was dressed in his gray coat and dark pants. He crossed the street on a red light and slipped. The delivery truck driver didn't see him." She paused. "It was quick. It was the way he would have wanted it. He didn't want to get really old and feeble. He died doing what he wanted to do. He's always missed Emily. He'd talk to her when he thought he was alone." Sparrow smiled. "And sometimes when he wasn't alone. Now he'll be with her." Sparrow reached for her daughter.

Finch put up her hands. "Oh no, he won't! He's gone—*dead*! We're here. I need him. He wasn't supposed to die. It's not fair!" She whirled and bounded down the stairs. The door slammed.

Finch stayed home that weekend. She would wake early, make her way downstairs and sit on the window seat, watching the flakes settle on the sidewalk. It seemed that any moment Uncle Dave would walk through the door, stomping snow off his feet. She remembered how his face lit up when he saw her. She had vague memories of being little and snuggling in his lap while he had his first cup of coffee. She had buried her head in his shirt and breathed in the pungent coffee smell, tempered with Old Spice. She had felt safe with Uncle Dave. The world was cold and empty without him.

Normally Finch would be worried about her mom and wonder how she would get along without Uncle Dave. But although Sparrow was sad and prone to tears, she busied herself with business matters and with finishing up her last term at Siena Heights. She said that Dave would want her to do that. Finch thought it had more to do with the professor, this Dr. Stewart guy who kept calling, who offered to take them both to dinner. No way was Finch going; she wasn't going to be a third wheel. Her mom came to life when Donald Stewart called, got a sparkle in her eye. How could she feel like that after Uncle Dave's death? The night Sparrow went out to dinner with Donald, Finch picked at one of the church women's casseroles, hating her mother with every bite.

Miserable and lonely, Finch returned to school.

On Monday morning Finch could not get out of bed. Shortly before eight Angie threatened her with water torture. Finch managed to roll out of bed and pull on a pair of jeans. When she came into the office late, Mr. Roland was bent over the filing cabinet.

"Finch, glad you're back." He turned and saw Finch's matted hair and swollen eyes. "You okay?'

"Yeah." Finch took off her mittens.

Mr. Roland walked around the counter and helped her off with her coat. "I'm really sorry about your Uncle Dave."

Finch burst into tears and buried her face in his shirt. Holding her coat with one hand, he patted her back with the other. Finch clutched at him and cried. He could smell her sour morning breath.

Finch sniffed. "You wear Old Spice, just like Uncle Dave."

Mr. Roland watched the door window. Someone paused in front of the door, then walked on. Mr. Roland drew away.

"I'm sorry. It's just so awful." Finch dug into her pocket for a Kleenex and blew her nose.

Mr. Roland touched his shirt, wet with her tears.

For the next few weeks, it was all Finch could do to drag herself out of bed. More often than not, she was late for work, five, ten, fifteen minutes. She would stare out of the window at the snow drifting on both sides of the road. She remembered sledding with Dave on the huge hill across from the golf club. She could see him trudging in from the snow, white covering gray, leaving wet boots to puddle on the floor. The memories did not soothe. She was caught in a cold space between the world of her childhood and the crush of her current life.

After complaints that the office wasn't opening on time, Mr. Roland made a point of getting to work by eight. Finch continued to come in late, pale and haggard, eyes vacant. He did not chastise her for tardiness, but kept a watchful distance. Finally he put her on the afternoon shift.

One frigid day Finch coughed most of the afternoon. Her eyes were red, her nose swollen. When it was time to close the office, it was snowing and the wind had picked up.

As Mr. Roland and Finch were putting on their coats, he said, "I'll drop you."

"It's okay. I can walk." Finch coughed.

"No, you're sick, and it's nasty out. I'll take you."

She nodded her assent.

The two drove in silence but when Mr. Roland stopped in front of the house, Finch turned to him. "I miss him so much."

"I know. I wish there was something I could do." He put his hand on Finch's shoulder.

"Oh, Mr. Roland." Finch fell into his arms.

Mr. Roland folded her into his chest and stroked her matted hair. Then he gently pushed her away and looked down the deserted street. "Do you have a picture of your Uncle Dave?"

"Oh, yes." Finch took a picture from her billfold. "I snapped this a few years ago. That's how I remember him, always sitting at the table, drinking coffee."

"He looks distinguished, with all that white hair, and I see a twinkle in his eyes."

"Yes—sometimes he acted like a grouch, but he really wasn't." Finch held up another picture. "I took this last summer, him with Mom. They're outside the store."

Mr. Roland took the picture. "Young mom."

"Here's a picture of her and me when I was just a baby. She looks older in that faded yellow sunflower dress and her hair pulled back."

Mr. Roland studied the picture. "What's her name?"

"Sparrow."

"Sparrow?"

"Yeah, I guess my grandmother liked birds. Named all her kids after birds, Sparrow, Jay and Robin. Mom always hated the name Sparrow, but she still named me Finch. She thinks finches are exotic." Finch managed a smile. "Kids used to tease me about being a bird. I'd rather have been Linda, Alice, even Jane—just plain Jane."

Revelation
February 1980

When the phone rang, Sparrow had just snapped off the lamp and snuggled into the quilt. It was 10:00 p.m., still early, but she had been exhausted since Dave's death. She had hired part-time help, but the effort of running the business and finishing up her degree was taking a toll. Sparrow could have managed if Finch had not been having such a difficult time. Her daughter was unreachable, resentful and angry. Sparrow consulted Ms. Sparks and came to the conclusion that Finch's anger covered her grief and, more troublingly, hid a growing depression. Now, each ring seemed to say Finch, Finch, Finch.

Sparrow picked up the phone. "Finch?" Silence. Sparrow clutched the phone.

"No, this is Robert Roland. Finch works for me in the Cashier's Office."

"What's happened?"

"She's okay, but I need to talk with you."

"What about?"

"Finch."

"You said she was okay."

"Yes, but there's another matter. We need to talk. Could I drive over and see you tomorrow?"

"Well…I guess so. The store closes at five."

"Good. I'll be there at five-thirty."

"What exactly is this about?"

"Sorry, I can't talk to you now. I assure you Finch is okay. I need to talk to you in person."

The phone clicked. Sparrow was irritated with this Robert Roland. He could have explained himself. Calling at ten at night was just plain rude.

Few patrons visited the shop the next day, giving Sparrow time to dwell on the abrupt phone conversation. At five she hung the CLOSED sign on the door and looked in the mirror—brown wool slacks, cream sweater, oxfords and heavy socks. She didn't have to look her best to talk with this intrusive man. Still, she dabbed on some lipstick and ran a comb through her hair. What could Mr. Roland want to talk to her about? Was Finch in some kind of trouble with a boy? No—not Finch.

Bob Roland arrived right on time and found a parking spot down the block from Booknook. He put on his parka and wool cap. As he trudged through the snow, icy wind nipped at his cheeks.

He touched the knob just as Sparrow opened the door. He pulled the cap from his head, revealing dark hair sprinkled with gray. Deep blue eyes sought hers. Sparrow gasped and clutched the counter for support. Bob moved to steady her, but she stepped out of reach. Wordlessly she turned and led him back to the oak table—to Dave's spot.

She opened her mouth to speak, but nothing came out. "Rob Roye?" She mouthed the words.

"Yes." His voice was firm.

"Why, why now?"

"Your daughter works for me."

"You're Robert Roland?"

"Yes."

Sparrow sank into a chair.

"This must be shocking."

Sparrow nodded.

Bob sat down opposite Sparrow. Neither spoke. Outside the wind howled. Frigid air seeped through cracks around the windows; the room chilled.

"Is she mine?"

"Is she yours?" Sparrow's head spun as though he had slapped her.

Bob cleared his throat. "There was something about her. I felt drawn to her. She reminded me of someone. Then I saw a picture of you holding her when she was a baby. You had on that yellow dress. Your hair was all done up on your head, and you looked older, tired and sad. Why didn't you let me know?" His words hung in the air.

"Let you know! You're asking me why I didn't tell you? I didn't know your name! You left town. You never called, didn't write. I went to the library and went through all the R-o-y's and R-o-y-e's in the Englewood, Colorado, phonebook. What was I supposed to do, call up and ask 'Do you have a son Rob? Was he in Milan, Michigan, this summer? If so, he got me pregnant.'"

Bob shifted on his feet, spread his hands. "I didn't think. Everybody called me Rob Roye. It was a nickname."

"But you left without a goodbye—not even a note."

"It was an emergency."

"You could have called."

227

"I was confused. When I finally sorted things out, I knew you weren't working at the drug store. I wrote you a letter, but you didn't answer."

"You wrote me a letter?"

"Sparrow, I'm so sorry."

He was older than she had imagined, with strands of gray hair, broader in the shoulders, but still slim — more handsome than she had remembered. Sparrow shivered.

The bell jingled. The two jumped. Donald flung open the door and stomped snow from his boots. "I'm here, Sparrow. A little early. Thought I'd help you clean up. Hadn't you better get some more light in here?"

Light flooded the shop.

Sparrow breathed deeply. "Donald, this is Robert Roland, Finch's father."

You Can't Run Away

*A*ngie had opened the window to let in the frosty air, but the bedroom still smelled of smoke, and now the room was cold. She sat on the bed in her pj's and winter coat, patting Finch's back. Finch was wrapped up in her mother's crocheted afghan.

"You can't just quit your job, Finch. You like it. And he's your dad. You've always wanted a dad. It's a chance to get to know him."

Finch peered out from her cover. "I can't believe it. I really liked him. I thought he liked me, too. I can't just say, 'Oh, hi, Dad,' and give him a big hug. It's all messed up. And he keeps calling *her*. I can't stand it! I'm just so embarrassed and mad at both of them."

"It's the Oedipal complex." Angie rubbed her hands together and screwed up her face, trying to remember. "Or is it the Electra?"

Finch sat up. "What do you mean—Oedipal, Electra?"

"You know, Freud. We studied it in psychology. Every little boy wants his mother for himself and a little girl wants her dad for herself. Mom said that when I was five, I said I'd grow up and marry Daddy,

229

and she would have to find another husband." Angie giggled.

"*Ugh*, you did not!" Finch buried her head in the afghan. Her voice was muffled. "You're just saying that to make me feel better."

"No! I really did. All girls go through it. You're just getting a double whammy 'cause he wasn't around when you were little."

"Uncle Dave is the one who was there. I was so scared. He made me feel safe."

"You, scared?"

"When I was little, sometimes Mom would hold me so tight that I could hardly breathe. Other times she'd be sitting with a book, not reading, just staring, and I'd have to shake her shoulder or even shout to get her to hear me. It's like she was somewhere else. I was afraid she'd disappear. Uncle Dave was the only one I could count on."

When Finch awoke the next morning, Angie was spread out on the bed, snoring softly, looking as though she had not a care in the world. Finch was tempted to kick the bed and disturb her slumber. Instead, she crept about, scribbled a note and threw on a pair of jeans and an EMU sweatshirt. She grabbed her coat and left the apartment without brushing her teeth or washing her face, leaving the door unlocked. She planned to slip the note under the office door before Mr. Roland got to work.

Fresh wet snow covered the sidewalks. Hands in her pockets, ears stinging from the cold, Finch tramped through the mushy snow, moisture seeping through her Nikes. Inside the Administration Building, she pushed the note under the office door. The deed done, she stood for a moment catching her breath. The door opened. Mr. Roland gazed down at her.

"Finch, what are—?"

She picked up the envelope, thrust it into his hand and ran.

"Finch, Finch!" Bob Roland started out the door and then thought better of chasing a coed down the hall.

He opened the letter. It read, "Mr. Roland, I am resigning my position. Under the circumstances I cannot give a two-week notice. I hope that it will not reflect badly on my employment record. Finch"

Bob crumpled the letter and tossed it into the wastebasket. He looked at the phone and thought about calling Sparrow. But she could do nothing, and calling would not endear him to her. He went to the door and reached for the knob, but pulled his hand back. Then pacing the room, he picked up the newspaper and flung it on the desk. Finally, he sat, opened the paper and attempted to do the crossword puzzle.

Outside, the frigid air did little to cool Finch's burning cheeks. A few students were on their way to early classes. Several spoke to her, but she did not see or hear them. Cars sped by, their tires spraying snow. Finch shuffled along, kicking the slush until her feet and jeans were soaked. Snowflakes settled on her bare head. She did not know where she was going, but she knew she was not going to class, nor was she going back to the apartment.

That night Sparrow, unaware of Finch's disappearance, sat on the bed. She had been shoveling; her arms and legs ached. She felt old. She dreaded the daily call to her unresponsive daughter. It seemed an exercise in futility. She thought if she heard the words "I'm fine" one more time she would surely scream.

Growing up, her daughter had been talkative and full of questions that Sparrow was unable to answer. Now that she was able to communicate, Finch had withdrawn into an impenetrable silence. If Finch could not talk to her, perhaps she could talk to someone else. But when Sparrow suggested that Finch see Ms. Sparks or another therapist, she had refused. Sparrow was beside herself with worry.

Then there was Bob, Rob Roye, Robert, whatever his name was—little more than a fantasy all these years, and now a huge presence. And in pursuit of her, wanting to understand. Understand what? That he had abandoned her and his unborn child? All those years she had dreamed of him, felt the passion of their two-week relationship, but had otherwise been numb. Now he was real, flesh and blood. And she was angry with him in a way she had never felt before.

Sparrow picked up the phone and made the call.

Angie answered. "She's not here. She left this morning before I got up. I don't know where she is. Is it snowing there? It's awful here—snowing and blowing."

Bob was watching the news in his pajamas when Sparrow called. "I didn't know who else to call...."

Bob did not tell Sparrow about the morning's confrontation. "I'll go look for her. I know the student hangouts. I'll call you back when I find her."

He dressed, pulling on a warm sweater and jeans. Letting the door slam behind him, he hurried to the car. He knew that he should have followed his impulse and gone after her, talked some sense into her. As he inched his car through the snow and onto the street, ice clumped on the windshield wipers. "Damn. I should have had those replaced." He turned the heater to defrost, stopped and chipped ice from the wipers.

Damp-haired patrons, smelling of steaming wool, packed the campus bars. Bare wooden floors were slippery with slush. Bob checked several bars, looking into every booth, with no results. A crowd lined the entrance to the Sidetrack; inside, it was mobbed with rowdy students. Scanning faces, Bob elbowed his way through the crowd. In a secluded back booth he found her with three young men. He recognized John, a lineman from the football team, someone he did not like Finch hanging out with. A soda untouched in front of her, fingering a half-drunk mug of beer, Finch leaned into John.

"Mr. Roland," John slurred.

The young man had his arm around Finch, his hand close to her breast. Bob restrained himself from grabbing him by the scruff of the neck. In spite of the situation, he smiled. There was no way that he could hoist up that young stud.

"What are you doing here, Finch?"

"It's a free country."

"It's late. You're underage."

"You have no say over me!"

John removed his arm from Finch's shoulders.

"No, I don't, but your mother does. She called me. She's worried. Okay, boys, the party's over. I'm taking Finch home now." He took hold of her arm.

Finch glared and flung his hand away. Then she shrugged and picked up her coat. To the boys, "Guess I have to go."

"You'd better put that on. It's a regular blizzard outside."

"No!" Finch marched to the car, wind whipping her hair, snow settling on her head. She got into the car and slammed the door.

Bob started the engine and turned up the defroster. "Take it easy."

Finch put her coat around her shoulders and stared straight ahead.

"I'll take you home."

"Where else, to the office, to your house?"

"Finch, I read the note. It's okay. You don't have to work for me. Later, if you change your mind, you can come back. I understand how devastating this must be for you, but I want to help you in any way I can."

"How could you do that to me? Embarrass me in front of my friends?"

"Those aren't your friends. You were in over your head. John has a reputation."

"I can take care of myself. You don't have any right to lecture me."

"You've been depressed, and you were missing all day. Your mom is upset. You may hate me, but your mom doesn't deserve this."

"Oh! You…you self-righteous bigot! Now you're concerned about Mom! Where were you when she was pregnant?"

"I do feel some responsibility toward you."

"You do, do you? Where were you when I was growing up, when I needed you?"

Bob breathed in the musty heater air, listened to the swish and then clunk of the wipers as they hit a bit of ice. He spoke softly. "I didn't know you existed. But now I do, and tonight, like it or not, you needed me. I don't want you getting mixed up with a bunch of guys who'll take advantage of you."

"The way you did my mother?"

"Finch, it's not what you think. We were just a couple of kids. Your mom was special."

"Not special enough for you."

Bob slapped the wheel; the car swerved. "Damn." Bob muttered. He drove more slowly, wiping the frost from the inside of the window with his hand, the wipers scraping against the windshield. When they reached Finch's apartment, he eased to a stop. Both hands on the wheel, he spoke softly, "What can I say?" He didn't say that, through the years, images of Sparrow had flitted through his mind, that the day he walked down the aisle, for an instant, he saw Sparrow's elfin face transposed onto his bride's.

Finch leapt out of the car, leaving the door open. Bob reached across and closed it.

He watched her run up the frozen walk.

Bob laid his head on the hard cold steering wheel. He ached to hold Finch, to melt the ice and distance between them. He always lost the ones he loved—his mom, Sparrow, Jeffery.

A day in 1966 was seared into his memory. He had told his wife, Maggie, that he had to work late; he had locked the office door and had not heard the knock or the click of the key. But he did hear Maggie's gasp. Then he turned and saw her, and four-year old Jeffery hanging onto her leg. A tall Nordic woman, she seemed to shrink. The light went out of her eyes.

"*Your supper,*" she said and threw a brown paper sack on the counter. "Come on, Jeffery. You and I are going home." She picked him up and carried him through the door.

"Daddy! Daddy! I want to have a picnic with Daddy!" His son's cries echoed down the hall.

"*You* and *I* are going home." That's what she had said, and it did not include him.

That night she packed up his personal belongings and set them on the porch. At twenty-seven, he had landed his first administrative position and lost his wife and child. The affair with the student had not lasted.

Cleaning House
April 1980

Winter turned to spring; cold gave way to erratic warmth and torrents of rain. Crocuses and daffodils bloomed. Finch did not go back to work at the Cashier's Office and continued to hang up when Robert Roland called. She found it difficult to concentrate in class and nearly impossible to study. Subsisting on oranges and ramen noodles, she lost weight; dark shadows encircled her eyes. Mired in self-pity, she spent much of her time watching TV or, on warm days, sunning on the deck outside her back door. When Sparrow begged her to go to counseling, Finch shocked herself by screaming, "I am not crazy." In one of Finch's rare receptive moments, Sparrow persuaded her to drop the physics class that she was failing. Seemingly unresponsive to Sparrow's nightly calls and weekly visits, Finch attempted to finish her remaining coursework.

While Finch languished, Sparrow tapped into the determination and energy that she had found when she first came to Adrian. Although Finch was constantly on her mind, there was work to be done and a certain comfort in doing it. She focused on keeping Booknook open. On a slow weekday Jennifer, her part-time employee, was capable of staffing the shop by herself, and Sparrow could take care of other business. Although she dreaded the thought of emptying Dave's home, feared the memories she would encounter, it was not good for a house to stand neglected. The job must be done.

It was still dark when Sparrow prepared to go to Dave's house. She ran up and down the apartment stairs, gathering cleaning supplies. When she opened the shop door, snow covered the street and the thermometer by the window read twenty degrees. With little warning, snow had vanquished spring.

She tossed the Windex, Mr. Clean, and Fantastic into the car. It seemed a long time ago when she had had to make do with vinegar and hot water. She must be rich now, she mused. When she turned the key in the ignition and held the gas pedal down, the cold engine sputtered. She tried again and yet again. Finally the engine turned over. She smiled. If she were truly rich or even middle-class, the car would have been in a warm garage and would have started right off. She got out and swished the snow from the windshield, then rubbed her hands together for warmth. When she reached Dave's house, she noted that the neighbor boy had not cleared the walk. She grabbed the shovel from the front porch and went to work. Wishing that she had worn warmer gloves, she stopped from time to time and rubbed her hands. She leaned the shovel against the porch, fumbled for the key, but dropped it in the snow. She groped for it, moisture seeping through her thin gloves.

Inside, a stagnant, frigid dampness greeted her. She turned up the heat and stood in the middle of the living room, hands under her coat next to her heart. The house was filled with Dave's presence. His recliner was open, and she could see the indentation that his body had made. There was a path worn in the dark shag carpet from kitchen to chair. His slippers were beside the chair; a half-filled cup of coffee sat on the side table. If it had not been for the mold growing in the cup, it would have looked as though he had gone to the bathroom and would return momentarily. She picked up the Adrian *Telegram* dated January 15, 1980.

He had been a private person. She felt like an intruder, as though he might walk in and scold her. How she wished he could! How she wished she had told him how much she loved him, how much he meant to her! So what if it had embarrassed him. At least she would have said it. She sat on the couch, eyes fixed on the empty chair, tears streaming down her face. After a while, sun peeked through the window, warming her face; she pulled out a tissue, wiped her eyes and blew her nose.

"Okay, Dave. I loved you, and you loved us. You can't deny it. I miss you. I'm worried about Finch and need you here to help me. But I'll do this. Today I am cleaning your house. I'm taking your clothes to the Goodwill." She looked around the room. "But I'm not going to live here. At least not yet." She gestured toward his empty chair. "It's still your house."

About noon Donald knocked. When there was no answer, he opened the door and cleared garbage bags out of the way. "Sparrow, Sparrow, where are you?" He walked down the hall to where Sparrow was vigorously sweeping. "Didn't you hear me?"

Startled, Sparrow whirled around, the broom upturned.

Donald chuckled. "Now I believe it."

Sparrow shook her head. "Believe what?"

"That story about you and the broom when Finch was little, you chasing those boys down the street. You look pretty scary!"

Sparrow assumed a warrior's position, used the dustpan as a shield and flourished the broom at him. "You'd better watch out."

Donald stepped back. "Please, spare me!" He held up a Subway bag. "I brought food."

Sparrow dropped the broom and opened her arms. "You don't know how hungry I am."

"Not half as hungry as I am." Donald held her and nuzzled and nipped her neck.

"How's it going? Tired?"

"I'm a little crazy. I feel his presence. I find myself talking to him, chiding him for his messes, telling him how glad I am to finally get rid of his old plaid shirt. You know—his favorite, the one I mended a hundred times. But the strangest thing—I never knew Emily, but I feel her presence, too, and it's like she is saying everything will be all right."

Donald held her shoulders. "If you say they're hanging around, they are." He kissed her forehead and ushered her into the kitchen. "Now I'm inviting you all to lunch."

A Meeting at the Clintonian Inn
May 1980

Sparrow had insisted they meet on neutral
territory, in Clinton, between Adrian and Ann
Arbor, at the Clintonian Inn, an historic brick hotel
with a restaurant and bar on the first floor. There
were tables in two rows the length of the rectangular
dining room, the outer row next to turn-of-the-
century narrow windows overlooking an empty
side street. A fringed white tablecloth and single silk
carnation adorned each table. The restaurant made
Bob think of a teahouse; he imagined they might
dine on crustless cucumber sandwiches. He would
have preferred to wait in the intimate bar with the
darkened oak counter, where he would have a view
of Highway 12. There he could have a beer, or maybe
a Scotch, while he watched for Sparrow. He needed
a drink. Instead, he sat at one of the small windowed
tables facing the entrance, long legs stretched out
into what would be her space. She'd been explicit:
this is where he was to be.

He was not certain that she would come and
sighed in relief when he saw her. She wore a sleeveless

pastel dress, fitted to the waist, accenting her small firm breasts. Pale skin, dark hair and tinted lips were familiar, but unfamiliar—not the timid girl that he had known twenty years ago. Head high, she walked to the table. He did not know that her hands were wet with perspiration, her heart pounding. Bob rose and offered her the chair across from him. When he sat back down, his feet brushed hers.

"Sorry," he said, pivoting his long legs into the aisle. "Thanks for coming."

Sparrow nodded.

"How are you?"

"I graduated."

"I know. Congratulations."

Sparrow laid a delicate straw purse on the white cloth. "Exactly what did you want, Bob—or is it Rob?"

"Listen, Sparrow, I'm sorry. I can't change things. I know you and Finch have had a hard time. You've made it clear you want nothing from me." He leaned forward. "I had to see you, talk to you. I've got to make sense of this."

Sparrow sat back in her chair. "You can't just walk into our lives out of nowhere. I don't know what to say to you. I don't even know what to call you. Who are you?"

"Sparrow, it was a long time ago. I haven't seen you in twenty years. I didn't know you were pregnant. Please, tell me what happened."

Sparrow's eyes sparked. "Isn't it a little late for that?"

"I didn't know! How could I know?"

"You wrote one letter and gave up!"

Bob's fist hit the table. "Guilty as charged!"

"May I take your order?" The waitress was young, a high-school girl dressed in jeans, bobby socks and loafers; a bibbed, gingham apron came to her knees.

Bob made a sweeping gesture with his hand. His voice cut through the restaurant. "No!"

The girl startled and hurried away.

Sparrow's eyes followed the retreating girl. "That wasn't necessary."

"What?"

"The way you treated her."

"What?"

"You yelled at her."

"I never yelled at her!"

Sparrow, hands in her lap, found the edge of the tablecloth. "She's just a girl. You hurt her feelings."

"I didn't mean to hurt her."

"You were just short of nasty." Sparrow fingered the fringe of the tablecloth.

Bob shook his head. "What did I do?"

Sparrow picked up her purse and stood up. "You were rude, abrupt, swished her away, as though she had no right to speak to you!"

Bob's hands thudded onto the table. "God, Sparrow, I've been trying to talk to her. She won't take my calls."

"The waitress? You've been calling the waitress?"

"Oh!... I thought you meant Finch."

Their eyes connected. They laughed. Sparrow sat back down and picked up the menu.

The girl returned, holding her pad and pencil at the ready. "Would you like to order now?" She looked at Sparrow. "You got any questions?"

"Ask the gentleman. He has lots of them," said Sparrow.

Bob spoke contritely. "Yes, please. What would you recommend?'

She grinned, revealing a mouth full of braces. "Chicken cordon bleu. That's the best."

They agreed on the chicken. Bob ordered a bottle of Chardonnay; they sipped the wine and made small talk.

"I'm updating the store…. I may do weekly book reviews for the Adrian *Telegram*. That should help business."

"There is so much I don't know about you." Bob sought her eyes.

"Yes, there is. And there is a lot you don't know about your daughter. Dave's death is bad enough. He was like a father to her. But then she finds out that you're her father."

"I'd like a relationship with her."

"She doesn't want one with you right now. She *doesn't* seem to want one with me."

"I'm sorry, Sparrow."

Sparrow nodded. "So am I."

The waitress brought two plates of steaming chicken and placed them on the table. "Be careful. The plates are warm."

"Smells good," said Bob.

Sparrow took a few small bites, then set her fork down. Her finger circling the rim of the wineglass, she watched Bob eat.

"Remember the Dairy Barn?" she asked.

"Of course." Bob took a huge bite of chicken.

"You'd wolf down a couple of burgers while I ate a half."

He took the last bite of chicken and wiped his hands on the napkin. "That's how I eat when I'm nervous."

"You're nervous?" She took a sip of wine.

"What do you think?"

Sparrow smiled.

"You don't know how naive I was when I met you. You were the first girl I made love to."

"I was? I thought you had all this experience. You seemed so sure of yourself."

He shrugged. "Pretty good act. If I'd been experienced, I would have known what to do. I was an ignorant kid. I was smitten. Thought you were terrific. It never occurred to me that you'd get pregnant."

He reached for her hand. Although Sparrow did not open her hand to him, she felt the heat of his touch.

The restaurant was not busy. A few couples came and went, but sat far enough away to ensure Bob and Sparrow's privacy. The tables were cleared and readied for the next day. The waitress dimmed the lights, and asked if they wanted anything more.

Bob looked around him. "Guess we're the last one. How about the bill?"

The waitress took the bill from her apron pocket and dropped it on the table, then turned away.

Bob reached for his billfold. "I suppose I'd better leave something extra for my rudeness." He pulled out Sparrow's chair and escorted her out of the restaurant, his hand on her back.

The town was asleep. Dim streetlights appeared to wend their way through the quiet village and down Highway 12. At her car, Sparrow turned. Bob flattened his hands on the car door, encircling her.

Sparrow was enveloped in his musky odor and memories of the long-gone summer. For a moment she leaned into his warmth. She slipped away. "I can't. I can't. There's been too much…. I don't know you."

Bob's arms fell to his sides. "Sparrow, please, please, give me a chance. We've time. Get to know me. Think about it."

Memories and Longings

*B*ob's memories of the summer of 1959 were dreamlike. He had turned nineteen the day he and his dad, Victor, rolled into Milan. A hick town, Bob thought, one flat street with a few stores: hardware, café, drugstore, and a movie theater. His home, Englewood, Colorado, a suburb of Denver, was a metropolitan area, and he'd just finished his freshman year at the University of Colorado. Victor made a good living, traveling the country refinishing lanes in bowling alleys. The summer of '59, he needed help, and Bob needed money. His dad was okay, not too bossy, and Bob didn't mind working for him, but he missed Maggie.

Her name was Margaret, but everybody called her Maggie. She wasn't exactly a girlfriend, more like a pal. He had grown up with her. They had ridden trikes together, then bikes, shot baskets and played softball on the school playground. When they were seniors, he had asked her to the prom. That winter, when their families were skiing at Breckon Ridge, they had almost become lovers, not because they were in love, but because they were comfortable with each other and hormones were flowing. Maggie's ten-year-old sister discovered them in the bedroom and said she was going to tell her Mom, but did not.

Bob had planned on getting a job at home that summer, but his dad's helper, Sam, went on a binge and ended up in the hospital. Bob had been pressed into service. He thought it would be a few dull weeks, sanding all the lanes in the area's bowling alleys, but it meant man's wages and he tried to think of it as an adventure. The day he saw Sparrow behind the drug store counter his misgivings vanished. He was intrigued with the sweet girl who seemed so fragile and wanted to smooth away her worries.

The night of their first lovemaking, they had gone to a movie—which one, he could not remember. He did remember the thrill of her hand in his, the sweat that joined them, of wiping his hand on his jeans while she discreetly wiped hers on her dress, and then the electricity of reconnection.

When he took her home, he had asked to go in. She put her head down and said no, that her mom would not allow it. He lifted her chin and kissed her. They walked around to the side of the house where the marigolds grew and found a patch of grass under a tree. He took his old cowboy blanket from the truck, and they sat on it. Sparrow asked about college. She said that her teacher thought she should go, but her mom would never let her, and it would be scary going away from home and all. He played with her ponytail until it came undone, then buried his nose in her curls, smelling her scent—sweet shampoo and Ivory-soap-clean. He had no plan to go all the way. She was not that kind of girl. But she was warm and soft, her body fitting to his, yielding to him. It had felt natural, right.

Afterwards, holding her in his arms, he apologized. "I'm sorry. I'm so sorry. It won't happen again." He knew it wasn't safe. He had no condoms, and he could not go into the drug store and ask Mr. Jensen or worse, Sparrow, for Trojans. For a couple of nights he maintained control, tried to satisfy himself by holding her, kissing her. On the third evening, they lay on the blanket again mesmerized by the stars, inhaling the green-clean scent of grass. He held her close and his hands, as though they had a mind of their own, began to explore the contours of her body. When he touched her breasts, his desire was so intense that he felt, if he did not have her, he would die. And she was willing. In spite of the fire within him, he had been careful to withdraw. He had assured her nothing could happen. Now, all these years later, he wondered which night she had conceived.

That night Victor had received a frantic call from his wife. She had been diagnosed with breast cancer that summer and surgery had been scheduled for early fall when Victor and Bob would be home. The cancer had grown more rapidly than they had expected; the surgeon had a cancellation and thought it would be wise to move more quickly.

Father and son left Milan at daybreak, stopping on their journey only to switch drivers, fuel up, and grab fast food. They arrived home the day of Bob's mother's mastectomy. The surgery did not get all the invasive, evasive cancer cells. The cancer traveled through her body like cars on the interstate. The minimal doses of morphine that the doctors allowed did little to relieve her pain. Bob could scarcely bear his mother's suffering. He thought the doctors were sadistic, torturing her with chemotherapy and radiation. He forced himself to stay close, tried to make himself useful, brought her ice and juice, a cloth for her head. He did the dishes and vacuumed the carpets.Through it all, Maggie had been there. She visited most days, and when his mom was too ill for company, Maggie watched TV with Bob and his dad. Then one night, when his dad was at work, Bob took her to his bedroom. It was not as exciting as he had hoped, but it was comforting, and he could sleep.

His mother had willed herself to live until summer when, in a quiet family ceremony in the backyard, she watched from her wheel chair as Bob and Maggie got married. While the young couple were on their honeymoon, his mother died. Perhaps it had been an omen for the marriage. For after her death, after the mourning, Bob found that Maggie was more of a pal than a mate. He began to dream of Sparrow, to wonder what had happened to her. And worse: a few years later a petite, shy co-ed reminded him of Sparrow— the way she cocked her head, her turned-up-lip smile. He had found her irresistible.

Confrontations

*F*or several weeks Bob had phoned Finch regularly, only to be rebuffed. Although she refused to talk with him, she had felt a certain satisfaction in his pursuit and was disappointed when he no longer called. When Sparrow called Finch and mentioned that she had gone to dinner with Bob the previous evening, Finch was stunned. When she hung up, she paced the apartment feeling as if her insides would implode. Finally, she marched across campus to the Cashier's Office.

Finch flung the office door open. Her voice a crescendo, she confronted Bob Roland. "What are you trying to do to my mother?"

Bob pulled her into the office, closed and locked the door. "What are you talking about?"

"I know what you've been doing! You had dinner with her last night. I know you did."

Bob sighed. "It's not a federal offense."

"You hurt my mother once, and you're not going to do it again."

Bob stepped close to Finch. "You are not your mother's keeper. She will see me if she wants."

Finch drew her hand back and slapped him on the face.

He seized her arm. "That's enough, Finch."

"Stay away from my mother!"

Bob held her close. "It's okay. We can work this out."

"You abandoned her. You didn't care that she was pregnant."

Bob's arms fell to his sides. "I didn't know."

"I don't believe you. You didn't care! We don't need you. We got along just fine without you. Mom raised me by herself. Now when she has a halfway normal life, you show up and ruin everything."

Shoulders drooping, Bob turned toward the light of the window. He did not hear the birds frantically chirping at a cat or see the cat jump from the tree. He was only aware of Finch's anger. He turned and sought her eyes.

"I didn't mean to hurt you or your mom. I do want to know you. But you won't talk to me, won't answer the phone."

"You're an old Casanova. Admit it. You liked me!... You flirted with me!"

"Finch, I didn't know you were my daughter."

"Doesn't matter. You're too old for me, and you shouldn't have."

"I didn't make a pass at you."

"Did you want to?"

Again, Bob turned away. "I loved your mother."

He could not speak of how he'd been drawn to Finch, how something sweet and vaguely familiar emanated from her. He'd noted the flush of her cheeks as she rushed into the office, the flourish of her hand as she picked up a folder, and her scent. That day in the car, when she showed him the picture of the girl in the faded yellow daisy dress, he had remembered the fragrance—Sparrow's ivory-soap-clean.

Brinnng, brinnng, Finch wrestled herself from sleep and tossed her pillow over the phone. She curled into a ball and held the blanket over her ears. The ringing stopped. She put the pillow under her head; the phone rang again. *Brinnng, brinnng.* She thought it must be her mother. If Angie were here, she would answer. Damned if she would pick up. The ringing stopped. Finch sighed and turned on her back; she was awake now. *Brinnng, brinnng!*

Finch grabbed the phone. "What!"

"What? What? Is that the way you answer the phone now?"

Finch recognized the voice—Clare Washington. She was in for it now. "I thought it was someone else."

"I don't care who you thought it was. That is no way to answer the phone, young lady."

"I know." Finch pulled the covers up around her. She would not apologize to the old goat.

"Do you have afternoon classes?"

"No, I finish at one."

"I called to invite you to lunch. I have to come to Saint Joe's for a bone-density test. Imagine that. With my build, they're concerned about bone loss. I'll pick you up shortly after one. Your mom gave me directions. I want to see your apartment…. Well, I can tell you just woke up. I'll talk to you later." The phone clicked.

Finch held her brick-heavy head. The apartment was a mess and Mrs. Washington was coming. The clock said nine-thirty. She had missed her nine o'clock class again. At the moment she hated the prim and proper woman. In fact, she hated everyone. Her stomach growled; she gave it a slap. Last week's orange sat shriveled on the nightstand. She poked it; it bounced and rolled across the carpet. Clothes were scattered about the room, making it difficult to distinguish dirty from clean. Empty beer bottles lined the windowsill. A partially filled bottle sat on the floor, inviting a kick. With perverse satisfaction, Finch imagined the pungent, urine-colored liquid oozing onto the carpet. She groaned, picked it up and poured it out into the sink.

When Finch and Clare arrived at Aubrey's, the noon crowd was thinning. They found a semi-clean booth near the gaming area where a couple of students were shooting pool. Clare wiped off the table with a napkin. She coughed, took a Kleenex from her purse and covered her mouth. Music blared; the cue stick slammed against the ball.

Clare jerked. "Oh, my, that startled me. It's noisy and smoky in here." She fanned her nose with the Kleenex.

Finch grinned. Fastidious Mrs. Washington was in a loud, dimly lit student hangout with skuzzy floors and tables. Let her squirm. Finch reached into her shirt pocket, pulled out a pack of cigarettes, and laid them on the table.

"You smoke now." It was a statement. But Clare's tone said that it was not acceptable.

Finch nodded, took a cigarette from the pack and offered one. Clare tapped the pack; a cigarette slid into her palm.

Finch gasped. "You smoke?"

"Used to."

Finch handed Clare the matches.

Clare put the Kleenex in her purse, sat back on her chair, lit the cigarette, took a couple of deep puffs and blew a perfect smoke ring in Finch's face. She stubbed out the cigarette and handed the matches to Finch, who laid them on the table next to her unlit cigarette.

The six-foot waiter peered down at them. "What would you like?" He smiled at Finch, who remained impassive. Clare returned his smile.

"What's good?" asked Clare.

"Burgers are best, real good." He leaned toward Clare. "You might stay away from the specials—got a new cook on today."

Clare nodded. "How about a cheeseburger and fries? How are they?"

"Oh, yeah!"

"Okay. What are you having, Finch?"

"I'm not very hungry. I'll just have a salad with ranch on the side." She glared up at the waiter. "Cook can't screw that up, can he?"

"Nope, doesn't make the salads. I do, and I promise it'll be good." He winked.

"That's all you're having?" asked Clare.

"I'll have a Diet Coke," said Finch.

Clare shook her head. "Coffee for me, cream."

She studied Finch. "So, you're having a hard time?"

"No!" Finch flipped the match cover open and shut.

"No?" Clare reached for Finch's hand.

"I'm fine."

"Oh, is that so? It's your first year of college, and that's an adjustment in itself."

Finch shrugged, withdrew her hand.

"You must be missing Dave."

Finch looked at the table.

"And your mom has a boyfriend."

Finch flared. "I'm glad."

The grinning waiter appeared and placed a Coke on the table. Eyes on Finch, oblivious to its sloshing, he plunked a cup of coffee next to Clare.

Clare wiped the spill with her napkin. "That young man is interested in you."

"I don't care." Finch skated the cigarette pack back and forth across the vinyl cloth.

"That's just it. You don't care. You're in college. You should be dating, having a good time. Instead, you're holed up in that apartment, smoking, drinking and *not* eating."

Finch slammed her hands on the table. The cigarette pack bounced onto the floor. The two sat in silence.

"A cheeseburger and fries for the lady, and a salad, made special for the young lady." The waiter placed a bowl with lettuce and tomatoes heaped to the rim before Finch. "I couldn't get everything in." He set a condiment bowl overflowing with grated cheese and croutons next to the salad.

Clare smiled. "What's your name, young man?"

"Alexander. Alex, call me Alex." He bent his long frame from the waist and scooped the cigarettes off the floor.

"How long have you worked here?" asked Clare.

"A couple of years. I'm a junior at Eastern."

"Isn't that a coincidence? My niece, Finch, is finishing her freshman year." Clare motioned to Finch.

"A lot of students come in here, but I haven't seen you." He grinned at Finch. "I usually work noons, like to keep my evenings free."

"What are you studying?" asked Clare.

Alex twirled the empty serving tray on his fingers. "I like anthropology a lot, but I don't think I can earn a living at it. So I'm getting a teaching degree—I like kids, too."

The restaurant was nearly empty. The young man looked at a chair as though he might like to sit down and chat. "What are you studying?" he asked Finch.

"Don't know yet. I like design." She turned away.

"Eastern has a great art department."

"Clothes, I like to design clothes." She fingered her fork.

"Great. Well, maybe I'll see you around." Alex walked to the register to ring up a customer.

"Why did you do that?" demanded Finch.

Clare shrugged. "He was clearly interested in you. He's cute—looks like a runner. I like him."

Finch stabbed the lettuce, brought it towards her mouth, but set it back on her plate. She picked up a crouton and popped it into her mouth.

Clare dabbed her burger in catsup and took a bite. "This is so good. Try it." She broke off a piece and handed it to Finch.

Falling In
July 1980

The summer after Dave's death was hot, unrelenting. Beckoned by the air conditioning, too lethargic to peruse the books, Booknook customers leaned against the counter chatting. Petunias bearing stunted flowers snaked their way out of Sparrow's window boxes and dropped their blossoms before they fully opened.

It was late afternoon, and Sparrow had forgotten to give the flowers their morning drink. Drooping heads on spindly stems cried out for water. She wondered if they would last the summer. Hefting the watering can, she thought of Finch, now out of crisis but irritable, tenacious like the petunias. As the water cascaded over the planters, the blossoms began to look toward the sun.

She let the cool water spill over her hands and pictured river rapids. She thought of canoeing. In high school she'd gone canoeing once with Mary, on the Raisin River, dark like the fruit. It had been warm and slow, the sun shining, and Sparrow had tucked the memory away for safekeeping. After Finch was born it did not occur to her that she could do anything as frivolous as canoeing. Being a good mother had become her mission and her penance. Now, *she wanted to go canoeing.* She laughed at the revelation: she knew what she wanted.

As a child Sparrow had learned never to express her desires. Once when she was not yet in school, as a special treat there had been chocolate chip cookies, her favorite, for dessert. Her mother had doled out one to each person. There was one left on the plate next to Sparrow. Sparrow hungered for that cookie. Finally, tentatively, she reached out her hand. As though waiting for this transgression, her mother rose out of her chair and smacked her hand. "You selfish little brat. What makes you think *you* can have that cookie?"

The turmoil of never, ever, getting what she wanted had taken its toll. She had suppressed her wishes until even she did not know what they were. Finch's birth had awakened her. She *wanted* to keep her baby. Nevertheless, Sparrow could not think of her own wants and needs separate from her child. It was in therapy that her feelings began to emerge. In the winter of the first year of her therapy, Sparrow had picked up Thomas Hardy's *Tess of the d'Urbervilles* from the used-book section. For several days she had the novel open at the register, barely able to tear herself away to answer a question or ring up a sale. Dave let it go; under no circumstance did he want to discourage Sparrow from something that *she* might like.

Sparrow loved and hated Tess. She marveled at Tess's bravery and strength. Tess had been sent away as an early adolescent to work and support the family. She was raped and had a baby, which she cared for single-handedly. Tess's life spiraled into utter poverty.

She could have, should have, asked for help, but did not. Sparrow was appalled by Tess's inability to advocate for herself. In therapy, she had railed against Tess's stupidity, her shame and not speaking up for herself.

She had been stopped mid-sentence when Ms. Sparks asked, "Does Tess remind you of yourself?"

When Sparrow had realized that she was pregnant, she'd considered suicide. She contemplated hanging herself, taking poison, throwing herself in front of a car. A gunshot to the head would be quick, but she had no gun. She retreated into a shell to wait for justice to be meted out. Instead, Dave had taken her in. After Finch's birth, when she could think again, she should have taken some action. She should have walked down to the bowling alley and asked some questions, gotten Rob's name and address. She should have had her mail forwarded to Adrian. Perhaps she and Rob would be together...or perhaps not. At least Finch could have grown up knowing who her father was. But at the time, Sparrow had not known to do these things, and if she had known, could not have done them. She had done what she could.

Sparrow had been shamed and rejected. She had gone into hiding. Determined not to let her own sin taint her daughter's life, she had lived for Finch. Hadn't she served her time? Now unmarried pregnant girls lived at home and finished high school. They paraded their swollen bellies down the street; families helped them care for their infants. Sparrow had done the best she could. Surely it was her turn.

Sparrow wanted to go canoeing. She had a choice, Bob or Donald. They'd both been vying for her attention. Bob would be at ease on the river; and he would be willing to go. Donald would be a less likely choice. He was not well-coordinated and spent most of his time indoors. As a kid, his greatest pleasure had been reading.

Sparrow had not been intimate with either man. It was exciting being with Bob, but she felt uneasy. She did not trust him. Donald was calm, cerebral. And he had not judged her for having a child out of wedlock. He seemed to understand her, and she felt comfortable with him.

Sparrow asked Donald if he'd like to go canoeing on the 4th of July. He ran his hand through his hair, pushing down his cowlick. "Why not? Let's make a trip of it. Drive up to Cadillac, spend a couple of nights and canoe the Pine River."

"Spend the weekend together?"

He touched her face. "I'd like to. Would you?"

"Yes—No—I'm not sure."

Donald held her hand. "Sparrow, we can get a room with two beds. Separate rooms if you like. Whatever you want."

Whatever I want, thought Sparrow.

On the morning of the canoe trip the livery was busy. A string of waiting canoes lined the dock. "The river's a bit high, not too fast, a couple of rapids, nothing to worry about," said the boy who handed them paddles and life preservers. "You can take off soon as this group is gone."

The two watched as a couple climbed cautiously into a moored canoe and the boy shoved the canoe out into the stream. The Pine snaked and curved, making its way over rocks and boulders. To Sparrow it looked nothing like the lazy Raisin River. "Let's leave our watches and stuff in the car," she said.

Donald stuck his wallet in his back pocket. "Never can tell when you might need it."

"Even on the river?"

They grabbed the picnic basket and Polaroid camera and rushed after the boy, who propelled their canoe effortlessly over the grass and down the bank. As Sparrow had seen others do, she strapped her sandals over the bar of the canoe and secured the basket with a plastic bag.

"You'd better strap your sandals on the bar," said Sparrow, stepping in.

"Nah, they'll be okay." Donald adjusted his cushion and settled himself awkwardly onto the seat.

The boy pushed the canoe into the water. Both paddling on the right, they started the three-hour trip down the swollen Pine. The canoe headed for the left bank. To compensate, Sparrow paddled on the left, but Donald continued on the right.

"Don, we're heading for the shore. Switch sides," said Sparrow.

The canoe bumped against a tree; Donald lost his paddle in the water. Sparrow grabbed a branch and steadied the canoe.

"Give me your paddle," Donald said. He took it and guided his paddle back to the boat, where he could reach it.

The bark of the tree dug into Sparrow's hands. "You're supposed to steer us." Donald held his oar across his knees. "Maybe I need a lesson."

"Haven't you ever canoed?" asked Sparrow.

"No."

"*No*? Why didn't you tell me?"

Water swirled around the canoe; Sparrow clung to the branch.

"I didn't think it was a big deal. You just paddle on the side opposite from where you want to go—right?"

"Sort of, but the one in back controls things."

"Do you know how to do it?"

"Mary did it. And I've only been once."

Donald scowled. "Was the Raisin River this fast?"

"No!"

A middle-aged couple came around the bend. "How're you doing?" called the man.

"Not so good," responded Donald.

"Looks that way. Need some help?"

A few minutes later Sparrow and Donald were weaving down the river. "Watch out for rocks and logs. Don't stand up. When you come to rapids, go right into them. Don't try and skirt them or you could tip," advised the helpful man as he and his wife sped by them.

Donald and Sparrow were not the only ones having difficulties. They watched as a canoe capsized in the rapids. The drenched woman screamed at her husband as they struggled to right their canoe. Donald and Sparrow concentrated on paddling. Birds sang from the trees bordering the river, turtles sunned themselves on fallen logs, and green and blue dragonflies flitted across the canoe. The water was clear and cool, the sun warm. The beauty was lost on them, however, as they were vigilant for obstructions.

At the first rapids, water surged over logs, leaving only a narrow opening. Sparrow froze.

Donald called over the sound of the rapids, "We can do it! Paddle faster! We'll take it head-on, like he said."

Sparrow closed her eyes and paddled, feeling the rush of the water as they went over. After that it was easier. They became a team.

Two hours into the trip, they found a sandy spot and tied up for lunch. There had been close calls. They had collided with the bank several times, gotten hung up on rocks, and had to lie down in the canoe to avoid branches. Although some canoers were drinking and snacking as they paddled, Sparrow and Donald had been so preoccupied with staying afloat that they barely moved lest they tip the canoe.

"I'm so thirsty," said Sparrow as she popped the tab off a soda. "You're so amazing, never been canoeing—look at us!"

Donald bit into his sub. "Sure, dehydrated and starving."

After devouring the sandwiches and candy bars, the two lay contentedly on the grass, watching the leaves sway above them, listening to an unseen woodpecker tapping on a nearby tree. Sparrow nestled into Donald's arms and dozed. Clouds hid the sun; it began to cool. Donald kissed Sparrow's cheek. "It's time."

"Sure, in a minute." Sparrow snuggled back in his arms.

"Come on, Sparrow. We need to get back!"

Sparrow rubbed her eyes and smiled, a full smile that lit up her face. "You make it sound like we're going off to battle."

"Aren't we?" He helped her up.

Sparrow put her arms around him and nuzzled his neck. The grass where they had lain was matted—inviting.

Donald caught her gaze. "We've got to go. I want to get you back in one piece." They gathered up the wrappers and soda cans and put them in a bag. Donald tossed his sandals into the canoe and looked up at the sky. "I think it might rain. We've got to get out of here."

The air turned chilly; it started to drizzle. They paddled on, muscles aching, wishing the trip would end. Around a bend, they came upon hard rapids. One canoe had just made it through; another had capsized.

"Be careful!" called the woman in the canoe that had just made it over.

"We can do it," shouted Donald over the roar of the rapids.

Forgetting their lesson, as they approached the rapids they slowed their strokes. They aimed for the center, the bow cutting through the middle. But they didn't have enough momentum. The current seized and flipped the canoe. Both fell clear, but Sparrow, caught in the rush of water, went under and could not touch bottom. Donald, clinging to a tree limb, grabbed her arm. She came up choking and spitting, holding the Polaroid camera. They watched helplessly as Donald's sandals—and worse—his wallet floated by, too far out to reach. A couple of young men banked their canoe and helped them out of the frigid water. While the three men righted the canoe and brought it to shore, Sparrow sat on the bank clutching the camera.

Donald dragged himself out of the water and took her in his arms. "Good heavens, Sparrow, you scared me!"

Shivering, holding the camera, she clung to him. A picture exploded from the Polaroid. Sparrow screamed and flung the camera down. They watched in amazement as black, wet, nothing pictures shot out. Finally, the camera emptied itself and lay quiet on the damp grass.

That evening they soaked their aching bodies in the warm pool at the motel, ate a simple dinner in a nearby restaurant and watched the fireworks over

Cadillac Lake. Back at the motel, Sparrow scurried into the bathroom and readied herself for bed. She cracked the door and peered out.

Donald held her hand and eased her into the room. "Don't you look stunning in your shortie pajamas!"

"Made them."

He encircled her in his arms. "You are one talented lady. One I've got to know better."

Although Sparrow had agreed to one room, she had requested two beds. Now she looked at the flowered motel spreads, then up at the obligatory seascape prints that hung above each bed. Although the vacuum marks were visible in the carpet, it felt gritty on her feet. She inhaled stale smoke and felt nauseous. She pulled away.

"Second thoughts?" asked Donald.

"It's the smell, the smoke."

"Do you want to change rooms?"

"Maybe it is second thoughts."

"Sparrow, I don't have to sleep with you. I don't want you to do anything you don't want to do."

"You really wouldn't care if I didn't sleep with you?"

"Of course I would. But I can wait." He took her in his arms.

Sparrow allowed her body to mold to his. Donald ran his hand down the small of her back and held her tightly. She felt his hardness. She kissed him, a lingering kiss, then traced his face with her fingers.

Donald whispered, "Which bed would you like, madam?"

Sparrow smiled and removed his hands from her back. "The one you're in," she said. And she led him to the bed.

267

Just before sleep, snug in Donald's arms, Sparrow whispered, "I wish you could have seen the look in your eyes when you pulled me out of the water."

"Hmm?"

"You—you looked absolutely stricken."

Donald caressed Sparrow's face. "I didn't want to lose you."

"Yes." Sparrow kissed his cheek. "But you lost your wallet."

"No comparison. I can get a new one. But there is only one you."

"And isn't it good that I locked my purse in the car?"

"Yes! We could have been out on the street. "

Sparrow laughed. "I am a woman of means!"

Donald wound his fingers through her curls. "I'd like to make you a woman of more means."

"More means?" Sparrow removed Donald's hand from her hair.

"Yes."

Sparrow giggled. "You're a bad risk: no wallet, no shoes. You looked pretty funny in bare feet, hopping across the gravel to the car."

"And I wish I had a picture of your face when that camera was shooting out film."

A delivery truck whizzed by Booknook, creating a slight breeze. Sparrow wiped sweat from her brow and ran dirty fingers through her tousled hair. She snipped straggly petunias from the pots and put them into a paper bag. Her fingers smelled of flowers and soil, a pleasant scent that reminded her of working in the garden as a child. It would be nice to have a yard where I could grow more flowers, she thought.

Finch rounded the corner and scowled at Sparrow. Her hair was pulled back in an uncombed ponytail; she wore no lipstick, and her shirt and shorts were rumpled and dirty.

Sparrow straightened. "Finch!"

"Where were you on the Fourth?" Finch's voice was accusatory.

"What are you talking about?"

"The store wasn't open!"

Sparrow laughed. "It was the Fourth of July."

"You weren't here!"

"Was I supposed to be?"

"You're always here."

Sparrow put her hand on Finch's shoulder to guide her into the shop. "I went canoeing."

"Not at night you didn't! You were with him, weren't you?"

A passer-by, a frequent customer, loitered on the other side of the street. Sparrow waved to her and grabbed Finch's arm. "You're making a scene. We will talk about this inside." She ushered her daughter through the door and hung up the closed sign. "What's this about?"

"I came home and you weren't here!"

"No, I wasn't."

"You didn't tell me you'd be gone."

"You didn't tell me you'd be home."

"You were gone all night!"

"I'm a grown woman!"

"But you were with him!"

"Yes, I was with *a* him."

Finch collapsed on a chair and buried her head in her hands. "I knew it. You're getting back together!" She flung her hands away and stared at her mom. "Are you?"

269

"Who?"

"You and Robert Roland!"

"I wasn't with your father."

"That professor? You were with that professor!"

Sparrow's face tightened. "Donald—his name is Donald."

"Why do you like him? He's so, so uptight."

Someone tried the door; Sparrow started. The person knocked. Finch glared at her mother, challenging her to answer it. Sparrow did not move. More persistent this time, the person knocked again. Silence, then footsteps echoed down the street.

Sparrow sat down near her daughter. "Finch, I'll always be your mother. But you're in college. And I'm still a young woman."

"But you've always been here. You and Uncle Dave, the three of us. And now he's dead, and I'm losing you." Tears rolled down Finch's cheeks.

Sparrow held out her arms and her daughter fell into them. The two rocked back and forth in time to the ticking clock.

"So, it was a bit of a shock when you came home and neither Uncle Dave nor I was here."

"Yes, yes," Finch muttered through her sobs. "Uncle Dave's dead. There are all these guys in your life. And I'm the one who should be dating." Finch gulped in a breath of air. "I worried about you all the time. It was awful, going off, leaving you. And now you don't even need me!"

Sparrow smoothed Finch's hair. "I'm sorry. I'm so sorry. When you were a baby, I wanted just to be with you. This shop was our nest. But like a baby bird, you had to learn to fly. I'd have stayed put, living through books, living through you. But Dave kept nudging me. You wanted me out, too. Remember when you screamed that I was a recluse? I was devastated. I knew I had to do something on my own. But I wasn't comfortable in my own skin. I wasn't a good example for you."

"It's not that. It's that you'd never talked about anything. You wouldn't tell me about my dad. There was this big scary mystery and you wouldn't talk about it."

"What more could I tell you? He was a fellow who came to work in Milan one summer."

Finch looked into her mother's eyes. "But what about him? Did you love him?"

Sparrow held her gaze. "When I met Rob, I was a kid, starved for love. I couldn't believe any boy could like me. But he did. He really did, Finch. The love that produced you was precious, but afterward I was too confused and ashamed to acknowledge that I was pregnant…. In the fifties, sweetie, you didn't do it."

Finch suppressed a grin. "Didn't do what, Mom?"

Sparrow grinned. "You didn't have sex. And if you did, you didn't tell. And if you got pregnant, you went away and had your baby. Rob never knew. And everyone thought it would be best if I gave you up for adoption. But when I looked into your pinched, little, red face, there was no way I would give you up."

"But why didn't you try and find him?"

"Oh Finch, I did. I looked for Rob Roye in the Englewood phone book. That's what he went by. I didn't know his name was Robert Roland. And he did write me, Finch. He did! My mother never forwarded the letter. He did care. But a lot of time has passed. We're both different."

"But you're going out with him?"

"I've seen him a few times, but I don't know how I feel about him."

"I don't like him."

"You might if you gave him a chance."

Finch shook her head.

"I don't think you'd like anybody that I'd date. You're too used to having me to yourself. But Robert Roland is your father. I doubt if he and I will ever be together, but that does not mean that you can't have a relationship with him."

The Picnic
August 1980

*F*inch and Gurns were both at EMU for the summer session, Gurns because he wanted to take a lighter load during basketball season, Finch because she hated home more than school and had credits to make up. The two were picnicking in the yard outside Finch's apartment. For months Finch had tried to avoid Gurns, not because she didn't like him, but because when she was with him, the bindings of her heart came free and threatened to spill out its pain. Angie had told Gurns Finch's class schedule, and he often showed up as class ended to walk her home or invite her to the student union for a soda or coffee.

The morning after she had talked with her mom, Finch had awakened to a stream of sunlight finding its way through the narrow bedroom window. She blinked and watched dust dance in its rays. Her heart did not have that bound-in feeling. For the first time in months, she was hungry. Famished. Then the phone rang.

"Just checking on you," Gurns said.

"I'm starved."

"I'll be over with food."

Sprawled on a blanket on the lawn, Finch told Gurns about the confrontation with her mother, how she had felt better afterward, but that she was still angry with her. As she talked about Sparrow, she became more animated. "So, just a couple of weeks ago, Sunday noon. I'm still in bed, and she is standing there. The place is a mess, and I'm a little hung over. She wants me to get up and clean. What business is it of hers how I live?"

Gurns was propped against a tree, legs spread, eating his sandwich. He caught a glob of errant mayonnaise with his finger and popped it into his mouth. "The two of you talked. You said you weren't so mad at her. Besides, she *is* a good mom."

Finch snarled. "I'm just an afterthought. She's *busy* with all her boyfriends." Finch took a bite of sandwich. "This roast beef is tough."

"It must not be too bad. It's your second. She could have aborted you."

"Illegal."

"Could have left you on a doorstep."

"Nah."

"Could have adopted you out."

Finch waved him away. "Okay. So, she wanted me—conversation ended." She stuffed her half-eaten sandwich into the paper bag.

"She took care of you."

"Are you trying to make me feel guilty?"

"Maybe. You've been moping around for months. Sure, you're missing Dave, but your mom is, too."

"No, she's not! She doesn't even have time for me."

"You're not so much fun to be with."

"Then why do you spend time with me?"

Gurns picked a weed from the yellowed grass. "You've been her whole life."

"Well, I'm not now."

Gurns sat up. "No, and that's a good thing. She's a smart lady, could have gone off to college, been a teacher, a librarian maybe. But she took care of you."

"That's not my fault!" The sun disappeared under a cloud. A dog barked.

Gurns reached for Finch's hand. "Did you think it was?"

Finch shoved his hand away, then clasped her hand over her mouth. The barking dog, a black Labrador, loped past the yard.

"Well, did you think it was?"

Finch placed her hands firmly on the blanket. "I don't know…. Maybe. She only seemed half there. It felt like maybe she wanted to be someplace else. But she never went anywhere—that's the weird part. Like it was my job to make her happy. But it never seemed like I could live up to it. And there was this big mystery. And she wouldn't talk about it. It's like we were meshed together, stuck in Booknook. And then my dad shows up. But I don't know he's my dad. She should have told me."

"Maybe she couldn't."

Finch whipped her arm through the air. "She couldn't talk about anything! When I got my period, she just handed me a box of pads. That was the extent of it."

"Wasn't her mom real mean to her?"

"What?"

"You told me that her mom used to yell at her, wouldn't let her go anywhere, just made her work. Sounds pretty cruel to me. And I'll bet she hit her, too. Your mom probably learned to keep her mouth shut, to keep her thoughts to herself. If you do that long enough, after a while you don't know what you're thinking."

"Oh, great wise one."

"I'm serious. That's what happened in my family. We were scared of my dad. If we said something the wrong way, he'd smack us. But we never knew what the right way was. It changed all the time. Once, when he complained the mashed potatoes were lumpy, Mom spoke up and he threw the bowl at her. She was lucky. It hit the wall, not her…. The night he beat me so bad, that night he was choking her. I thought he was going to kill her. I jumped on his back and tried to stop him. But he took a mop to me, just a plain old mop, and he kept screaming and hitting me until a neighbor pounded on door. The next day I came to school all bruised up. That's when they took me away. They'd 'a let me stay with Mom, but she wouldn't leave him. After all that she'd been through, she couldn't leave him!"

Finch reached for Gurns's hand.

He took a deep breath. "That's what I mean. She'd been so beat down that she couldn't speak up against him, couldn't leave him. And then I was the one thrown out. Like I was the bad guy, and I had to come back to school and face everyone. And I couldn't talk about it. He'd ripped every word out of me. But I was so angry, and I couldn't fight him, so I fought with everyone else." Gurns took another deep breath and spoke softly. "If Mr. Rice hadn't seen something in me, taken me in, got me on the basketball court, encouraged me, talked to me, always talked to me…"

Gurns picked up the sack and smacked it between his hands. "I'd have turned out just like the old man."

Mayonnaise dripped from the bag.

"Oh, Gurns, I'm sorry."

"Me too…. But what I'm trying to tell you is, your mom was beat down, too. Sure, she got herself in a mess, but she was just a kid, and she found a way to keep you."

"Aren't you mad at your mom?'

"Mad? I was. But she did the best she could. It just wasn't good enough."

"And you think my mom was?"

Gurns smiled. "Yeah."

Finch shook her head. "For a guy who said he couldn't talk, you sure have a lot to say."

"Would you rather I'd be like I was in fourth grade?"

Finch shrugged. "You were pretty nasty to me." She paused. "After all you've said, I don't know if I should bring this up. But remember when you called me 'Bastard Girl'?"

"Not one of my proudest moments."

"I didn't know what it meant 'til I looked it up in the dictionary. You really hurt my feelings."

"I'm sorry…." Gurns shook his head. "But I didn't know what it meant either. That's what my dad called me."

"He called you that? And you didn't know what it meant?

"I had a crush on you."

"No! What a way to show it."

"I told you I was pretty messed up. Besides, you got me back good."

"What do you mean?"

"The gym shorts."

"How'd you know? The note?" Finch busied herself brushing crumbs off the blanket.

"Gees, it was written all over your face."

Finch looked at him. "I've been meaning to apologize."

"So?"

Finch grinned. "I'm sorry."

Gurns brushed his pants off, stood, and pulled her up. "Apology accepted. Want to go to a movie?"

"Only if you're paying."

Finch was cleaning her apartment. She had vacuumed, dusted and done the dishes, but she was stymied. The floor had not been mopped since Christmas; it was filthy, and she was out of cleaner. "Vinegar, that's it!" she said. She remembered her mother scrubbing the counter and floor with such a solution. She dumped a half bottle of vinegar into the bucket, added hot water and got to work. Dirt, spaghetti sauce and other food particles pooled on the floor. When she finished, she was amazed that the gritty brown linoleum was now sparkling beige. She was tired, but felt the same sense of satisfaction that she had felt as a child when on Saturday mornings she and her mother cleaned their apartment. She washed her hands, dried them on a soiled dishtowel and checked the tuna noodle casserole bubbling in the oven.

Right on time, Sparrow tapped on the door. Finch opened it with a flourish. Sparrow hugged her daughter. "Wow! The place looks great. And what do I smell?"

"Guess."

"Vinegar."

"No, tuna noodle, like you make."

"Oh…yes, nice! But it does smell like you dumped a bottle of vinegar in here."

Finch sniffed. "Just like home."

The two had finished their meal. Finch had cleared the dishes, and they were drinking tea, making small talk, Sparrow asking about school and Gurns. She sipped the last of the tea from her cup and smiled at her daughter. "This was good, Finch, delicious!"

"Don't get used to it. I had a reason."

Sparrow Laughed. "How much money do you need?"

Finch shook her head. "Mom, I've been thinking. You never talked much about yourself, about how it was for you growing up. I've never met my grandparents. I thought maybe...."

Sparrow clasped her daughter's hand. "What would you like to know, Finch?"

"All of it. Everything."

Reconciliation
October 24, 1980

*O*ctober, Riverside Park. Most of the trees had changed their dress from green to gold and orange; the oaks were clad in vivid red. Capricious yellowed grass grew in clusters; evergreens added a contrast of brilliant green and blue. An Indian-summer sun warmed the small wedding party. Birds flitted from tree to tree, providing the music. Adrian's mayor was reading a love poem. The vows were yet to be said.

Sparrow had chosen a simple full-length cream-colored dress. Three pink roses with ferns, tied with a pink bow, comprised her bouquet. Donald, his arm around the bride, wore a sleek new suit, with a rose boutonniere complementing her modest bouquet. Finch stood apart, on the opposite side of Sparrow, holding a single red rose. She had insisted on wearing her black pageant gown. Although black meant mourning to Sparrow, she did not mind Finch wearing the color. Sparrow was well aware that her daughter needed time to work through her feelings. In fact, it was only when Finch had told her, "Marry him. You need a life," that Sparrow had given herself permission to follow her heart.

Maria and Anton were dressed in their Sunday best, Maria's heels sinking into the soft ground, Anton's shirt soaked with perspiration. Angie, stunning in a short red sheath, stood next to her parents. Beaming her satisfaction, Clare sat at a picnic table. Through two decades, she had rescued, tutored, advised and hounded Sparrow. Clare loved her, but could not help thinking of her as a project well done. Dave's absence was her only regret.

Vows were murmured and sealed with a kiss. There was laughter, hugs and congratulations. As though she were a spectator, Finch walked to the table, sat and surveyed the scene. Her mother, dropping her husband's arm, came to Finch and knelt, her gown brushing the dormant grass. "Finch, I love you." She held out her arms.

Finch hugged her. "I wish Uncle Dave could be here."

"Me too."

"Yeah, he'd be happy for you."

Sparrow touched Finch's cheek." I hope you are."

"You'd better get up, Mom. You'll get your dress all stained." Finch pulled her mother up. "*Go, go*! And, and be happy."

Sparrow kissed Finch on the cheek and turned to join her husband. The group dispersed to their respective cars to attend the wedding luncheon at Mr. Ed's. As Finch and Angie neared Sparrow's Impala, Finch looked across the lot. "You go with your folks. I'll be there in a while."

Angie's gaze followed Finch's. "Are you sure?"

"Yeah."

Finch watched the others leave and then strode across the parking lot to a black Thunderbird glistening in the sunlight. Clouds swept across the sky, changing the car's color to a dull gray. Her voice harsh, she spoke through the open window. "You couldn't stay away."

"I didn't mean for anyone to notice," said Bob.

"Nobody but me. How'd you know?"

"Your mom told me. She didn't want me to read it in the paper." Dark circles made his blue eyes look gray; his salt and pepper hair was disheveled.

Finch exhaled slowly, silent.

"I hope I didn't spoil it for you." He waited.

Finch said nothing.

"I know you're angry with me, and well you should be. It's too little, too late to be your dad, Finch. But is there a chance that we can be friends?"

The volcano of her heart erupted. "No!" But then she whispered, "I don't know…. I always dreamed of having a dad. Then you show up, and I feel weird with you." She paused to gain control. "Mom goes and gets married, and I have a step-dad. I sort of have two dads, but it feels like I've lost my mom. It's always been just me and Mom, well, and Uncle Dave, too. " She rested her hands on the window seal.

Bob put his hand over hers.

"You're not anything like I imagined. Everything's all screwed up. And Mom doesn't need me anymore!" She turned to leave.

"No, don't go." Bob thrust the door open and stepped out, towering above her. "Listen to me. Your mom loves you. Donald could never take your place with your mom."

"No?" She sighed. "He tries to be so darned nice."

Bob put his arms on Finch's shoulders. "He *is* a nice guy. He may not be your dad, but he cares about you. You have an opportunity to make that family you always wanted."

Drawn by the comforting scent of Old Spice, Finch laid her head on his shoulder; "When I was little, I made up a fairy tale about having a dad."

Bob patted her back.

Finch whispered, "So…so, what about you?"

"Well, what about me?"

Their eyes connected.

His voice was soft. "Perhaps one day, you could tell me that fairy tale."

"It's about birds."

Finch's Journal

December 1980

*M*om *said I should go to therapy that it had helped her. But I told her I wasn't going to talk to some stranger. Then she said I should journal, thought it might help me understand stuff. Like she didn't mess up her life? I asked her about how it was when she was a kid and shock, shock, she told me. I didn't realize how scared she was. I feel real bad about that, but somehow I feel better knowing, like some cracks in me are getting filled in.*

Gurns got me to thinking about abortion. Then when I was in the library, I checked out Cider House Rules. I couldn't put it down. There were all these poor women and girls even who got pregnant. And it wasn't their fault. They didn't have contraception back then and some were raped. There were only risky back-alley abortions that could maim or even kill. But there was this "hospital/orphanage" where a few women could go to have abortions or they could give their babies up. It made me think of what Mom went through.

Okay, so it wasn't the dark ages when Mom had me, but in 1960 abortions were illegal and her mom kicked her out. When she was nineteen, just my age, there she was with a two-year-old. If she could have explained things to me, I don't think I'd be so screwed up. But she sort of closed up and all those years she's living in a fantasy world, not quite there. She finally gets it together and goes to college Then Rob Roye comes back as Robert Roland and is in love with her. But she's in love with Donald Stewart. Weird!

All my life Uncle Dave was in love with a dead woman. Okay, she had been his wife. But he was living in the past. And all that time Miss English was pining over him. He liked her, too. They didn't have to get married. But they could have been friends. What a waste, two old, lonely people.

And me, all my life I'm yearning for a father. I'm looking for him everywhere, at Booknook, on the street. It's all inside me, taking up space. Then I go to college, end up working for this guy, and I get a crush on him. And then I find out he's my dad. Not exactly what I had in mind.

Then Mom marries Dr. Stewart. And I can't talk to him. He told me to call him Donald, not Doctor or Mr. Stewart. I could never call him Dad. They're all over each other—holding hands and kissing. That's awful when you're not used to your mom being with a guy. I'm not going to live with them. I'm not going to listen to their night noises. They're fixing up Uncle Dave's house to move into. It seems wrong, Donald there instead of Uncle Dave. But Mom loves him and it's good to see her happy.

So, I'm stuck with Robert Roland as a "father." He calls once a week, on Sundays about noon, figures I'll be up by then. Asks me how I am, what I'm doing. I asked him why he calls like that, so regular. He says that's what he did and does with Jeffery. He says he couldn't be with him a lot when he was growing up, just vacations, and he wanted to have a relationship with him. He wants one with me, too. (Where was he when I needed him?) I do have a brother. Well, a half-brother—just two years younger. One I've never met. I imagine Bob phones Jeffery first and warms up for me—the difficult one. He's invited me to dinner a couple of times. I can hardly get any food down. It's a waste of his money, but it serves him right. Jeffery—Jeff?—is coming for Christmas, and I'm going to meet him. It might be okay having a kid brother.

Would you believe I just met my grandparents? Mom sent Grandma an invitation to the wedding, but she and Grandpa (sounds odd saying Grandma and Grandpa) didn't come. Later Mom called them. I don't know why. If Mom had been as nasty to me as her mom was to her, I'd never speak to her. Grandpa answered the phone. He congratulated Mom on getting married and graduating college. Mom invited them down to meet me and her husband and see Booknook. They came. Shock, shock! Grandpa was all bent over with a cane. He's disabled with some back thing. He didn't say much, just kept smiling and looking at Mom and me. Except that I have straight hair, he says I look a lot like Mom. (Of course he'd notice my straight hair.) Grandma is a grim little woman, with gray hair in braids wrapped around her head. I'll bet her hair comes down to her ankles. I think maybe she's a little crazy. These old people may be blood relations, but they are strangers—not my family.

This I know, Mom and Uncle Dave and I were a family. Oh we weren't like Angie's family. We were different. Uncle Dave wasn't my dad. He didn't live with us but he loved us and was there for me. I'll always miss him.

Clare says I have to be busier, get involved in school activities, date. Angie's mom wants to fatten me up, enchiladas, burritos, sopapillas. We've got her beans and rice molding in the fridge.

School's okay. I'm working as a waitress at Aubree's. Alex put in a good word for me. He hardly knew me, but he vouched for me. Guess he likes me. He's fun, but I haven't gone out with him.

I've been hanging out with Gurns a lot.